THE BOOK OF CHANGES

Books by R. H. W. DILLARD

THE DAY I STOPPED DREAMING ABOUT BARBARA STEELE (*Poetry*)

NEWS OF THE NILE (*Poetry*)

AFTER BORGES (*Poetry*)

The Book of Changes

a novel by R_ıchard H. W. DILLARD

DOUBLEDAY & COMPANY, INC., GARDEN CITY, NEW YORK

1974

Library of Congress Cataloging in Publication Data

Dillard, Richard H. W.
  The book of changes, a novel.

  I. Title.
PZ4.D577Bo [PS3554.I4] 813'.5'4
ISBN 0-385-07157-4
Library of Congress Catalog Card Number 73–16619

C O P.1

All the characters in this book are fictitious, and any resemblance
to actual persons, living or dead is purely coincidental.

"Lobetanz" (Ch. 1) and "September Morn" (Ch. 3) appeared originally,
in different form, in Vol. III, No. 9 of "Plume and Sword," March, 1963.
"The Dowlong-Drungways Murder Case" (Ch. 6) appeared originally,
in different form, in Vol. IV, No. 2, of "Plume and Sword," 1963.

A stanza of the poem "Words for My Students," which appears on
p. 222, first appeared in *The Hollins Poets*, ed. by Louis D. Rubin, Jr.,
published by University Press of Virginia, copyright © 1967 by University of Virginia.

for

George Garrett

William R. Robinson

John von B. Rodenbeck

In som wynters nyght whan
the firmament is cler and
thikke sterred, wayte a
tyme til that eny sterre
fix sitte lyne-right
perpendiculer over the pool
artik, and clepe that
sterre A. . . .
—Geoffrey Chaucer
*A Treatise on
the Astrolabe*

ACKNOWLEDGMENT

The author wishes to thank the Ford Foundation and Hollins College for the grant and leave of absence which enabled him to complete this novel.

πάντα χωρεῖ καὶ οὐδὲν μένει

—Heraclitus
according to Plato

When Wheeler first had his idea he saw in a flash
a stupendous cosmic pattern: a single electron
shuttling back and forth, back and forth, back and
forth on the loom of time to weave a rich tapestry
containing perhaps all the electrons and positrons
in the world.

—Banesh Hoffmann

"O no!" said Otto.

—Robert Louis Stevenson

. . . . . . ! ! ! ! ! !

—Ronald Firbank

THE BOOK OF CHANGES

It opens with a snap, a flash of light as if you had flicked a wall switch and the ceiling lamp had popped into sudden and suicidal light, the orange filaments fading suddenly like a sunset or a cat's hooding eye.

It begins that way. And with a sense of snow's slow sift under the door, crawling across the floor with the steadiness of glacial flow. Cold as hard in the room as a wall or the links of a chain.

And sounds around you in the dark. Scuffles. A muffled snort. A sob. A single cry: "O no!" Someone, something pushes past you in the iron-cold air. You dare not make a sound.

A memory crosses your eye, imprinted there as clearly as the shape of a bulb's demise: snow, the leaves of the tree, its white blooms; the sun's slow crawl from west to east; snow blind, sand blind, your fingers eager as antennae; her skin pimpled like a goose.

You are in the dark.

In at the beginning, you are aware of an end, that something is at an end, something to be seen, to be solved, the end of something that means a great deal to you.

More, my friend, than you know.

"Ah, no," he said, "but think on it a moment and I'm sure you'll see."

"To be sure," I said. Then, "Ah, to be sure."

At that moment my reveries were interrupted by Gregor's return, which was announced both by a curiously familiar odor and a low and most annoying rumble which each exhalation of his breath produced. Motioning to us with his shoulders, he led us across the dark hall to a deeply polished, if scarred, double door a full ten feet tall, which, with effort, he opened, revealing to us the Baroness at her reading, illuminated only by the pale echoes of the setting sun. The Baroness was sitting erect in her chair in a black velvet gown, her thin figure almost blending into the Morris paper on the wall, which was, as Sir Hugh was later to inform me, signed.

We seated ourselves on a curved lounge opposite the Baroness, and while waiting for her to reach the bottom of her page, I found ample opportunity to examine the room itself. Behind us was the double door which Gregor had just closed and on the wall a large and pleasantly faded print of Mozart as the shepherd Corydon. To our right, two large French windows, one open, revealed the broad flat lawn leading down to a row of yew trees which even then were growing dim with dusk. The cold air entering the open window gave such a chill to the room that our breathing was graced by frothy puffs of vapor which danced under our noses and before our lips. Conversation in such circumstances becomes indeed an aesthetic delight. Behind the Baroness were two windows and, between them, miniatures of her parents: her father and mother in poses typical of the friction which led to his mysterious death and her ingenious suicide by self-garrote. To our left was the ornate fireplace, barren of fire, over which hung a large painting which was, as I was later to learn, of the Baroness's great-uncle Helmut's execution executed by her uncle Teilhard (he was some years younger than the Baroness's seventy-four), who had only recently entered a monastery after being turned away at seven nunneries. And in the shadowy corner of the wall behind us with the door hung a dark portrait of the Emperor

Otho the Great, of which the world has heard so much and so very little, his figure foreshortened by the angle of my gaze so as to appear almost dwarfish, and an evil grin seemed to snarl across his lips and move in the last sinking sunlight.

Two wing-backed chairs stood before the fire, and I was examining, from, of course, my seat, several large scratches on their gleaming legs when the Baroness, ending permanently my exploration of the room and its contents, spoke.

"There," she said, "there," as she closed the pale thin volume with her pale thin hands and placed it with care on the pale thin velvet cushion on the precise black velvet of her lap.

"One is so," she continued, "soothed by Pomfret in such times as these, these terrible, most terrible of times." A long reflective silence, then, "And you did come, my dear friend, you did come to me, my dear boy, in this hour of trial." She nodded her head toward us and seemed to await a reply, but before either of us could utter even a sound, she continued, "Kérem, ne kiabáljon . . . ah, but do forgive me. How thoughtless of me to forget. Inexcusably stupid, but do forgive me."

"But of course," replied Sir Hugh briskly, his breath dancing on his lips, his fingers lacing and unraveling before him, "and . . ."

"I've been reading Pomfret. Quite a blessing, Pomfret. And, of course, there's cousin Ludovic's verse. Were it not for dear Ludovic . . ."

"Indeed, but . . ."

"You do know the dear lad's latest," she asked, "*Der mutwillige Speichellecker?*"

Sir Hugh accepted the proffered slim lavender volume from the Baroness, opened it, and began to pound his feet on the floor while painfully humming out the rhythm.

"De-de-dum-dum-de-de-dum, ah, no, de-de-dum-de-dum-de-dum." Then, to me, "Reminds one of the earlier Tennyson. . . ."

"Or, perhaps, Austin," I offered, but only to Sir Hugh's annoyance (I had, of course, forgotten his strong feelings toward that so recently honored poet whom we called "the other Alfred").

The light had become so dim that Sir Hugh's small round glasses were literally skimming the page, and I noticed that a full moon, which glistened on the already frosted lawn, offered the sole available light. The Baroness was snoring softly in the darkness, her head tilted ever so slightly toward the open French windows, through which a sound of heavy breathing and a grassy scuffling were clearly audible.

I had so often insisted to scoffing acquaintances (one hesitates to use the word "friends" here) that Sir Hugh was capable of great physical exertion should the need so require, that I was less startled than elated and vindicated when he, bounding from his end of the lounge, leapt to the open French window and slammed it to. An object which had been lying on the sill thudded into the room as a dark, hairy figure rammed into the window and rebounded onto the chill turf.

Sir Hugh knelt briefly and stood up again with a small book.

"Poetry," he mumbled. And then, in his best declamatory manner,

> "Mon âme est une Amazone qui,
> Comme une cathédrale moisie,
> A perdu une des saintes biches
> Et gardera toujours le niche.
> Ce manque le rend plus bonne archère
> Mais moins à moitié mammifère."

At that, the Baroness awoke and, in a state of some confusion, cried out, "French poetry! Now who could have left that there?"

"Who," said Sir Hugh, choosing his words with some care, "indeed?"

After a pause pregnant with implication, Sir Hugh beckoned me to the window, and there, on the lawn, I saw what perhaps no human eye had ever seen before. In the light of the full moon, which hung over the yew trees casting a crystal glare from the lawn into our faces, a great black figure, a wolf's if I may venture my opinion, was dancing, head thrown back, reared on its hind legs, its bushy tail weaving an intricate and hypnotic rhythm. Its eyes flashed red in the moonlight, and saliva beaded silver from its gleaming fangs to the glistening grass. Its feet seemed to hang trembling over the ground, suspended by faith, beauty, and the cold magic of the moon. At regular intervals, timed by some inner necromantic metronome, the beast, which in all its strangeness seemed somehow familiar, let forth great shattering howls. I trembled involuntarily and turned to Sir Hugh.

He stood, transfixed, his eyes held by that spinning vision, and could only say, his voice colored by awe and a trace of fear, "A gavotte." Then, "A veritable gavotte!"

Just then, a cloud covered the moon and cast us into darkness, and when it had passed, the dancing figure had disappeared. The silence of the room was broken only by the Baroness's subtly regular snores.

Rather than awaken her peaceful slumber, we moved quietly out of the room, the double doors requiring the efforts of us both before they opened, closed the doors heavily behind us, and sought Gregor, who proved nowhere to be found. Sir Hugh did find and lit a lamp, and we moved cautiously out of the hall and into a corridor opening into the interior of the vast house in search of a guest room. My memory of our wanderings is as dim now as that dark house was then in the lamp's wavering light. I recall only hallways, curving staircases, large and looming pieces of ill-defined furniture, a suit of sagging armor (headless with the casque hung crazily on its spear's point), portraits that leered out from distant walls (one of them, a young woman's, seemed to wink and even to beckon in the fluid light of our passing), one large painting of a small boy holding up an arm from which the hand had just been lopped (the blood making a quavering smear across the entire scene, so realistic that I actually remember slipping in a pool of it on the smooth floor underfoot), and doors, all of them locked, many of them furiously clawed and scarred, and one of them, finally, open.

It led to the guest room we sought. As we entered, Sir Hugh holding the sputtering lamp high, we discovered that thick layers of dust furred the room: the chairs, the desk, the covered bed, the floor save for what appeared to be some sort of animal track running from the door to the open window. Disturbing as little dust as we were able, we climbed into the large bed, pulled the heavy brocaded curtains around us, and, without removing our clothes, spent the night crouched in fitful and frigid slumber in the center of the dust-patterned counterpane.

Pudd awoke. Easier said than done. To awaken. First the eyelids, left then right, his fingers tugging them open, peeling them apart, the dry glue flaking down onto his cheeks. Then the tongue, stapled with fur to the roof of his mouth, so that, staring at the ceiling, at the yellow bars of light crossing out the crisscross of cracks evenly, moving with the sun across the room, he could at last groan articulately and spit the heaviness of his head onto his chest.

The soggy pillow was balled between his left foot and the wall, the sheet peeled half off so that Pudd's head rested on the bare mattress at the foot of the bed; his right leg, bent at the knee, hung to the floor. Pudd lifted the leg, raised it erect over himself toward the ceiling, a pale leg, wet with sweat, muscled, wired with fading red hair. The toenails needed clipping.

His eyes, still gummy with sleep, moved up the leg, the crooked knee, the ankle, the toes, across the ceiling, drifting through the cracks and bars, to the dressing closet, door open, mirror exposed, reflecting the bed, the extended leg, and hazily, half only, the jaw and the veins which, like an echo of the ceiling, mapped the tip of his nose.

21

A woman's pale-gray nylon stocking hung over the edge of the open door; one shiny black shoe, high-heeled and open-sided, lay at the foot of the door under the pointing toe of the stocking, and among the smells which reached Pudd's nose was the heliotrope shadow of her perfume. His leg descended and his body heaved erect. Pudd was naked. His feet splayed out as he crossed the litter of the room, stepped over his trousers, and stopped before the mirror. He studied his bare flesh, wet with the heat, running to fat, pale with the absence of the sun, reddish in splotches, a headless corpse waiting only to be found, boxed and covered over in a potter's field.

Too tired to stoop and bring his head into view, Pudd pulled the stocking down over his shoulder, turned and walked out of the room, through the wandering dust balls in the narrow hall and into the bathroom. The bathroom window was closed, the air stuffy and damp, a towel wadded on the closed red lid of the commode along with a pair of black nylon bikini panties, with a white and coy pussy cat etched on them, stained with love. He had been staring at the mirror for some time before he realized, focusing himself, that printed across it, in orange lipstick, surrounded delicately by small orange posies, was the single word, in letters two inches high, OBSCENITY.

His razor blades, all stripped of their red-and-black paper wrappers (scattered into the sticky bottom of the tub), were lined up across the bottom of the window, propped on the sill. His face stared wearily out of them all, blue and distorted and unfamiliar, a row of ugly strangers who turned away from him in disgust as he turned back to the mirror.

His face, dissected by the orange letters, was gray and red, his teeth yellow, the watery green of his eyes and the red strands of his falling hair. He had not shaved for three days. He closed his eyes. He pulled the stocking from his shoulder and tugged its open end over and onto his head, the sweat on his forehead making a squeak and tug on his flesh. He looked then again into the mirror at the gray face rendered in squares and dots, a poorly inked newspaper photo which metamorphoses the father of the year into a deformed monster, a badly made-up creature from a cheap Florida horror film—the mashed nose, the rubber lips, the pained eyes—a strange face but no uglier and no more unfamiliar to Pudd than the other faces he had seen in the mirror and in the gleaming razor blades, the face beneath the stretched nylon.

He turned to piss, pushing the towel to the floor and dangling the black panties from a fingertip. When the urine came, it came painfully, and in his agony Pudd pulled the black panties over his stockinged head. Finished, he shook himself and moved back out of the room, down the hall, but turning into the kitchen, where he sloshed out a streaked glass at the sink and hunted in the litter of empty bottles for one with an Alka-Seltzer in it as the door buzzer sounded. He walked back down the hall, not speeding his pace, to the entrance door, opened it, and stared through the mesh of nylon, black and gray, at the small figure standing there.

"Wire for Mr. Pudd." The boy in the tight blue uniform, cap in hand, stared at Pudd's nakedness and then held his gaze rigidly on the masked head as Pudd tore the envelope open, unfolded the telegram, and peered at the pasted strips:

WOULD APPRECIATE SINCERELY YOUR APPEAR-
ANCE THIS MIDNITE STOP JUDGMENT HAS
COME STOP GONE STOP NOW ONLY FINAL
BLESSINGS OF PAIN AND RELEASE REMAIN
STOP

S. HARDING

He crumpled the paper into a ball and bounced it among its moving dusty shadows in the hall. The boy's hand remained extended, his eyes fastened to Pudd's head, as from the muffled mouth came a lilting, silvery voice, the voice of a maiden aunt, flustered by the chaos of this modern world, a pale echo of the charm of a long since departed old order:

"I'm afraid," it piped and trembled, "I've left my change purse behind, young man. O this heat, I'm afraid I shall faint."

The door slammed shut on the boy's open face, and Pudd shuffled back down the hall and into the bedroom. The clock above the bed read 4, so that eight hours remained before his appointment. He sank wearily onto the bed, his left hand idly squeezing a thick rubber band under a fold in the sheet. Raising then his right hand, he spoke, his belly tensing to the task, resonantly, filling the closed and dusty world:

> "He that trusts to you
> Where he should find you lions, finds you hares;
> Where foxes, geese: you are not surer, no,
> Than is the coal of fire upon the ice,
> Or hailstone in the sun."

He peeled the panties and the stocking off his head, balled them up, and hurled them into a dim corner of the room, then dizzy with the air, however stale, continued, rising to stride across the room, posing himself erect and proud before the mirror, his headless body filled with life as the lost head boomed into the room:

> "Would the nobility lay aside their ruth,
> And let me use my sword, I'ld make a quarry
> With thousands of these quarter'd slaves, as high
> As I could pick my lance."

Talk of Fun!
Where will you beat this?

—Winston S. Churchill

I should perhaps mention here that the reason we had been summoned with such urgency to the Trutz-Drachen country house was that a great number of young women in the surrounding villages had been brutally murdered and partially devoured, always under a full moon. The Baroness, needless to say, was somewhat apprehensive and, thus, cabled Sir Hugh, who had then some reputation in higher circles as an amateur detective, to come, despite the cramped traveling conditions caused by the Crown Prince's approaching birthday, and solve this appalling mystery. The events of the preceding night were, then, as one might suppose, of considerable interest to Sir Hugh and, indeed, to myself.

The night itself, I might add, offered some events of a less substantial nature which were of interest, if not to Sir Hugh, who would not hear tell of them—a warning finger to his lips whenever I tried over the next few days to broach the subject by way of a curious sidelight on the week's business—certainly to my own inquiring mind.

I speak, as one might have supposed, of my chilled and somewhat feverish dreams of that alien late summer's night. My first impressions, as I lay (or rather, crouched) at the foot of that vast and dusty bed in the dark, were of odors: first, a musty odor, or should I say a musky one?, a scent that caused an image of hair or possibly fur to cross my mind (I seem to recall then a dream of my lying with my head in Mama's lap, or possibly Nanny's, as she stroked my limp locks into a semblance of place with that harsh brush which had always given such a refined sense of pleasure); and then a simpler smell, one of garlic or perhaps wolfsbane, a breathy scent, lippy and full-lunged, long-traveled. My next impressions were of a curtain's opening (I have always been thrilled by theatrics), of an irregular motion, of a rising and settling (of sand? of dust?), and whisperings then, low whisperings, two light delicate voices. I recall stirring in my sleep and being struck by a sudden silence as of held breath, but I soon slumbered again, soothed by more whisperings, more risings and fallings, and a regular rhythm, steady as clockwork or the sea's sure slapping at the shore—not a rocky coast, but rather a silvery soft beach under a noontime sun.

I would mention none of this, for it offers evidence only of the disordered state of my nerves at the time (and, I might add, for some time after), save for the curious vision that followed these first garbled impressions. It seemed to me that I awoke for one startled moment, filled with an unutterable fear, feeling myself tossed about, choked in a cloud of dust, beset by odors that were frighteningly familiar and totally strange, and surrounded by sounds that may only be described properly as bestial—growls and grumbles, the fearsome carnivorous slap of flesh on bone and flesh. I thrust my hand into my greatcoat pocket, fumbled for and found a sulphur match, snapped it into sudden flame against my shirt collar, and saw, through what appeared in my stupid state of half-sleep a flounced female undergarment of some kind that was draped carelessly over my head, the strangest and most inexplicable sight I have ever seen: what appeared to be an enormous, shaggy, faceless head of unshorn hair shaking over the slim back of a young woman (I would guess), that back leading down by way of an entrancing arch to a fine double round of pearly posterior, but from those feminine delights sprang a disjointed pair of thin, pale, sparsely haired but decidedly male legs, extending back from the back toward me, crossed, as Sir Hugh so often crosses his legs at the Club when he is engrossed in a particularly delicious memoir, at knee and again at ankle. The toes were particularly long, long-nailed and repulsive. The horrid beast continued to utter its now arrhythmic cries as the match touched my thumb in its death throes, and I fainted dead away.

I was troubled by no more dreams that night, only by fits of violent sneezing which awakened me into the dusty dark sporadically. We were aroused just at sunrise the following morning by a heavy thumping sound from the direction of the window. Sir Hugh, a finger to his lips, his greatcoat lying between us in a heap, his clothes wrinkled and misbuttoned as if he too had had a bad night, spread the bed curtains apart, and we peered into the room.

Gregor, covered with what, for lack of a polite word, one must describe as gore, was crawling across the floor, following the animal track from window to door. Sir Hugh quietly closed the curtains and, after we had heard Gregor open, crawl through, and close the door behind him, said, "Mustn't say anything about this, eh? Wouldn't want to embarrass the poor fellow."

We were both covered with a coating of dust, especially me, so that we looked rather like two manikins, formed of dust and risen at some primal behest from the very substance of the room itself. Sir Hugh was a perfect gentleman, who would of course make no mention to me of my unpleasant appearance, and so I, equally of course, made no mention of his. He rebuttoned and reordered as I brushed and pounded myself. The atmosphere of the room was positively gray when I finished. How that dust had come so thoroughly upon me in the night I have never ascertained, for the heavy bed curtains would surely have protected us from the drafts of the open window. But I have decided, to my own satisfaction at least, that the dust's odd behavior and our long fast, for we had not eaten since leaving the abbey at St. Michaelsburg early the day before, were together responsible for my vision of the night before, that and no succubus or inkling of mental disorder on my surely sane part.

Back in passing fair order again, we set forth in search of the Baroness and of sustenance. I had never known Sir Hugh to go so long without food, and I believe to this day that had he been required to engage in any further strenuous activity after his bold leap to the French windows on the evening last, that activity might well have spelled his doom.

We made our way briskly back along that labyrinth of halls, passing wide windows through which the early sun cast its bright and beckoning beams, past large paintings (mainly of pastoral scenes, innocent nymphs, foiled satyrs, smiling patrons), an ormolu clock pacing off the passing of the infant day, a suit of shining armor with one of its iron gauntlets carelessly misplaced, bowing butlers and beaming maidservants, all of them pointing the way along the gleaming halls, down the gentle curve of the staircase, across the wide entrance hall, and, much to my surprise but (much to my surprise) not apparently to Sir Hugh's, into the oak-beamed kitchen, where the Baroness sat at her breakfast before a large, round, rough-hewn but smoothly maintained working table. At her request, we joined her.

At breakfast, I could tell by the way Sir Hugh carelessly smeared great daubs of Marmite on his bread, ignoring entirely the ministrations of the hovering myriad of serving girls and especially those of one of them—a tall young thing with her hair pulled back into an enormous bun, her face flushed if a bit mottled, dust dappling her hair and long scratches down the backs of her legs—that he was deep in cogitation and that a solution was near.

After she had told us of another vile murder which had occurred during the night, the Baroness would only repeat, "Van egy detektiv regényem," and stare with apparent fascination at Sir Hugh's swinging jaw.

I, too, found the outward manifestations of Sir Hugh's raging inner needs somewhat hypnotic, so I forced myself to look away, across the undulating surface of the huge table toward the clustered servants, but I focused eye and ear beyond their shiftings and shufflings and the hum of their morning's gossip until I was able to see the clues in the case spread out as cleanly and clearly as a butterfly on a pinning board, gold and vermilion.

I listed them: the murders, the clawed doors and furniture, the French poetry, the dancing wolf, the moon, the dust (my eye wavered for a moment, entangled in the dusty bun of the serving girl the Baroness called Ottavia or Ottilia, sensing for a second a whiff of garlic and possibly something else before I forced myself back into the abstract pattern and concrete substance of the case), and above all the ancient gypsy's muttered warning. I felt I almost had the answer. I knew there was only one small element missing. If I could only find it, I knew that the answer in all its shimmering illusiveness was mine.

I thought back to our arrival at the door, of Gregor opening the door, of . . . , of . . . , and suddenly I had it, but just as suddenly Sir Hugh clapped an enormous slab of coarse brown bread and Marmite into his mouth, and with bulging eyes and violent chewings, he leaned across the table, grasped the Baroness's pale thin hand, and, in a shower of Marmitic crumbs, made a wondrous series of quite unintelligible sounds, punctuated with painful gulps and nods of his head. When, finally, he had swallowed the last of his breakfast, he came round the table and said, with his old confidence and familiar poise, to the Baroness (he was still holding her hand), "I believe I've quite solved your problem for you." He then stooped, placed his lips next to her ear (Ottina gasped), and whispered into it at some length.

I observed the expression on the Baroness's face change from one of puzzlement and worry to one of serenity and ease, and I knew by that placid metamorphosis that once again all of my careful analytic musing had come to nought. I swore at that moment never to reveal, to Sir Hugh or to a waiting world, the foolish results of my thinking; I do not think I could have stood one of Sir Hugh's quiet smirks, much less the gaping guffaws of some of our acquaintances at the Club. "Magyarországon," the Baroness was saying as she arose, crossed the room, and returned carrying a large jar of calf's-foot jelly, "minden háziasszony maga teszi el télire a gyümölcsöt és főzeléket."

She, in harmonious unity with sun, servants, and ceiling, beamed as she gave us the jelly, and when, later that morning, we were preparing to leave for home, her gentle snores could be heard echoing down the halls from her reading room.

Gregor was standing at the door as we left, his jowls caked with dried and flaking blood.

"Cut yourself, eh?" Sir Hugh said playfully as we passed through the door and into the fresh morning.

"You know," he continued to me in one of those moments of genuine intimacy that have always given value to our relationship, "one would have wondered about that Gregor were it not for . . ."

"Of course," I replied.

At that precise moment, as we were later to learn, ten thousand dervishes under the white banners of Osman Azrak hurled themselves against the left and center of the British Army at Omdurman. And, too, there was the approaching birthday festival for the Crown Prince, which needs, of course, no explanation.

Albert Longinus was depressed from his eleventh year by the intolerable burden of his surname, as if it requried of him a classic calm, an insight into things honed by cool reason and carefully acquired antiquity. As he grew older, the years clawing at his skin like furious Harpies, stiffening his bones with the surety of Medusa's gaze, the burden on his spirit also grew, attained the weight of Rome's weathered stones with little of their control or grace. He was a small man with eyes small and set close to the tight sides of his narrow nose; he spoke as if he were continually on the brink of a massive and cleansing sneeze, an explosive corrective to the stuffed quality of his life and times, a purgative which never came; his voice was tight and breathless. "I have come," he would say, his fingers nervously trembling on the frayed lips of his green windbreaker pockets, "for the wash." And now the truth is out, for Albert Longinus was a routeman for the Wet-N-Spin-M-Clean Laundry and Dry Cleaning Company of Newark, New Jersey, where he had worked for seven years, uneventful and colorless, level and drab as the dull and wasted buildings of Newark itself.

Sodom and Gomorrah had nothing on Newark, New Jersey, especially not in that pause of winter when the sun rose and set gray and flat, and light and dark blurred together into monochromic evenness. And the things that went on in those shadowy rooms only Albert Longinus and an occasionally brave paperboy who accepted the invitations of darkening blondes in pink and torn peignoirs to come in out of the cold while they searched for some change, only they knew.

One afternoon, nearing three-thirty of a cloudy afternoon in the third week of January of an indeterminate year, Albert Longinus moved on his scarcely serene rounds onto the street named Ugly and climbed stiffly out of the bright green (but dirty with the grime of the cities of the Jersey Flats) truck with its loudspeaker blaring out, "We're Gonna Wash That Crud Right Outta Your Wash," and walked into, folding the empty laundry bag over his left arm, the Dagon Arms Apartments, where his pinched nose wrinkled with the ancient smell of cheap fried fish and a haze of room deodorant, now as much a part of the place's very essential being as the cracked wallpaper or the fleeing roaches. Up the stairs then, walking with tired precision, mounting up to the third floor, where he tattooed the intricate seven-beat knock of the laundry on the door of apartment 3-7B.

Rap-tap-tap-rap-rap-tap-tap.

And she opened the door almost before the beat was out and on the wood, as naked as drunken Lot and as shameless. Albert Longinus covered her torso with the white laundry bag even as he averted his gaze and gasped a hasty and squeezed "I have come for the wash."

There they stood, immobile as stone, carved marble, cold as late January, until she took his extended and clenched hand in hers, frozen and small, and pulled him wordless and stiff into the dim apartment. Then she kicked the door shut with one slim leg from behind the still smooth laundry bag, moved forward giving all that blankness form and substance, clenched Albert shoulder and hip, hung on him like old Proteus himself but with no change of shape or essence.

"Hot dog," she said, her voice warming the chill air and the chill in Albert's bones like fiery Yaanek at the boreal pole, and then again, "Hot dog," gripping frail Albert hard and harder as they both fell a laundry-bag sandwich to the hard wood floor and rolled like a weighted ball, humped and humping, bumped and bumping, across wood and frayed wool to end up between couch and stuffed chair, wall and fading air. "Hot dog!"

And what would the neighbors say on the other side of that peeling wall at the scuffling and growling, the grunts and guffaws which ensued?

Nothing, for the entire floor was empty of tenants, the entire building condemned as unsafe and unsanitary without Albert's or the laundry's knowledge, the whole block intended for a slum-clearance project, a parking lot for the municipal stadium (new home of the hapless New York Behemoths of the NFL) planned in the nearby vicinity.

But then, what was this clinging pale creature clutched so tenaciously to Albert's bosom? Some ghostly succubus draining him dry? Some night thing venturing into the late Newark afternoon emboldened by the scent of her prey? A social worker lost in the empty walls, her clothes gone for fuel, leaping now for aid and dreamed-for succor?

Not so. Actually, known to Albert only as Miss Parker, an employee of the now closed Weaving Mill, she was by day that quiet weaver, but by night was of the Loose and Easy Three, a trio of strippers known around Newark and as far as New Brunswick for their elaborate act in which they passed back and forth among them one pasty and a tiny hand fan from the Jovial Funeral Home of Rome, Georgia, to a weave of colored lights and the thumping beat of five teen-agers, required by law to wear cut-down horse blinders and face the crowd (those sweating bald heads, eager faces, the few enchanted women in the shadowy last rows) even as they ground out the familiar sounds of a strip version of "Three Little Words." Miss Parker by day and Ginger Snap by night, she was flesh and real, active and alive, and she said once more, wedged head down, feet up, between the rungs of the rocking chair by the window, "Hot dog."

PUDD MOVES THROUGH THE DARK

First, there was the bus. Pudd seldom traveled to work on the subway, felt uneasy in the underground holding the burden of his leather case among those empty faces and open, excited evening tabloids, hated the climb up to the street, the kiosk opening directly before the high flat wall with its turrets and pacing watches, calling softly and far away, one to the other, exchanging memories of women and cigars and the shock of sudden death. Pudd preferred the bus and the walk down the dark block, its varied buildings forming a tawdry and multiform shield between his progress and the gray wall.

The bus seats were hard, and the jiggling hurt Pudd's head and kidneys, as did the erratic movement of neon outside the bus windows in the night, no single sign remaining stationary long enough for him to make reasonable words of the letters, the figures, blinking and trembling, blue, green, red, and yellow, an audible whirring in his brain, punctuated by the hissings and rumblings of the bus, the hacking cough of the fat bus driver (the sound of a withered and pale consumptive shaking and jiggling that parfait flesh), and the whispered giggling of the girls.

The girls hurt as much as the bus itself, as much even as the subway, but Pudd could never be sure when they would be on the bus, smug and plump and dark in their smooth skin, whispering and pinching each other's round arms, touching lightly their breasts (their own and each other's), rising and rubbery firm or liberated and nippled through loose cotton cloth, sharing their secrets obscurely with the night and their tired-eyed fellow travelers, making a mocking and mysterious conspiracy of their voyage home from the halls of night school.

They hurt because Pudd had no restraint, swelled painfully and obviously even as he would lug his heavy case up from the floor and balance it on his lap, for he could not keep his eyes from them, the confusion of arms and smocks, tits and tails, lips and legs, as ultimately dissatisfying and confused as the neon world beyond the damp windows.

This night there were fewer girls than usual, only six or eight, bunched oddly to the back of the bus. Their hair was long and loose, seemingly uncombed, and they wore blue jeans and loose blouses, loose-limbed and, to Pudd's practiced eye, generally loose. ("Not a bra in the bunch," he would have thought, had he not been so busy tugging the heavy case up from the floor at his feet and across his agonized lap.) They were carrying textbooks and notebooks, and their talk was of professors and classes and films. Pudd was embarrassed at his undeniable interest and turned his eyes back to the jarring and jiggling night beyond the glass. The single word TOOT caught his eye in red neon before the whole erased its parts in a rainbow blur.

Pudd yawned. A mistake, opening his mossy teeth, drawing in the damp air and exhaling his own stale inner confusions into the already confused air where they mingled with the whispers, the flashing lights. And Pudd's eyes, blinking after the yawn, watering, fixed suddenly on another pair of eyes focused into radiating rings of thick plasticky eyeglasses, opened as wide as his own mouth had been and staring with the concentration and fury of a rat cornered in the bright parking lot of a supermarket, caught in the concentric rings of the headlights of a dozen automobiles, their female drivers' ankles pimpled and atremble with watery fear. Pudd froze then, too, his own eyes pulled into those plastic circles, drawn into those dark beads, the narrow face and pinched body, taut with fear and hatred, a little man's, almost (not quite) a dwarf's, pimpled and skinny, knobby and sharp, those eyes reading his own eyes, searching the lines and blotches of his face, seeking answers, vainly flicking, the head jerking with them, winding the eyeglasses up and down, back and forth, across Pudd (his arms straining the old cloth of his black jersey, his legs, balanced on his toes, holding the heavy case and concealing the too obvious evidence of his lust), searching vainly for answers to questions which disgusted Pudd, inarticulate questions in those eyes, those bony fingers pressed onto the bus seat on either side of the yearning figure.

Startled, awake, his eyes struggling to turn to the girls, their number diminished now by the passing blocks to one (and she, a hatchet-faced young woman with a huge bun of hair, a fierce look in her eye, her bosom shielded by a portable typewriter case and a propped shorthand book hiding her hips, a figure tight as a drawn bow or stretched muscle). And then to the glaring signs, their pace also diminished as the bright center of the city grew farther past. He even looked to the advertising signs but was foiled by a stammer of red on yellow—TRY TOTO, TRY TOTO, TRY TOTO, TRY TOTO, TRY TOTO.

Pudd reached his right hand into his jersey pocket, a tube of cloth pulled flat over and by his belly, and pulled out a letter, crumpled and worn, having been pulled in and out of its frayed envelope again and again to be read aloud at bars, to women in his narrow bed, to be laughed at loudly and with tears, pulled it out, opened it and thrust it before his face, letting the envelope fall onto the floor, not stopping to pick it up, and giving his eyes free run of the familiar page, allowing them to escape into the small, carefully typewritten letters, into the lines which they knew so well and where they could hide from their angry and frustrated captors.

Sir:

This is my last attempt at a reasonable and calm correspondence with you. I am almost through with you. I have had almost enough. But, for one last, desperate time, I shall repeat what I have told you in my preceding letters in the faint hope that they were lost in the mails. As you will notice, I have carefully used your Zip Code on this letter and so I am sure you are now holding it in your muscular hand.

Some months ago (and I have the canceled check, I once again assure you, and Xerox copies as well), I sent you a two-year subscription order (for 24 copies) and a $15.00 (fifteen dollar) check (which earned me 2 extra issues—a total of 26). I never received a single copy of PUDD, not copy one, but, as I said, I did receive the canceled check.

I would still, despite everything, like very much to receive PUDD regularly in my box (in plain wrappers), for I sincerely believe as your ads suggest that building my physique is the key to success and happiness as a human being, but if you do not want to send me the magazines you owe me or to refund my fifteen dollars, I shall reluctantly be forced to turn the whole affair over to the Better Business Bureau.

Yours firmly,

O. N. Otto
O. N. Otto
1001 Sator Lane
Sonoma, California

ONO/ono

And then, through the comfort of the familiar and hilarious letters, rising through them like a figure through fog, was a face . . . Otto N. Otto's . . . o no, the face was not that of Otto Notto but was the pimpled face which had so nearly trapped him, circling eyes now bulging out like the rubber bulbs of squeezed goo-goo dolls, pop pop, with rubbery surprise—the face wet, the nose runny with the damp, right before Pudd, between him and the letter, spittle clearing in its throat, some spraying out onto Pudd's nose, and the beginning of a whine, sing-song, the keening of the thousand lost, million betrayed, widows and motherless children, men with harridan wives, the skinny, the pimpled, the varicosed fat, Otto Otto, beautiful brides with fever blisters ripening on their lips, aging actresses still plagued with acne, but not the genuinely deformed, the crippled, the blank mindless, the startled dead, no trace of the numb surprise of the cancerous or the sullen coma of the condemned felon, only the whine of the trivial, cranking itself wetly up in Pudd's face, before his swollen nose:

"I believe you dropped your envelope, Mister . . . uh . . . [his eyes narrowed in the glassy circles to become triangles, arcane isosceles twisting with cleverness] . . . Pudd." A pause, then, "I could not help [a clearing of his noisy throat] but notice. The, ah, the envelope. The, ah, the address."

Pudd's eyes recoiled, turned in on themselves, but they still could see those triangular eyes as he took the envelope, his hands automatically performing their practiced ritual, the folding, the inserting, the replacing in his jersey, as his ears heard the voice continue, mingling with the driver's "Ninety-sixth Street," as he began to rise, "What is so sweet," low and wet, as Pudd grasped the handle of his heavy case, "as a rose," gurgling, desperate, in haste, "unblown," as Pudd arose, his stout belly bumping the little man aside, his voice booming into the nearly empty bus, no girls:

> "Go no further; not a step more; thou art
> A master-plague in the midst of miseries.
> Go— I fear thee. I tremble every limb,
> Who never shook before. There's moldy death
> In thy resolved looks— Yes, I could kneel
> To pray thee far away."

The little man, coiled back on the grimy bus floor, his glasses cocked crazily on his face leaving the eyes flat and lidless, still silently questioning, still imploring, hissed at the wide black jersey back of Pudd, who walked up the aisle as the bus slowed and stopped, stepped through the door, and, raising his left hand up, fist balled at the stars, at the sounds of the departing bus, at the block-distant invisible shadow of the prison wall and its moody, pacing watches:

> "If he survives one hour, then may I die
> In unimagined tortures—or breathe through
> A long life in the foulest sink of the world!"

And he walked briskly, waving his free arm in the air to balance the weight of his case, past dark windows, some few lighted, dusty showcases for pets, tobaccos, artificial limbs, one small hardware shop with a display of files in its window, and the two bars: the one gloomy one where sodden drunks sang Irish ballads in sharp and flat uncadenced voices, and Schwartz Carl's Hot Bar with its smoky red interior, the small stage behind the bar where three sluggish women undressed each other to the music of a scratchy jukebox, the outsized His Master's Voice dog (head cocked in perpetual wonder and attentiveness) by the always open door.

Pudd lingered for a moment at Schwartz Carl's but, remembering the lateness of the hour, his appointment, and the scornful fury of Septimus Harding at his every error, he hurried on down the street, weaving like a tipsy tightrope walker with the weight of his burden, moving through the dark toward the prison wall, his own small private door, and the quiet, clean privacy of the dressing room.

> *Even yet, though my thoughts*
> *were ultimately much absorbed*
> *in the task, it wears, to my*
> *eye, a stern and sombre aspect.*

—Nathaniel Hawthorne

The only sound, aside from our quiet if tense breathing, which disturbed the stillness of the dim and musty room was the somewhat unsteady ticking of the large and ornately carved clock, graced with bold scenes of Bruce at Bannockburn, in the corner of the room by the tattered battle flags still clinging to their worn oaken poles and the faint hissing of the fading coal fire which glowed in the massive fireplace before us. Pale moonlight mingled with the trembling ruddy flickers of firelight, and, in the gilt-framed (bedecked with twining bulges of flowers and flat leaves) and tarnished mirror over the polished mantel (reflecting itself the warped reflections of the glass above it), I could make out the thin, worried face, made more obviously thin by the tiny round glasses perched uneasily on the pointed and bony nose, of Sir Hugh Fitz-Hyffen.

We had been sitting there, swimming silently and smoothly in our respective thoughts and those confused shadows, for nearly the two hours since dinner (cold porridge and oat bread), hours of suspension and suspense, made interminable by the knowledge that, at precisely midnight, the arrival of the Dowlong-Drungways murderer would be announced by our ancient but hearty host, Sandy Mc

Mc-Mc, the crusty Scottish laird whose known ancestry extended far back beyond recorded history, whose venerable name had survived even the shame of proscription, and whose known progeny thrived in every land under the British flag. The murderer was to be drawn there irresistibly by the cunning of the thin, frail man before me, his long legs, wound knee and knee, ankle and ankle, extending from the great wing-backed chair, plush and huge, to the bumper on the hearth, prematurely old in mind and body (he was then but twenty-four), the man fated to be the last of the Fitz-Hyffens, my dear friend and wise mentor, Sir Hugh himself.

For their own safety, the servants had been dismissed and sent down the winding Scottish highroad into town, and, somewhere below, the laird himself, in the blazing kilts of his clan, waited to open the door at the summons of the brass knocker (a heavy thistle hinged at the center of a brazen cross) to be wielded by the insidious murderer of Nigel Dowlong-Drungways, the young and oddly handsome heir to the Dowlong-Drungways fortune, that fortune amassed in the West Indies by Nigel's father, Lord Fairfax Dowlong-Drungways, reputedly a slave trader but unquestionably the iron and stern captain of colonial enterprise.

It was Lord Dowlong-Drungways who had requested Sir Hugh, upon the advice of our old and mutual friend Mc Mc-Mc, to investigate, Sir Hugh already having achieved a modicum of fame as an amateur detective for his part in the baffling case of the Cheshire Snatch (little dampened by the disheartening *finis* he privately wrote to the misnamed case of "Jack the Ripper"), and, indeed, to bring the cringing villain to the bar of uncringing justice. At that time, a mere if crowded three days before, Nigel was little known to the world. One remembered, in truth, only his recent and widely disapproved marriage to the beautiful and scandalous girl who, as we were later to learn, was known in her disreputable and artistic circles as Plump Esther Plum, the girl who had startled Brighton in the October before her wedding by tickling Lord Alfred Douglas's chin and who had attended the year after that event the funeral of

Lady Wilde attired in a dress as scarlet as her husband's blushing face.

Since our arrival at Mc Mc-Mc Manor, however, the paradox of Nigel Dowlong-Drungways, fleshed out with facts and tinted with the lurid tincture of gossip, loomed ever larger in our minds as the key to his death. Young Nigel had been tall and lean, his face hard to the point of asceticism; he had been diligent and hard-working, having taken a first at Oxford and having spent a successful year as foreman of one of his father's Jamaican plantations. The marriage, but a year before his death, had been the initial indication of another nature's lurking beneath those cold exteriors; hints of wildly mysterious lawn parties under the full moon, of nudity, of salmon poaching, of mad dancing to the savage drumming of Humber Baboo, the suave and darkly handsome black servant whom the young Nigel had acquired in the Americas, completed the enigmatic picture of this young man given us by shocked presbyters of the small Scottish village. How he met, wooed, and won Plump Esther Plum remained a mystery to us even as we sat in the gloom of Mc Mc-Mc Manor awaiting the one person who had solved the puzzle of Nigel Dowlong-Drungways, who had sundered the intricate knot of his nature with the single blow of a blade, his unknown (to us) murderer.

The clock clanked and clattered out twelve strokes, and I saw the knuckles of Sir Hugh's thin hands shine tautly through his skin as, involuntarily, he clutched the arms of his chair.

"Tea?" I heard his strained voice say from between the wings of the chair, his lips distorted as they moved in the wavering mirror image.

"Of course," I replied, only to hear Sir Hugh's immediate laugh.

"Your manners," he said jovially. Then, "Our guest," as he subsided back into his chair. I marveled at his control, for once again politeness had conquered hunger. Sir Hugh, thin as he was, required enormous amounts of food to stimulate his thought, this gnawing need causing his gentlemanliness to undergo the severest of strains for hours before each meal. Tonight, however, his clever plan to trap the murderer had foiled the satisfaction (the oat biscuits and tea laid out painfully beside him for a small supper on the tiny, darkly gleaming table between our chairs and directly before the third and intriguingly empty chair facing the fire) of his hunger, for his plan, so startlingly subtle in its simplicity, had been to place the following notice in the local paper, published that noon:

> Would the murderer of Nigel Dowlong-Drungways be pleased to join me for a light supper at Mc Mc-Mc Manor this midnight? I have something of interest to us both to show you.
>
> Sir H F-H

"What," I had at the time asked, "have you of interest to," a pause, "him?"

"These," had been his sole reply, holding up before my eyes, glittering and new, a pair of handcuffs.

Distantly, that midnight, I heard a far-off knocking and a voice with a curiously forced Scottish accent singing. I strained to hear and, through the oriel window on the far side of the room, heard:

> "Gudewife, when your gudeman's frae hame,
> Might I but be sae bauld,
> As come to your bed-chamber,
> When winter nights are cauld;
> As come to your bed-chamber,
> When nights are cauld and wat,
> And lie in your gudeman's stead,
> Wad ye do that?"

"Sir Hugh," I said, "isn't that . . . ?"

"Hush" was his answer, his eyes fixed, as even the distorted mirror revealed, on the tray of waiting oat biscuits.

This answer, oddly enough, set in motion a chain of recollections and reveries in my mind, and I thought back to our first look at Nigel

Dowlong-Drungways, lying in state on a particularly large and round mahogany table in the grand hall of the Drungways, the family's Highland seat, his face composed and at peace, the dagger wound in his chest mercifully concealed, at Lord Fairfax Dowlong-Drungways' tasteful command, by his stiff shirtfront and folded hands. The murder weapon, on the table by his side, had been, indeed, a dagger, West Indian and with a stuffed black Voo-Doo figure dangling from its handle. Only Humber Baboo, of all those present, had professed to have seen its like before; he had said no more.

Sir Hugh had spoken to the bereaved widow that night, surprised but not disappointed that she wore a scarlet gown, dipping daringly low at the bosom and lower still in the back. Her arms were as round as her eyes, her skin was pale, and as one might have expected, she was pleasantly plump, in fact enticingly so.

Referring to her attire, she managed, between gently chesttrembling sobs, to say only, "Nigel would have wanted it this way."

Watching her speak, the clear mistiness of her eyes and general firmness of her, one surmised, soft lips, one could easily believe the rumors concerning Roger Daphnis Farqhart, the man whom Nigel Dowlong-Drungways had, according to report, openly accused of "rogering" his wife. One could even understand Farqhart's following Esther from London, his refusal to surrender her or even to admit that he had, in fact, lost her to another man—Farqhart the rake, evil in demeanor and appearance with a cruel face framed by slick black hair and a pointed beard; Farqhart, reputedly dubbed "Schwarz Roger" by some degenerate descendant of King Ottocar of Bohemia, rumored to have participated in a black mass in Soho and to have performed a strange surgical experiment on the chest of a young minister in Sibiu.

When the police reached the dying young Dowlong-Drungways, as Esther soon told us, he spoke only once to those assembled around him in his drawing room, where he lay on the floor on papers spread by the thoughtful Humber Baboo to protect the rug, saying only, "Hush, Esther, hush!" Then, after a painful pause, suddenly and with enormous warmth of feeling, "The Black Man . . ."

I was remembering the look on Sir Hugh's face as he heard Esther speak those words, as he stared across the body of young Nigel, past Humber Baboo, who was discreetly serving canapés to the mourners, at the flushed and satanic face of Roger Daphnis Farqhart, when Sandy Mc Mc-Mc burst into the room through the open hall door, causing me to start from my reverie and Sir Hugh, unwinding his legs as he moved, to leap from his chair.

I should add here that Sandy Mc Mc-Mc spoke in a rich Scottish burr, so thick as often to be unintelligible, which I shall make no attempt to reproduce here for the sake of that clarity which is so essential to an account of this nature.

"Sir Hugh, Sir Hugh," he shouted, and then, much to my amazement, broke into a fling, his kilts flapping about his lively knobby knees. Still dancing, his face flush and damp with perspiration, he began to sing:

> "O gin a body meet a body
> Comin' throu the rye . . ."

Sir Hugh moved toward the bouncing laird, who stopped dancing as suddenly as he had started and, with a sly grin, said, "Did you ever hear now of the three Macgregors, the queen and the lowland locksmith?" Then, apparently much abashed, he allowed his head to droop and his arms to hang loosely by his sides.

"You're not wanting," said Sir Hugh, his voice calm and calming, "to tell us something."

"Hoot, hoot, hoot," said the laird's tired voice, "I failed thee," and then, "I failed to open the door." Then only silence.

"He knocked," said Sir Hugh.

A nodded hoary head.

"Fear?" I queried.

"No," Sir Hugh responded with a frown, "pride."

Mc Mc-Mc began to sob.

"No Mc Mc-Mc," Sir Hugh continued, "has ever opened a door

for himself. I am sorry," a hand laid light on the laird's shaking shoulder, "I should have known."

Our venerable friend, suddenly looking his many years, tugged at his filibeg and began to weep unabashedly as I sympathized with Sir Hugh's worry and admired the courage of his kindness, for, unless the case were settled that very night, we would be forced to miss our train and Sir Hugh his birthday appearance in the test matches in London. As Sandy Mc Mc-Mc's sobs subsided, Sir Hugh, an expression of confusion and increasing doubt creasing his face, turned and began wolfing down the butterless oat biscuits on the small table before the waning fire.

Standing there in that wavering light, listening to the frenzied chewing and swallowing, punctuated with sighs and actual groans, of Sir Hugh, I was suddenly startled into total alertness by a heavy pounding which echoed through the hollow halls from the front door below. At Sir Hugh's fingered signal, I leapt out of the room and down the winding stairs, past the dim portraits of generations of scowling Mc Mc-Mcs in battle dress or leaning on knurred staffs, to the door, threw back the brass latches, flung the door inward, and stared into the foggy darkness.

The damp and blustering figure, his gray mustaches aquiver and jowls red and veined with excitement, of Lord Fairfax Dowlong-Drungways stamped into the hall.

"You," I managed, backing toward the curving stairs.

"Yes, damme," he replied, glancing wildly about, "I've news for Fitz-Hyffen."

"I understand," I said, leading him up the steep stairs, across the wide hall, and into the dim room where Sir Hugh, one hand resting lightly on the empty serving tray, and Sandy Mc Mc-Mc silently sat.

"Mc Mc-Mc," nodded Lord Dowlong-Drungways pleasantly. Then, with a rising inflection, "Sir Hugh."

Sir Hugh arose, extended his right hand, his left dipping unobtrusively into the pocket where I knew the new handcuffs lay, and stepped to Lord Dowlong-Drungways, the two, such a striking contrast in bearing and stature, shaking hands in the manner that the elder of the two had acquired in the Americas.

"Nigel," said Lord Dowlong-Drungways.

"Yes," said Sir Hugh.

"But, no," came the reply. Then, "You see," a pause in which all of our breaths were stilled, "there was a mistress."

Sir Hugh, his mouth popped open, sat suddenly back, arms and legs unbecomingly akimbo.

"She," he managed to say. "An American," another pause as Lord Dowlong-Drungways's face reddened even more, "but she is known as Pearl de Paon, a young thing, plays the virginal and sings with the voice . . . the voice, I must say, of an angel, but a demon child, scarcely fourteen . . . eyes, limbs." Then, brushing his face with a large becrested handkerchief, "Both lithe and clever . . . exceedingly so for her years." He would say no more.

As later we, at Sir Hugh's suggestion, stepped out of the house into the cold and wet night, wrapped now in tartan rainwear from Mc Mc-Mc's amply endowed closets, proposing to visit the enchanting and precocious Mlle. de Paon, an event occurred which so changed the course of our lives that we never met that mysterious creature, not even after Lord Dowlong-Drungways, in the goodness of his nature, took her into his childless and lonely home as his ward, giving her the best of everything in memory of his lost son. In the darkness, as we stood discussing our mode of transport, one of the servants of the house, who had been returning woozily from the village and the Memories of '45 Inn, ran up to us, shouting almost incoherently about a dead man and a black man just down the road.

Needless to say, at a cry of "Quick, gentlemen," from Sir Hugh, we, all of us, broke into a run, Lord Dowlong-Drungways lagging behind, hindered by his gout, down the twisting drive to the rutted highroad, where, by one of the deep ditches on the sides of the road, a large and dark figure stood, staring down into the ditch at another figure, elegantly dressed but sprawled awkwardly, its head crushed nearly beyond recognition. Humber Baboo, as the erect figure proved to be, turned to us in the gloom, an enormous and bloody stone held in his black, strong hands. A cavity yawned in one of the stone pillars which stood sentinel on either side of the drive leading up to Mc Mc-Mc Manor from which, apparently, the death stone had come.

"Farqhart," muttered Sir Hugh, staring down at the crumpled figure in the ditch and then looking at the stone in Humber Baboo's capable hands, those hands with the stone rising ominously.

"Picked it up, eh?" Sir Hugh said quickly, looking up at the grisly stone now high above his head. Then, to us, "Nasty accident."

"Yes," continued Sir Hugh, stepping carefully back, his hand rising to afford a prop for his pointed chin, "an accident." Then musingly, "Or, perhaps, one should call it," an effective pause, heightening the drama of this already histrionic moment, "justice."

The faint whine of the pipes sounded then, floating up to us, over the round hills, from the village, as Lord Dowlong-Drungways, panting and grunting, hobbled up, stared for a moment at the crushed corpse, and turned to Sir Hugh.

"Who?" he said.

Sir Hugh, smiling grimly, spoke, quietly and firmly, to him. "I don't," he said, "think that we need be troubled any more by the Dowlong-Drungways murderer."

As Sir Hugh paused, Humber Baboo, forgetful in the excitement engendered by that moment of awesome truth, released the fatal stone, which fell with a leathery crunch to the gouty foot of Lord Dowlong-Drungways. Even now, I am often awakened in a cold sweat from sleep by the recollection in some otherwise innocent dream of that hideous shriek of pain.

In the early, following, dawn, after a sleepless remainder of the night, Esther Plum, as she preferred to be called ("Nigel," she explained, "would have wanted it this way"), called for us and accompanied us to the railway station in an elegant barouche driven by Humber Baboo, tumescent with pride in his resplendent Dowlong-Drungways livery, sneering at the few gaping Scottish peasants that we passed along the way.

The morning was so misty that, from our coach window, we could scarcely see Miss Plum, even with her sleek scarlet wrap, or the towering Baboo beside her.

"Luck at Lord's," she called out, having the grace to remember, as the express began slowly to move out, its driving wheels spinning for an explosive second on the slick tracks. As the train began to gain speed, we faintly saw (or seemed to see) Humber Baboo place his arm around her waist, his large black hand in startling complement to her blazing scarlet, no doubt, as Sir Hugh remarked, to steady her in her grief—their bright figures in the mist, so sombre was it, the one ever glowing point of light gloomier than the shadow.

And in the suburbs, beneath a blue suburban sky, on a warm spring afternoon with wavering butterflies and the steady hum of June bugs, walking slowly because of the weight of his paper bag with its gaudy orange reflecting strap, a young paperboy, past puberty but not far, was making his rounds, folding, snapping the small green rubber bands in place, and tossing the papers in easy arcs across lawns and curving flagstone walks onto stoops, each stoop alike, each lawn, each curving flagstone walk. Curly-haired and towheaded, freckled and grinning wide to one and all, this boy brought the news: STRANGE ODORS PLAGUE CITY, PEACE STILL IN SIGHT BELLIGERENTS ASSERT, EXECUTION SCHEDULED, RECORD BROKEN IN LATEST ATTEMPT, SILVER HANDS ON DISPLAY AT PROSTHETICS CONVENTION, SLUM CLEARANCE ON SCHEDULE, and NEWARK MOTHER PUNISHES CHILD WITH PORTABLE ELECTRIC MIXER.

History in the making, as it were; time's relentless motion, ebb and flow, caught in black and white and rolled out for this small boy to deliver. The news this day was little different, the usual, but the afternoon was to prove momentous for the boy, the beginning of something which would mark him forever.

Such events are always simple at first. History makes itself slowly and reveals itself as slowly, the claims of all best-selling prophets to the contrary. A peek here, a glimpse there, something doing, and then suddenly the whole truth, exposed and shameless for all to see who have eyes to see.

The boy had finished, or nearly finished, collecting the money owed him on his route the Saturday before, but one door had not opened, had remained closed despite the giggles and squeals which had issued from behind the impassive wood whenever he had rapped.

This simple event marks the beginning of the adventure, of the unveiling, and introduces Miss Shirley Ease, the initial agent of truth.

Miss Ease had always paid promptly upon demand in the weeks prior to her refusal to open up, at least to the boy's demanding rap, and she had always seemed a nice enough sort to him. Her hair was of a bright platinum color, and she did chew gum even as she talked, a trait, the boy had been taught in third grade, which was undeniably bovine and inexcusably impolite, but she always paid and even bantered about the weather in the winter when the snow made walking a slippery (if delightful) chore or in the summer when sweat often ran in rivulets down the boy's cheeks. She was, she had said, a receptionist and aide for and to Dr. Oswald H. Omwake, M.D., whose office, she said, she literally ran for the poor man. He was a proctologist or gynecologist, she said, but she never could get it quite straight which, but then six of one and a dozen of the other, as she always said with a wink. She liked her paper so that when she got home in the evening, she said, she could soak her feet in a hot tub with bubbles and nothing else at all on, she said, and read the news. She always took her bath, she said, at paper time for that reason, and she had mentioned that the door was always open and perhaps he would like, she said, to bring the paper in to her sometime when he had the time. That would be a pleasure, she said, but the boy's route was long and far from his home, so he had had to apologize and say that no, he couldn't.

There was, in fact, nothing at all unusual about Miss Ease that he could see, until the other day when the door was so unaccountably locked and the giggles and squeals had flowed out to him around it. But he thought little about the occurrence and went on to collect the rest of his route so as to be able to get home early enough to do his chores before dinner.

Simple enough, but when you don't collect one day, you must the next—a simple truth history had already revealed to him. So when he reached 2100 on the street called Life, he carried the paper up to the door rather than tossing it and knocked on the familiar wooden panels. Rap-rap-rap-rap-rap, pause, rap-rap. The ancient tonsorial signal of youth across the countryside.

No answer, so he knocked again, and this time the door opened just a crack, and the familiar voice of Miss Ease, although a bit strained and hesitant, asked, "Who is it? It's not you again is it, Leon?"

"No, ma'am," the boy replied, chipper and efficient, holding no grudges. "It's just me, the paperboy."

A silence, the door remaining open ever so slightly, followed that exchange of information.

"I missed you Saturday," he continued, "and I've got to collect. I hope I didn't get you up or anything."

"Oh," said Miss Ease, and opened the door wider with the clatter of a small chain's removal. "Just a minute, kid, huh?" Then she added, "You can come on in and wait in the cool."

The boy didn't feel particularly hot, but he stepped politely into the room beyond the door. He stood for a quiet moment waiting for his eyes to adjust to the dark, for dark it was and musty. All the blinds were tightly closed, and, as his eyes made the slow transition, the boy became a little bit nervous.

The room was in considerable disarray; that was the first impression his narrowing pupils gave him. There were ashes and the butts of cigarettes piled deep in saucers and ashtrays around the room, more of those receptacles by far than there was furnishing. Two chairs, a small coffee table, a sofa, on the sofa satin sheets in bunches and wads, large gold coins that he yearned to inspect but dared not

53

(probably just gold foil, candy perhaps, he thought) scattered around the sofa, two pictures on the wall (one of an Alpine scene complete with a tiny Heidi and two goats with an Alp-uncle in the foreground, and the other of three women who seemed to be dancing and wearing very little), and one tufted footstool.

"Sorry about the mess, kid," said Miss Ease from the next room, "but I been home sick all weekend and I haven't been able to pick up or anything. It seems like I've been flat on my back for months."

The boy did not reply, and then there she was in a pink peignoir with white panties and brassiere clearly visible through the folds, holding out seventy-five cents in change and saying, "Here."

The boy stood stock-still, eyes agape and mouth slowly opening, stuck fast on the white and pink cloth, the skin, Miss Ease's navel like a little scar, a dimple, a fairy's mouth. He said nothing, did nothing, stared, and could not move or look away.

"Hey, kid," said Miss Ease, "not today, huh? Like I said, I'm on sick leave and I feel awful bad. Some other day, huh?"

She pressed the three quarters into his palm, folded the small hand around the coins, and pushed the boy back to the door and out of it. He did not resist, walked out like a stunned calf on the chute at the abattoir, and stood on the stoop staring at the bare arm as it gave him a last push and retreated back inside the door.

"Gee, kid, I'm sorry," said Miss Ease. "I sure don't mean to be rude or anything, but some other day, huh? When I ain't sick?"

The walls were dead white, as smooth and unwrinkled as reams of paper, whiter than newsprint, slick and shining and clean, broken almost imperceptibly by four corners, the ceiling line, and the fine lines of the flush doors. Pudd had no power here. It was his room, and he sat on a white metal stool in the center of it, hunched on the cold stool, red and raw, naked, one arm hanging limp, the hand resting on his case, the other hand cushioning his testicles from the cold metal. It was his room, this chill, white cube, but in it he could open no doors, could only wait for the familiar whir and click before a blank section of the wall would slide open, a signal for his next action.

It was all familiar to him, the clinical whiteness, the routine. He was at ease. He had come this night through the usual door in the walls, small with a grilled iron window, had used his own key, put his back against the door and bulged it in, heavy and complaining, and shoved it closed with a boom that caused shivers in the cell blocks, hairs to prickle on even the guards' necks, and a moment's cold silence to fall through the hot, dark air. He had pocketed the heavy key in his jersey with the frayed envelope, walked across the gravel to another door which opened before him and shut after him, and climbed the narrow dark stairs, stumbling once where the stone had crumbled, up into the old tower, the ancient part of the prison where honor and ignominy had so often met the same end in history, to wait finally before a blank wall in the impenetrable dark.

The brightness of his room was a shock; he always blinked continually for the first few minutes in it, his eyes struggling for a grip on the glare. This time the shock had seemed even worse, but he had followed the routine without complaining or faltering, had waited for the wall to close behind him, for the click of another door opening before him, had shed his clothes and hung them carefully on the hooks in the small closet, had put his shoes on its floor and stepped back as the door sealed the wall again.

Another whir and click, and Pudd stood up, walked toward the new opening, still cradling his tender organs until he needed both hands to open the white drawers and remove the jerseys, tights, and hoods, clean, pressed, and neatly folded. He closed the drawers, turned, and walked back to the stool, listening to the closing door and to the sounds of another panel sliding open behind him revealing a mirror; he did not turn to see.

He placed the pile of clothes on the stool and began to dress, first the white cotton tights, up over his knees and around his belly, his legs now white and smooth, the muscles shapely, the groin a healthy bulge, and then the jersey, over his head, pulling it down to meet and slide into the tights, then pulling the knit sleeves down to his wrists, shifting his body, flexing the cloth into a proper fit. And then the hood, over his head, tucking it all round into the neck of the jersey, tugging at it until the eyeholes were centered properly and the nose tucked through the hole and able to breathe again.

He turned to meet himself in the mirror, eight feet tall, containing him full and all, a white figure of a man, smooth and taut, his bare feet and rough hands red and out of place, but his head in place, the jaw sinister and strong, hard and firm, the nose too red, and the eyes dark and illegible. Satisfied with his double's trim, breathing in, he thumped his chest twice quickly and turned back to the stool. On it lay another hood, another jersey and tights, these a black mesh, nylon, a fine mesh, smooth to the eye, but upon closer examination a black net which passed light only weakly, diffusely. This black suit Pudd pulled on in the same order as the white, so thin that it slid over his body smoothly, making him look no bulkier than before, but ominous now, a substantial shadow of the white inner self, heavy and somber. He stared in the mirror again and, as always, knew himself for what he appeared to be.

The mirror closed, and from another door Pudd took the black boots and pulled them on. There would be now only one more door, so he knelt beside his case, laid it over gently on its side, snapped its latches, and opened its lid. The interior was blue velvet, soft and thick, its sheen rich and dark against the white floor, and in cushioned grooves lay the ax, its heavy head and glistening edge, the handle in three pieces, ready to be screwed together into a balanced whole.

Pudd grunted very slightly as he lifted the head and examined it, let his vision touch the blade edge lightly but not his thumb, for once he had touched it very gingerly with his thumb, as gently as a butterfly's trembling on a lily's lip, a spring breeze on a baby's cheek, and had drawn blood, a red stain that blossomed on his white jersey thumb, that had soaked through the black mesh and smeared the handle of the ax. Harding had been angry, very angry, and Pudd had never touched the blade again before a performance. He lifted out the first piece of the handle and, holding the heavy head, blade up, on his knee, screwed it into place. The handle was of an aluminum alloy so that he could hold and turn its pieces quickly and easily. He screwed the other two parts onto the handle and, easing the head to the floor, handle up, tightened the joints and then the safety sleeves which screwed and locked over the joints. He stood up then, squeezed his hands around the handle, gripped them, and swung the ax up until it poised over his head, straight up, unwavering, no tremble in his arms or legs.

He lowered it after a moment, leaned it against the stool, and stooping, reached into the case, removed his gloves and pulled them on, black leather, supple and skin tight. He straightened up again, faced about, and looked at a door opening in the wall, revealing a long, dim corridor and two small figures, two men, one in a blue-serge business suit and the other a policeman, uniformed, his buttons shining, but with no cap, the handle of his pistol bright with polish and disuse at his hip. Pudd lifted the ax, balanced it on his right shoulder, his right hand on the handle, his left arm cocked on his hip, and walked toward the door and the men, a black figure, but at the door, the fine stipple of white gleaming through the black mesh, silhouetted against the white interior, a hollow figure, the white wall seeming to shine through the black mesh as if there were nothing at all inside.

They walked down the hall, the three abreast, the door clicking shut behind them, their heels popping a rattling rhythm down and up the hall before and after them. The warden, small and gray in his blue suit, his head shiny and bald, spoke to Pudd with a voice quiet and clipped:

"You are fit, I assume. You'd better be this time. This time is special. You'd better be perfect. One slip and you are through. I can tolerate no more errors. I am a patient man. But I am also known as a just man. I am patient, and I have been patient with you. I am just, and I have been and shall continue to be just with you. Do your task cleanly and well, and I shall continue to be patient. Make an error, even the smallest of errors, and you are through, over, finished, out —stamped, sealed, and delivered."

He snapped his fingers against his thumb, one more sharp pop in the echoing hall. They continued to walk at a steady pace. Pudd's eyes shifted sharply to the left and down to the glistening bald head and the thin, gray neck of Warden Harding.

As they reached a wall at the end of the long corridor, it opened inward, and they were able to enter the anteroom of the amphitheater. It was small and gray, no seats, no windows, no ornament of any kind. Through the closed door before them, Pudd could hear dimly, through the rushing blood in his ears, the rumble of muffled drums, the ceaseless rumble of the long dead roll. The door opened, and the warden, then the policeman, and then Pudd, slowly, ever so slowly, paced out into the bright light and hot air of the crowded amphitheater.

The room was large, one wall curving with the outer wall of the old tower, a semicircle of banked seats, row on row, faces with wide eyes, the faces of old men and eager women, of children pop-eyed and open-mouthed, of police officials and professionally bored reporters, and all eyes were on Pudd, black Pudd and his heavy, glistening ax.

The drum roll quickened and grew louder as a door at the opposite end of the wide stage from Pudd opened, as two guards in dress blue stepped in and turned facing each other on both sides of the door, and reached a loud plateau as the prisoner entered, dressed in a plain white robe, falling straight from the neck with long sleeves loose at the shoulder and tight at the wrists, her hair long and blond as cornsilk, her eyes sharp green and bright, her lips tight and still. She crossed the wide stage, a cassocked priest humming at her heels, walking quickly to keep up, and she stopped at the block, looked down at it and, then, startled, worried for the first time, around the stage, around the room, her eyes flitting from face to face and finally lighting on the warden's bright skull. He walked over to her as she began to speak, Pudd following, and she continued to speak, quickly and angrily, to the warden until Pudd stopped beside the block, swung his ax off his shoulder and lowered it to the block, for as it touched the block the drums stopped and she was suddenly speaking to the silence and the whole room, her voice like flawed crystal, thin but ringing pure:

". . . French. I was promised velvet on which to kneel, and I was promised a sword and swordsman to whom I would not have to bow. No common ax shall touch my neck. I am betrayed in my confidence. I will not have it. I will not."

The warden was upset, pulled his flustered hands in and out of his pockets, nervous and annoyed before the silent audience. He whispered to the prisoner and then turned suddenly to Pudd: "Have you ever used a sword?"

Pudd slowly, as he was always supposed to move on the stage until the delivery of the blow itself, nodded his head no. "And, sir," said the policeman, sweat popping out on head and hands, "I don't think we have a sword heavy enough."

"Then, get one," hissed Harding.

A long, silent pause. Midnight passed. The room was quiet, but members of the audience shifted in their seats, the warden fidgeted, and Pudd looked steadily at the prisoner, whose eyes never left his. A long, unbroken moment. He saw her small ears through her fine hair, her eyebrows, her narrow smooth nose, no sign of her body's form beneath the heavy robe, hands delicate and clenched, and her eyes, always her green clear eyes, unblinking, expressionless, never leaving the eyeholes of his impermeable hood.

A sword was found and brought, a tall sword, blunt-ended, heavy and unpolished. A guard carried off the ax as Pudd stared after it and hefted the sword in his hands. He wanted to test one of its double edges with his thumb, both, but dared not. They looked dull, broad and unhoned; the handle was metal and plain, no figures, gems, or carved faces. The warden and the prisoner whispered together, and she knelt before the block, her back to the audience, her face to the flat, gray wall. A guard undid her robe at the collar and opened it down over her shoulders, leaving them bare and the hair spilling over her smooth, white back.

"She refuses to put her head on the block," the warden whispered. "Strike horizontally, and do not miss." He walked quickly away with the priest and the policeman. Pudd and the prisoner were completely alone at the center of the stage.

The lights dimmed, leaving a bright spot around the block. The drums began again. Pudd's body and his hands were soaked with sweat; his eyes blurred with the salty sting. He raised the sword, rested the flat of the blade on his shoulder; the drums quickened. He took an open stance, his feet spread beside and a little behind the prisoner, to the left of her heels. The robe slipped of its own weight on her shoulder, and he could see a breast, firm and smooth, the nipple swollen and cochineal. No sweat slicked its rounded surface. Pudd raised the sword, tightened his grip. A guard hastened from

60

the darkness and parted the prisoner's hair, letting it slide over her shoulders, baring the nape of her neck and draping her exposed breast in silken waves; he left as quickly as he had come. Pudd swung the blade down to shoulder level, cocked straight back toward the audience, sighted at her neck with his stinging eyes, and swung.

His muscles whipped the sword around hard, and it hit with a crack. He had swung high and opened the back of her head, splitting it and almost wrenching the sword from his hands. The drums stopped and then sputtered to life again as Pudd pulled the sword back, bloodied and dull. The prisoner had fallen forward to the block, but she jerked erect, the back of her head open, gray, draining a colorless fluid and leaking blood, the whole back of her robe suddenly red with it, staining the floor behind her. A woman screamed in the audience, and in the rush of drums and the rising noise of the darkened crowd, Pudd swung again, quickly and hard.

This time he struck the neck, knocking the prisoner forward to her knees onto the block, but with the head still not severed, hanging on by tendons and a shred of flesh. The drums stammered and rattled; a stick dropped on the hard floor and clattered out into the circle of light. Pudd raised the sword, blood dripping down onto his hooded head and shoulders, and struck again, over and down, severing the mangled head and its tangled mass of hair and also the prisoner's right hand from her arm, which had been lying on the block beside her head where she had fallen.

The prisoner's body staggered back and up, turned headless to the screaming audience, blood spouting from the split throat down and over the hard breasts, the stained robe hanging about her hips, stepped rigidly once, twice, and fell, splayed out, a pool of blood forming at the neck, another at the bleeding wrist.

The drums stopped at last and Pudd stood motionless, the sword fallen at his feet. He listened to the chaos of the crowd, a chiaroscuro of horror and delight; he once thought he heard a dog barking and barking, but he could not trust his pounding ears.

The warden stepped gingerly across the bloody floor as the house lights came up again. He stooped and grasped the slippery hair of the severed head, but it came away in his hand, hung a blond wig draining onto the floor until he dropped it behind the block and grasped the head again, this time with both hands, by its close-cropped and gray-white hair. He turned to the audience and held it high, the face, that of a cruel and embittered old woman, lined and twisted, hateful and hating.

"God save us all!" he cried in the usual fashion. "So perish all who dare oppose the rule of law!"

The doors at the rear of the amphitheater opened, and the audience began to push its way up and out. Pudd remained standing, motionless and unmoved. The warden walked up to him, still holding the head awkwardly by its short hair, its eyes glaring into Pudd's.

"Pudd," he hissed, tears of anger on his cheeks, his bald head flashing, "you are through. As an executioner, you are a nothing!"

Needless to say, Albert Longinus was less steady on his feet on exiting the Dagon Arms Apartments than he had been on entering. He walked across the sidewalk and climbed into the truck. Fortunately the musical loudspeaker ran on its own battery, so that, despite the draining basso groan of the continuing song, the truck started immediately and began its slow voyage into dark and nighttime Newark. Albert tossed the empty laundry bag into the Dirty part of the truck even though Miss Parker had had no wash to be washed.

In the night, Newark is as oppressive as by day, dirty, dark, ominous in every shadow and dark alleyway. Albert was thirsty, and he was behind on his rounds. There was nothing to do but go back to the garage, check in, and get an early start in the gray morning to come. He switched off the loudspeaker in the middle of a growled "Crud," and drove silently and stealthily the rest of the way through the New Jersey night.

The garage of the laundry was closed when Albert pulled up, so, leaving the motor idling and the lights very much on, he got out of the truck and opened the garage door with his own key. He ran back to the truck after swinging the door up and away, and drove quickly into the dark interior. Again with the motor still idling and the lights still on, he ran back, shut the garage door, and turned on the overhead lighting system.

Dirty yellow light filled the large and greasy room with its row upon row of green trucks and the empty loading platform. Albert pulled his truck up alongside the platform, turned off the engine, and turned to the unloading of his wash. Seventeen heavy bags, lumped on the platform, dirty towels and shirts, sheets and bedspreads, pillowcases, underwear, blouses and dresses, play togs and uniforms, all dirty, all waiting to be cleaned on the morrow, Albert's precious cargo safe at dock.

Only one full sack had a note, a torn piece of paper with the usual message:

> Dear Mr. Laundryman,
> No starch in the pyjamas please as it makes my husband nervous and irritable so he cant sleep nights which effects his work and also makes him lie awake and think of new ways to "bother" me all night long so I dont get any rest neither.
>
> Thanx.
>
> Mrs. Quickly

A fake. Albert's practiced eye, seven years in the training, caught that immediately. He could always tell a joker by the style, the handwriting, the pulpy tablet paper, something; how they got these notes into his truck he did not know, but they were always there, or usually—at least two or three times a week, a ringer. And on the backs of the notes, other messages, some obviously also frauds, others real notes, forgotten by the prankster, enigmatic clues to the unknown hand or hands, delphic, sibylline, a code he had not yet managed to break.

He turned the note from "Mrs. Quickly" over to find writing in another hand, a masculine hand, no backslant as on the other side, firm, upright, eminently sane. It was a book list of some kind, normal at first glance but then somehow askew, distorted, with books Albert did not know or did not recognize, disguised, concealed, metamorphosed. He read the list entire:

THE GLASS COLIN by Cage Wilson
THE WRONG MOSS by Stanley Angel
FEEL SLAVITT by David Free
PAINTED GERTRUDE by Lace Stein
THE DEER MAILER by Norman Park
GULLS OVER CRONAN by M. Memphis Minton
OTTO OF THE SILVER PYLE by Howard Hand
THE SAX OF FU MANCHU by Hand Rohmer
THE TIN JAY by William Can Smith
BELLOW by Saul Herzog
HOWL by Allen Ginsberg
BUCKDANCER'S DICKEY by James Choice
THE GOLDEN RUBIN by Louis Weather
THE WRONG STANLEY by Angel Moss
THE FLOATING JOHN by Opera Barth
THE BRAZEN JOHN by Head Cowper Powys
JOHN THE GREAT by Otho Keats
BAD DAY IN BADENBECK by John Roden-Baden
THE BOOK OF DILLARDS by R. H. W. Change
FRED'S RIDE by Ossian Hoyle
IT IS TIME, FRED by Lord Chappell
JAMES JIM by Lord Conrad
DO, GEORGE, REMEMBER ME by Lord Garrett
RICHARD TODAY by Lawd Wright
ROBERT OTTO by Prince Louis Stevenson
THE RIVET IN GRANDFATHER'S NECK by James
    Branch Cabell

The list entirely read but no clearer, Opera Barth just did not sound right, but the others seemed reasonable enough. He sat down on the edge of the platform and began to read the list again, one last, slow, and careful time before going home and putting it in his scrapbook of fraudulent messages, where it might, he thought, make more sense in context, although most of the others didn't.

He was interrupted, however, by a loud cry just at his left ear, shrill and demoniac, and a fierce cackle that froze the marrow of his bones quite to the quick.

"Ah ha," the cry said, "caught you red-handed, you laundry thief. Put up your hands or you're a dead man."

Albert vaulted off the loading platform and spun around, landing with his back to the truck. Above him in the yellow was a wizened old man with one eye, the other a gaping socket, alive with jerking muscle as he turned his good eye one way and the other.

"Who are you?" he cried, shrill like a ravening bird.

"Nobody," said Albert, disgusted as he recognized the night watchman, an old man, cousin to the manager's wife, hired more out of pity than genuine nepotism, allowed to carry a pistol but loaded only with blanks, old, helpless, and more than half blind.

"Ah ha," the old creature shrilled again, and leapt from the platform, landing head first in Albert's chest, knocking him back into the truck and down onto the greasy floor.

"Burglar," he cried, "Thief," and "Robber." And they tangled and tussled on the gummy floor, writhing in the grease, staggering almost erect and falling back, the old man's bony fingers and slicing fingernails probing at Albert's eyes, clawing his ears, and tearing the back of his shirt to ribbons, his knee firmly in Albert's groin, grinding and unrelenting, and his jagged gums popping around Albert's nose and face.

Finally Albert managed to stand up, back against the truck, the old man slung on him like an angry squid, all over and around him, leviathan and behemoth in his fragile form. Looking around wildly, Albert managed to fling the old man off, to hurl him onto the platform and the laundry bags with a force sufficient to pound an ordinary man windless and limp, but the old man seemed renewed and

66

returned to the attack, grappling at Albert and pulling him to the platform and then up on it.

They wrestled on, one up and one down, the reverse, over and under, tumbling and bumbling among the laundry bags. Once again Albert lifted him high in his arms, the old man's fingers groping at his ears, leaving raw slivers behind them, and hurled him to the bags, and again the old man rose up renewed.

They grappled on the edge of the platform, teetering on the edge, wavering over the truck and the hard concrete below. Albert squeezed the old man to him, feeling the thin ribs cutting into his chest and arms, and then turned him loose. Surprisingly, the old man did not press the attack immediately, but fell back on the laundry bags, panting. Albert stood over him, hot and angry, torn and tired. Then suddenly, the old man sprang at his legs, biting at his groin, teeth tangling in his metal zipper, and Albert had to roll back and over, an obscene somersault, the old man flopping over after him, teeth still clenched, like an enormous and ugly codpiece. Then Albert crawled to his knees with the old man still attached, and on up to his feet, and he shook then like a wild stripper doing the grinds and bumps of her life, the last and wild swan dance of a demented Tempest Storm. The old man hung on for shake after shake and then finally let go, leaving Albert's zipper dangling and his underwear exposed. Albert quickly picked him up as he began to crawl for the laundry bags, squeezed him, back to Albert's chest, and held him aloft and kicking.

The old man squirmed, his hands raking at Albert's sides, and filing his fingers to blood and bone, but Albert held on until soon the old man's struggles subsided and he hung limp in Albert's arms. Strong with rage, bold with anger, Albert raised him aloft and hurled him across the bags and into a large metal door opening into the drying rooms. The old man bounced off the door, jarring its lock and opening it. A blast of hot air smote the room like a titanic fist, hurling Albert across the platform, over onto the roof of his truck, and off onto the floor.

He crouched in the shelter of the truck, watching the dust whirl and roar about the large garage, carrying loose items of laundry torn from the bags across the floor and among the green trucks. Soon the dim yellow light was blanked out in the wind, hot and littered with dust and grit, cloth and paper. A piece of paper smacked into Albert's eyes, and he pulled it off. It was still light enough to see that it was the strange book list. He tucked it into a jacket pocket and turned to run across the littered and twisting garage. He reached the outside door after bouncing from truck to truck, falling and crawling, and wrenched it open to fall out onto the sidewalk, tumbling over in another somersault into the gutter.

He managed to stand up and start running down the street, clutching his fly together and hunched over against the alien night. The open hollow behind him howled and bellowed into the Newark streets, but he did not go back to shut the door.

Auranthe (Mrs. Conrad) Franconia of 2102 Life Street was the first to call to her neighbors' attention the strange goings on at 2100 Life Street, the home of Miss Shirley Ease—goings on having to do with the paperboy, a neighborhood favorite, that fine and earnest lad.

She reported to her neighbor on the other side, the widow Mrs. Olivia Limpy, across the privet hedge one long warm evening, that the paperboy seemed to be delivering Miss Ease's paper to her door by hand, that he seemed to take a long time doing it, and that when he left the premises, he was usually whistling and often did a little step (she demonstrated) on the curving flagstone walk.

Mrs. Limpy, needless to say, since the early and sudden death of Mr. Limpy in 1937 during the Court Packing Crisis had left her childless, was concerned and promised to pass the word along.

And she did.

The word circulated up and down the block, wandering from hedge to fence to kitchen, making its way down into the center of town and through a maze of circuits and switches and finally back across the street called Life by way of telephonic impulses along the lines. Pete Peters heard of it on the way from the bus stop to his front door, but was careful to tell his wife Mary only after their little Maggie was safely tucked in and half, if not fast, asleep. But she heard, nonetheless, and Betsy Harding bore the news to her dad and mom, Warren and Nan, who well might have missed out on it otherwise, what with the neighborhood suspicion, seldom voiced but always understood, concerning their exact racial status. Even Daphne Sanders got the word at the supermarket from Mrs. Limpy, although in less trying times the respectable widow made a point of avoiding both young Daphne and her "trial husband" Mike Venning.

The word got around, eventually to every house on the block on both sides of the street, except maybe to the old corner "mansion" of the seldom seen Alfred Omega, for no one really knew just exactly what he did or didn't know (although it usually seemed to be a lot). So it was no surprise, then, when, on one late spring evening at the Our Own Block Home Improvement League and Environmental Protection Association, which was meeting in Mr. Oscar Wilde's colorful living room at 2114 Life Street, the subject broke into the open, came, in fact, onto the floor for action.

Miss Shirley Ease was, like the Hardings, not a member of the League. The Bartholomews, Fred and Frederica, had moved once that she be invited to join, but the motion had been tabled after a lengthy session of lively if futile debate. Miss Ease just didn't seem right somehow, with her airs and occasional carryings on. So there was little difficulty involved when a morally aroused Mrs. Limpy broached the subject. The ground was, after all, familiar.

"I suggest," said Mrs. Limpy, "that that hussy, and you all know just who I mean, is seducing that darling little boy, and you all know it."

The meeting professed to be shocked.

Debate followed, punctuated by heated demands that the parliamentarian (Mr. Z. B. D. James, the well-known writer of western novels) make ruling after ruling, and, as was most often the case, debate engendered little more than hard feelings. Mr. Oscar Wilde scurried about the room, passing peanuts, his homemade *quiche*

Lorraine, and refilling the glasses of root beer and Cold Bear wine. But all to little avail, as debate continued and voices and tempers rose.

Dr. St. John John, in a statement of dubious sincerity, said that he would hesitate to (splitting his infinitive) first cast a stone at her, but the mood of the meeting was such that his words cast little weight themselves, although his neighbors on his side of the street (not, it must be said, Miss Ease's) appeared generally to be in agreement with him.

Finally, Mrs. Limpy settled the debate she had begun by making a motion. "I propose," she said, "that we form ourselves into a committee of the whole and call on Miss Ease right this very minute and ask her to her face to explain herself and her disgraceful behavior."

"I second the motion," said Mr. Herbert Hoover, who had always wanted to call on Miss Ease, but had been restrained by shyness, being a bachelor of forty-three and a virgin to boot.

The motion, after having been reworded for clarity several times, passed unanimously, and the Committee of the Whole to Call on Miss Ease moved out of Mr. Wilde's living room, through his yellow hallway, out of the door, down the curving flagstone walk, and, like a loose-limbed parade (each member his own drummer), down the street to the very door of Miss Shirley Ease.

Mrs. Limpy and Mr. Franconia led the way, and Mr. Hoover and Mr. Michael Venning brought up the rear. Mr. Hoover was particularly pleased that Mr. Venning had come to the meeting instead of his companion, Miss Sanders, for, ever since the day when he had seen Mr. Venning hanging a pair of pink nylon bikini panties on the clothes line back of their house and, dizzy and flushed, had had to rush into his own house before he could take himself in hand, he had been particularly shy of the attractive Miss Sanders. But for Mr. Venning he felt a bond, a fellowship of sorts, inexplicable but real, and he sought out his company at the end of the procession both as a result of his shy feelings toward Miss Ease and as an expression of that good fellow feeling.

"How nice to see you," said a startled Miss Ease after answering Mr. Franconia's stern rap on the door. "Won't you come in?" She removed her gum and placed it carefully behind her right ear.

The Committee allowed as how they could conduct their business outside, especially since Miss Ease's stoop light was on and was shedding its light over the lawn in the gathering dusk. They asked her bluntly then about the boy and his strange behavior.

"What are you doing to him?" demanded Mrs. Limpy.

Miss Ease was at first offended, but under the pressure of the entire neighborhood assembled, she relented.

"He told me about his life," she said. "He's an orphan, living with his grandparents. They don't have much money, not even enough to buy him any presents. Just food, clothes, and the rent. Why, he hasn't even seen a movie."

The Committee stirred and was moved.

"Go on," said Mrs. Limpy, still stern but beginning to gather a little dampness in the corner of each eye.

"So I found a way I could give him a little pleasure," Miss Ease continued.

The Committee moved forward a step as one.

"I, well, I, you see, the first time was by accident, but he liked it so much, you could tell, that . . ."

"Go on," said the Committee as one.

"Well," Miss Ease inhaled and continued, "I do a little modeling act for him. I, I show him clothes that he wouldn't be able to see anywhere else."

The Committee breathed a communal sigh of relief, but Mrs. Limpy dissented.

"Show me," she said.

After further debate back and forth, Mr. Hoover in a shadowy affirmative from the rear of the Committee, Miss Ease was persuaded to give a sample of one of her little modeling acts. She retired, some were later to say angrily, to her house, and reappeared some minutes later, spotlighted by her stoop light in the now nighttime darkness, wearing a pink peignoir, semi-transparent, a white brassiere (Cross-

Your-Heart) and white panties, not scanty in the least, but underwear nonetheless. Garter straps hung down on her bare thighs from under the panties.

At the sight of those, to him, arcane devices, Mr. Herbert Hoover fainted dead away.

"Well, I never," said Mrs. Limpy, finally getting her astonished breath back.

"Nor I," said Mr. Franconia, polishing eyeglasses quickly, but not quickly enough, for Miss Ease had gone back in, shut her door, and snapped off her stoop light, leaving the whole Committee literally in the dark.

THE CHINESE MOONSTONE SECRET DOCUMENTS
SPY ADVENTURE

> *So the years pass, and repeat*
> *each other; so the same events*
> *revolve in the cycles of time.*
> *What will be the next adventures*
> *of the Moonstone? Who can tell?*

—Wilkie Collins

The room was in Police Headquarters, tall-ceilinged and echoing, facing out over busy and bustling Wain Gate, and by leaning far out of the window, farther, I might add, than I, despite the comparative vigor of my middle years, would ever dare lean or even scarcely imagine leaning, one could most likely manage to catch sight of nearby Lady's Bridge and the sluggish River Don making its murky way through the active heart of Sheffield, no doubt a trial for it, before making its way north past Doncaster to its rendezvous with the distant Ouse and ultimately the Humber and the cold and, in that year, bellicose North Sea.

Beside that window, framed dustily by it and the weak sunlight, sifting through the soot of a late autumn's afternoon, seated facing each other in two identical oaken swivel chairs, were, what to the untutored eye might appear to be, two identical old gentlemen, their heads stooped forward, pointed and bright-veined nose to pointed and bright-veined nose, round eyeglasses to round eyeglasses, knee to knee to knee to knee. But, of course, as I trust everyone in these curious modern times has learned by now (or will certainly soon), appearances are most often deceiving.

One of the old gentlemen was, however, just that—an old gentleman, Octavius Guy, a retired police inspector, eighty-six years old, bright and sprightly, stooped with age but unbowed by that passage of time, superannuated perhaps, but superior to that obsolescence nonetheless. But the matching figure was no old man at all, was rather my good friend and long-time companion, baronet and amateur detective of no little note, bright and sprightly, stooped unnaturally by his forty-three years but by no means rendered stupid by that same token, none other than, as you may well have surmised (and correctly), Sir Hugh Fitz-Hyffen.

Although the passing years had rendered us both, by military standards, unfit for active service in His Majesty's cause beyond the sea, we were able nonetheless to render service at home with an appropriate but altogether more appropriately discreet patriotic fervor. And that, quite simply, explains our being in, of all places, Sheffield on this November Wednesday afternoon. Armed with my revolver, Sir Hugh's Yorkshire phrase book, and our mutual resolve to do our respective parts in the war effort, we had traveled by crowded train the night before from London to Sheffield, at the request of young Anthony Quiz-Brightling, a distant relation of Sir Hugh (his uncle, a stepson of Sir Hugh's great-aunt Jezebel by her third marriage to the short-lived but lively Reginald Quiz-Brightling of the Quiz-Brightling soap-flakes fortune) who was just then involved at rather high levels in some confidential business for the Foreign Office (having transferred over to that office after Churchill's recent resignation as First Lord of the Admiralty in the cabinet shake-up had rendered his services unnecessary at the Admiralty), the nature of which business was to be revealed to us soon in the awkward confines of this police office with its single desk, its stiff chairs and imposing safe, wherein lay, we supposed, the secret of the day's events. And there we sat, bored by the slow progress of time in that room but eager at the prospect of the revelations to come and of tea, both of which were guaranteed a hearty welcome both by myself and by the always ravenously interested Sir Hugh.

The presence of Octavius Guy was, however, as mysterious to us as the larger mystery in regard to which we had been summoned. We had, of course, heard of him; who, indeed, had not? The name Inspector Guy had at one time been on the lips of every schoolboy in the land, and it still was of considerable currency in circles concerned with crime and its swift detection. Not since Sergeant Cuff himself, if one overlooked the sensational successes of Sherlock Holmes (a name which I dare not utter around Sir Hugh without fear of bringing to his mind the appalling circumstances which he had uncovered as an adolescent in Whitechapel), or the more recent scandalous carryings on of Gridley Quayle, had one detective so thoroughly captured the public mind. But we knew, too, that he had long since retired to Wath-on-Dearne near the mining village of Swinton to tend his begonias and swap long tales of an evening with Constable Walker, his alert neighbor and dearest friend. What, then, was he doing in this room, and what bearing had his being there on the case at hand? I wondered in silence as he and Sir Hugh enjoyed their quiet conversation by the wide window.

Excluded from that conversation by the circumstances of seating, I arose and wandered about the room. Its furnishing offered little of interest to me, so I perused the few large pictures which, if not exactly graced its walls, nevertheless hung on them.

There were four framed pictures, two on each wall perpendicular to the walls containing window and door. I began on the wall to the left of the door. The pictures seemed dully appropriate to their surroundings. The first was a photograph of a collection of "Murder Weapons," among them the usual dirk, razor, pistol, rope, wrench, hammer, and several less likely ones—a quill pen, what appeared to be a citrus fruit of some kind, a leather-bound copy of *The Poetical Works of Mrs. Hemans*, a shuttlecock, and a locket opened to reveal a tiny portrait of a cross-eyed infant. There was no explanation given for any of these weapons.

The second picture was entitled "The Physiognomy of Murder," and it contained four smaller pictures, each of which had its own legend. The first was a rather crude drawing of a stern-visaged woman nursing a baby in arms. The baby was wrinkled and had the look more of a small monkey than a human child. The legend simply read, "Mary Bateman, The Yorkshire Witch," although a phrase had been added under it in ink which had turned brown with age: "the skin was stripped from her body and sold in pieces for charms." The second face, that of a Neanderthal man had it not been for its remarkably domed forehead, was simply labeled "Charley Peace." The third was apparently of a woman, for it was of a completely veiled head, and it was labeled "Henrietta Robinson, a descendant of King George III." The fourth face was that of a dwarfish individual, his head curiously twisted like that of a squeezed lemon, his lips in a snarl, his jaw stippled with a two day's growth of wiry beard, his eyes so filled with hate that I involuntarily recoiled from the picture. There was no legend under that last photograph.

The two pictures on the opposite side of the room were more difficult to understand. The first, untitled, was what surely was a photograph, perhaps a single frame from a photoplay, of an executioner, completely dressed in black, his features shielded by a black hood which revealed only his jaw, his bulbous nose, and his incredibly empty eyes. He was holding a bloody and enormous sword at an awkward angle, a tipless sword unadorned by ornamentation, and the whole picture left one with a feeling of terrible awkwardness and an incredible blankness, a void approaching what those few Swedenborgians I have allowed myself to know would call vastation.

I hurried on to the last picture, after taking a quick glance at those two calm gentlemen, both emblems of security, poised themselves so securely by the window, and regaining by that glance at least a semblance of the balance I had felt before my inspection of that third picture. The last picture was absolutely puzzling to me, however, not unnerving but certainly difficult to explain. It was a nineteenth-century etching, or a good reproduction of one, a tavern scene, a large number of people in the room, a fat bald barman on the left, a group of ordinary people standing in the middle, a cluster of tables on the right, and to the far right a group of laborers examining some picture on the wall. In the foreground a small boy is sitting on the floor clutching a box in his arms, his legs spread before him in an inverted V, and in the background are three soldiers at a table, drinkless and dreaming, behind them a confused mass of vaguely drawn drinkers. Under the print, in the white margin, in the same hand as the note under the picture of Mary Bateman, appear the words "La défaite de Reichenfels." Why these words should be in French, why, in fact, the picture should be on the wall of this room in the Police Headquarters at all, these questions frankly baffled me, but just as I was turning to Sir Hugh to ask his opinion, the door opened and Anthony Quiz-Brightling entered, accompanied by a cheerful red-faced constable wearing glasses as round and as small as Sir Hugh's and Octavius Guy's, and they were, the two of them, accompanied by a much younger constable pushing a mobile table on which the tea was spread, so that my questions remained unspoken and have so remained until this day.

Tea proceeded apace, unmarked by untoward or notable incident, only Sir Hugh's vigorous assault on the cream tea cakes, Octavius Guy's repeated request that someone pass him the gooseberry preserves, and the bespectacled constable's evident relish for what he loudly referred to as "jam-butties." That constable, as no doubt you have decided on your own, proved to be none other than Guy's friend Walker, whose presence further heightened the mystery surrounding the room and the day.

After tea, we all settled back as well as we were able in the room's sparse furnishings, ready for Quiz-Brightling's explanations to commence. Octavius Guy pulled a rough and worn meerschaum from his pocket, stuffed it with shag tobacco, and lit it, but as he began to smoke, Constable Walker muttered, "A flame on one end; a fool on t'other," no doubt in response to some ancient argument, and the two glared at each other angrily until young Quiz-Brightling cleared his throat audibly and began to speak.

"We have here," he said, "a rather sticky problem, or rather, as you may well have surmised, two rather sticky problems, which, because of their stickiness and their unfortunate juxtaposition in time and place, have become glued, as it were, into one sticky problem of unusual tacticity." He cleared his throat again, wiping his no doubt sticky fingers on the linen napkin, enstenciled S.P.D., which lingered in his lap from tea. "And, frankly, gentlemen," he continued, "I'm stuck."

Octavius Guy exhaled a reeking quantity of tobacco smoke into the air at that moment as Sir Hugh sneezed, and Constable Walker turned his back on them both and glared out the window.

"First," said the visibly shaken Quiz-Brightling, "I must pledge you all to absolute secrecy regarding what I am about to tell you," a chorus of mixed assent around the room, "for the future of your country and perhaps of the very world itself is at stake," a gasp, mine I'm afraid, "and we may well be the only people in the world able to deal with its future adequately at this moment."

Sir Hugh and Octavius Guy pivoted on their swivels and peered into each other's eyeglasses, each no doubt seeing the other's watering (the smoke was getting intense) eyes and his own eyes as well, reflected in the other's eyeglasses.

"But, before I get down to details, I must," young Anthony went on, "offer you some background, four items.

"First, this report from France: Joffre's great offensive has regrettably failed despite the success of our army at the Third Battle of Artois. This information, together with the news that the Tsar has taken supreme command of the Russian army, that the Bulgarians succeeded in taking Nish only five days ago, and that Townshend will begin his advance on Baghdad tomorrow, puts us, all of the Allies, in a position of extreme crisis.

"Now, given this state of crisis, seven distinct and separate events come together to form a coherent picture of the forces which have managed to plunge us into this holocaust of war and which are, even as we sit in this room in these comfortable chairs," a groan escaped my lips, Sir Hugh and Octavius Guy turning to glare at me, "shaping themselves into an ominous pattern which will shape the course of the war and the world for years to come.

"Number one: the discovery by the French of the cruel treatment of the Abbé Oudin."

Quiz-Brightling lifted a large manuscript from the table behind him and opened it to a marked place.

"Allow me," he continued, "to read to you from an advance copy of *Rapports et Procès-Verbaux d'Enquête de la Commission Instituée en Vue de Constater les Actes Commis par l'Ennemi en Violation du Droit des Gens*, forgiving as you allow my rough translation into English.

"I continue," he continued, "by reading from pages eight and nine: 'Abbé Oudin, an old man of seventy-three, afflicted with asthma, was arrested and locked up in his cellar without food till the following day, with his maid, Mlle. Côte, aged sixty-seven, and MM. Mougeot, Arnould, Poignet, and Cuchard. On the 8th they were taken to Coole, where they had to pass the night—still without food. Then they were marched to Châlons-sur-Marne. On the way to Châlons the aged priest, who had been belabored with rifle butts and reduced to complete exhaustion, was unable to go further, so they put him with his maid on a butcher's cart, which the other prisoners had to drag along. . . .

"'From Châlons they were removed to Suippes, and taken into a house to be examined. The abbé, who could scarcely stand, was seized by the shoulder and roughly shaken by an officer, who questioned him in an insulting tone. He came out from the examination dazed and tottering, and was then made to spend the whole night in the rain, in the courtyard of a school.

"'On the 11th they reached Vouziers, and were kept there till the 14th in a stable, where they had to lie on sodden sawdust. The 13th was a particularly atrocious day. Soldiers, especially officers, came in large numbers with the deliberate purpose of amusing themselves by tormenting the curé. They spat in his face, flogged him with their horsewhips, threw him in the air and then let him fall on the ground, kicked him or slashed him with their spurs all over the arms, thighs, and chest.'"

"Huns!" said Constable Walker, then, almost inaudibly under his breath, "Huns."

"It is not, I fear, quite that simple, Constable," Quiz-Brightling responded, "pray, let me continue," and he did:

" 'After these abominable outrages, M. Oudin was reduced to such a condition of weakness that his groans were hardly audible. On the 15th he was taken to Sedan, and in a hospital there he almost immediately succumbed.' I don't believe that I need add any further comment to that ghastly account."

"None at all," said Sir Hugh and Octavius Guy in remarkable unison.

"I could, however, add that the old maid was herself tied to a carriage wheel and rolled in the mud, but that would be beside the point."

"Of course," the duet replied.

"But," continued Quiz-Brightling, "to continue, the second remarkable event was that in Dinant sixty thousand bottles of wine were stolen from the cellars of one M. Piret. The coincidence, if it were coincidence, would, I am sure you would agree, be overwhelming."

We all nodded agreement, myself a hairsbreadth behind Sir Hugh.

"It is no wonder," I ventured, "that Kipling has referred to the brutes as 'lesser breeds without the Law,' " but Sir Hugh silenced me with a frown, a frown mirrored on the ancient face opposite his.

"Third, gentlemen," Quiz-Brightling said, reasserting his dominance in the room, "is the appointment of the Grand Duke Nicholas Nicolaievich as Viceroy to the Caucasus.

"And fourth," he hurried on, his voice rising in pitch and intensity, although maintaining its level volume, the result of an excellent public-school education, "is," a glance at Octavius Guy, "the reappearance of the giant yellow diamond," Guy drew in his breath sharply, then coughed furiously, almost strangled by the bitter smoke from the pipe which he had forgotten to remove from his lips, "known as the Moonstone," a pause, "here in Yorkshire."

As Octavius Guy regained his composure, Quiz-Brightling continued his account. "In China, Yüan Shih-k'ai is making his bid for power, opposed in Yünnan by Ts'ai Ao. But Ts'ai Ao, we have reason to believe, is not his most formidable opponent. For one thing, the forbidden Jong Tong has raised its head again, led by the mysterious Madame Fang-Loos, although I must admit that she has dropped from sight in recent weeks. But, even more frighteningly, dare I suggest that Madame Fang-Loos is none other than Fah Lo Suee and that the renascence of the Jong Tong may be attributed to none other than the Council of Seven of the Si-Fan?" He paused, then said, carefully, "Gentlemen, I do so dare." The small hairs on the back of my neck prickled and rose.

"Two other events connected with those," said Anthony Quiz-Brightling by way of conclusion, "are that three mysterious Hindoos in the company of an enormous Baluchistani known only as Ali Aliynfri have shown up this week in Sheffield, and, need I add, Edith Cavell was executed by the Germans this very year. Think on it, gentlemen, and I'm certain you'll see the enormity of what I am suggesting and, therefore, of the task that lies before us."

I must, in fact I am impelled to admit by a gnawing fear that I have never properly understood the enormity of the events of those two days in Yorkshire, that I almost asked a question of young Quiz-Brightling, but the immediate comprehension which lit the mutual faces of Octavius Guy and Sir Hugh choked the words in my throat. How now I wish I had continued, but the past is, after all, past, and my narrative requires that, undaunted, I press on into that jungle of gnarled and swarming events, seeking at least a way through if not an answer.

Octavius Guy was the only remaining participant in the Moonstone's previous appearance in Great Britain and thus was the obvious choice for a consultant on the case. Constable Walker was invited along to support the aging Guy in his efforts. And Sir Hugh Fitz-Hyffen was requested to participate because he was surely the only first-class operative available in wartime England who was unknown to the enemy's intelligence offices. That much at least was clear. But why Sheffield?

"But why, you may be asking yourselves," Anthony spoke up just then, "Sheffield? Because, gentlemen, the course of events, both accidental and controlled, has seen to it that in that safe," pointing to the enormity in the corner of the room, "lies both the Moonstone," another choking gasp by Octavius Guy, "and a sealed document, the only one of its kind in the world, written by a hand the owner of which is now dead and his name with him, which contains a piece of information which ties the whole business together and which, gentlemen, I swear to you, can and will, once opened by the Prime Minister, who will arrive here tomorrow, shorten this awful war in which we are involved by a full three years," stunned gasps this time around the room, Octavius Guy choking and sputtering once again, "and, gentlemen, our job is to see that both that document and the Moonstone are safely here when the Prime Minister arrives tomorrow morning."

At that moment, just as we were, all of us, about to pledge our fealty to the task, there appeared in the window a hideously grinning face, a stunted body turning around it like the moon about its mother earth, the face constant and unchanging, that horrible grin, a jaw stubbled with two days' growth of beard, the eyes burning with unleashed fury, and then the entire apparition disappeared, only to appear less than a minute later, just as before, the body turning up and over and around, the face immobile and floating like some deadly species of barrage balloon. And then it sank to appear no more.

We, again all of us, rushed to the glass and peered out, only to see a caravan moving slowly down the street, a trampoline stretched on its roof, that trampoline topped by a bounding body, and the words in gaudy gold painted on its vermilion side: OTTO THE ACROBATIC GERMAN DWARF, the whole thing followed by a procession of street urchins, shouting, "Hun go home, Hun go home, Hun go home," as the entire parade passed on, turning into Castlegate and out of sight.

When we turned back to the room, I noticed that a large square of yellow paper had appeared on the center of the now disordered teacart. I pointed it out to Sir Hugh, who picked it up, held it to the waning light from the large window, and allowed us all to see that it contained only four large symbols, which I reproduce here:

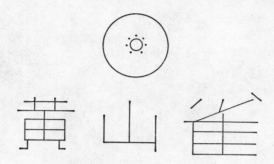

"I see," said Sir Hugh, speaking suddenly alone, his voice thin but sure, as if none of us quite existed for him any more, not even his fading double, Octavius Guy, "that there is more here than immediately meets the eye."

At that moment, the sun suddenly set, and we were in the dark for good and all.

The home of Albert Longinus was an apartment, a flat, rooms on the third floor of an elastic-wear shop in dreary Newark. Though never really at home in New Jersey, Albert did feel relatively at ease in these rooms. He had fixed them up comfortably, a few stuffed chairs, a bed, tables, lamps, pictures of antiquities on the wall as a kind of masochistic gesture to the weight of his past. Here he repaired from the vicinity of the laundry and its disaster, torn and worn, weary and spent.

He undressed, took a hot bath, soaked and groaned and floated in the steam and water in the deep tub, dried himself off, put on his pajamas, and retired to bed with his new ersatz note and his scrapbook of the old ones. In order to be able to approach the new note with a fresher eye, or so he told himself, he decided to read over some of the more relevant-seeming of the older ones. He stung and smarted all over his head, hands, and back where the torn flesh rubbed on the clean cloth. Even mercurochrome didn't help very much. He lay back on a mound of goose-feather pillows, his only real luxury, and opened his heavy scrapbook.

The first of the really puzzling ones was on the back of a note about stains by a Mrs. O. Nan Jerky, a crude and clumsy joke. It was typed on what appeared to be some sort of official stationery:

> I have absolute proof that Roosevelt is still alive in Antarctica, witnesses, photographs, wire recordings, but the clerks in the Pentagon won't let me get near the Joint Chiefs of Staff. They are the *real* powers in the government, the clerks, mild mannered, meek, weak chinned (I make much of that) and unutterably unscrupulous. He is in Antarctica in Little America where he was flown by Admiral Byrd (of the *Virginia* Byrds, *FFV*, that is what Truman was trying to tell us about *Byrds* in *Congress*) who was then murdered, or else he is there too; my information isn't exactly clear on that. He is down there plotting an even NEWER DEAL! It is too horrible to consider. If only the Joint Chiefs of Staff knew. I think he has many scientists with him. They are trying to gas me; I smell odors every day around my house. I wear a wet handkerchief around my head and nose at all times, asleep and awake. I have unbearable sinus infection. I cannot go on longer. If only this

And there the letter ended, if letter it was, for the note to the laundryman had been torn off at that point. It had been the first one, and in some ways the most frightening, but Albert could see no direct connection between it and the new note. Nor, for that matter, between it and any of the others.

Albert turned on to another one, a few pages on, past ads for nonexistent stores, pages from the ends of obscene novels that he could never find mention of elsewhere, and a photograph of happy children pouring honey on the ground around the head of a partially buried little playmate. He found small comfort and less knowledge from the one he was examining:

> I am so happy here, away from the children and Fred. I hope they are happy, too, safe in Abraham's bosom, held

snug and close and warm. They were always cold, poor things, shivering and asking me to make them warm. Even Fred at night when he was asleep and his guard was down would cry out, "Cold, mommy, cold. Fix. Fix." And what could I do, what with Fred's being out of work and the mine's being closed down and all? I ask you, what could I do? Well, the winter gets colder and colder, and you know what I did. You must have read it in the paper. They had all cried themselves to sleep. I took the iron which had been sitting on the stove for heating, only we didn't have any coal or wood, and I hefted it in my hand. I guess I was trying to pretend it was warm. After that it all gets kind of hazy. I remember standing over Fred and hitting him in the head. He never felt a thing. Only twitched like he always did when he went to sleep, like his arm always did when my head was on it when we went to sleep in each other's arms. It mashed his head terrible, but it was quiet, didn't wake anyone, so I did it to each of the children, one by one. Not a one of them sweet darlings made so much as a whimper. So then I got some oily rags out of Fred's old truck that we didn't have the money to run any more, and I lit them with the last Ohio Blue Tip we had and burned the house down. I am only sorry that the fire spread and burned up the Lukins place too, but I have real solace that they are all good and warm and not crying now, for there wasn't a mean bone in one of them, not one.

This one was written in a woman's crabbed hand, in crayon. On its reverse was a short note about how Mrs. Vanderbilt's daughter's seven ball gowns had been wrinkled by the deliveryman last time and threatening to make it "genuinely hot" for him if he so much as creased a ribbon this time.

And then Albert found the book list, not the new one, but the old one he had composed himself from all of the random book titles he had found scattered among his collection of notes, his composite list tucked between the pages of the scrapbook, but not attached because he had never arrived at a satisfactory arrangement for the titles, one which would reveal the hidden and meaningful pattern in their collective disorder.

He had tried grouping them for a time in categories of his own making, but that had failed. *God as Idea* might for example seem to fit nicely with *God Is a Humorist* and *The God of the Labyrinth*, but what was their connection with *A Bloody Shovel* or *2BRO2B*? And did *Time to Fight* have anything to do with *Vindication of Eternity*? And what did *The Strange Mushroom* have to do with anything at all?

So he surrendered, or at least gave up for a time, and arranged the books alphabetically by author, an arrangement which, if not entirely satisfying, nevertheless seemed to bring about many interesting juxtapositions and gave to the whole mass of titles at least an imposed sense of order. He settled back and read the list one more time, hoping to find at least a clue as to the meaning of his new book list and its disquietingly unfamiliar titles:

THE 33 BOOK TITLES, BY AUTHOR

Abdul Alhazred — *The Necronomicon*
Mir Bahadur Ali — *The Approach to al-Mu'tasim*
Gilbert Austin — *Life, Being and Language*
Rosie M. Banks — *A Red, Red Summer Rose*
Felix Clovelly — *The Adventure of the Wand of Death*
Sir John Crabtree, Baronet — *Memoirs of a Visit to the Courts of Europe*
Carlos Argentino Daneri — *La Tierra*
Pierre Delaland — *Discours sur les ombres*
Mervyn Dillard (ed.) — *Of the Deflowering of Maids*
Andrew Field — *The Flawed Pretense*
John Fincastle — *God as Idea*
Fréderic et Amélie — *Poésies*
Justin Geoffrey — *People of the Monolith*
Robert Hitchinson — *The East Is Whispering*

Jaromir Hladík — *Vindication of Eternity*
Z. B. D. James — *Thundering Pistoleras*
Alroy Kear — *The Eye of the Needle*
Sebastian Knight — *The Prismatic Bezel*
Charles Latimer — *A Bloody Shovel*
Pierre Menard — *Les problèmes d'un problème*
Ludwig Pursewarden — *God Is a Humorist*
Herbert Quain — *The God of the Labyrinth*
Clare Quilty — *The Strange Mushroom*
Laban Shrewsbury — *Cthulhu in The Necronomicon*
Gerard Sorme — *Methods and Techniques of Self-Delusion*
Orville Sundheim — *The Beast in Revelation*
Father Surin — *In the Dusk of the Dawn*
General Richard Thoresby, Ret. — *Time to Fight*
Kilgore Trout — *2BRO2B*
Van Veen — *Letters from Terra*
Cora Velasquez — *Men—My Delight*
Hon. Mrs. Victor-Smythe — *Men Are Animals*
Ludovic Vuelph — *Der mutwillige Speichellecker*

The list proved as enigmatic as ever. The same questions arose and remained unanswered. What had a book like *The Adventure of the Wand of Death* to do with *A Red, Red Summer Rose?* The first was obviously hideously obscene, while the second was as obviously charming, religious, and serene, but there had to be a connection. Chance was no longer ever enough for Albert when meaning was so obviously just on the tip of his tongue or lurking between the lines on every printed page in his collection. Were "tierra" and "terra" the same place? If he even could know the answer to that one, he would feel so very much relieved. Chronology (the order of his discovery of the titles) had failed, and now the alphabet was doing little better. Perhaps he would toss them all in a hat on separate pieces of paper and try a new random order, let chance have the chance to make amends for itself. Or maybe he would go to the library and try once again to find a copy of *Methods and Techniques of Self-Delusion*, wherein he was convinced the whole answer lay.

Albert flipped on, his head aching and his stomach queasy, looking for relief but finding only the note that he had really been looking for, the message about Newark, written on what appeared to be parchment in an antique hand. It had come after two weeks of ads for elastic wear which Mr. Moshe, Albert's knowledgeable landlord, had said present technology could not produce, and a smattering of teen-age love letters about abortion, suicide, incest, and orgy. It was ostensibly from the Newark Welfare Orphans Home, and the note on the front was an ordinary one about lost diapers and torn rompers. But the back was different and chillingly strange:

> I fear I have forgotten how to pray, my lips move but no words, only gibberish, emerge. Not tongues, for tongues I know, only gibberish. I fear too that soon I may be forced to gaze unguarded upon the visage of Ghatanothoa and be petrified like this city itself. They are here. They are real. And they are returning—the Old Ones, subterranean, hideous. The ground trembles daily. There are foul smells in the air. Awful events are ordinary. A woman is delivered daily of the head of a cow. The newspapers are filled with lies. Nÿogtha is beneath the pavement. His amoebic substance already oozes into deep cellars and dark places. The ground has often given beneath my feet as I walk at night. I find this passage in Chambers: "There are so many things which are impossible to explain!" He knew. He knew. Flying things passed off as swamp gas or flying ships. Fools! The answer is so close to home. Underfoot. Examine *De Vermis Mysteriis*. Here is the answer to your UFO: "*Tibi, Magnum Innominandum, signa stellarum nigrarum et bufaniformis Sadoque sigillum.*" Is that not answer enough? But there is more to it than research. There is direct contact, voices issuing from a crevice in the cellar of my own building. A dark and unutterably deep voice, a low bestial growl forming words, the voice of the Thing That Should Not Be, Toto, Otto, Nÿogtha. It spoke with no tongue,

but it said the name, over and over, "Newarkk, Newarkk, Newarkk." I write the Vach-Virag incantation here and now:

Ya na kadishtu nilgh're . . .
stell'hsna kn'aa Nÿogtha . . .
k'yarnak phlegethor . . .

The earth shakes as I write, muffled by the passage of heavy trucks, but I can hear, I can feel. There is no escape for me. Newark is older than history. The dirt in its cracks and corners is obscene in its age. Newarkk, seat of the Old Ones, awaits their return in filth and darkness. Is there no one to tell? I feel myself aging as I write. My hand grows gray and wrinkles as I look. The paper ages. The ink browns. My skin begins to flake away revealing nothing but scaling bone and mold, gray, puffed and swollen, living, dead, decay. The pen is impossible to hold. The incantation has failed. He has heard his name scratched out on paper and has come. Do not, for God's sake, ever look into a mirror again!

The script was antique as was the parchment. Bits and pieces had flaked away, and there were curious stains near the bottom of the page. Albert had not looked into a mirror for some days after finding this message safety-pinned to the note from the Orphans Home, but he had learned how ubiquitous mirrors are, how he lived in a world of reflections: spoons at breakfast, the coffeepot, the sides of his electric razor, windows, puddles, his customers' eyes, the glass over the truck speedometer, the sunglasses of the policeman who had stopped him for speeding. It had, of course, proven impossible. He had been surrounded the whole time by countless images of himself, never alone, ever mindful of his own frightened face.

Why had this letter so convinced Albert, when it was so much more obviously fraudulent than any of the others? He did not know, but he broke out into a cold sweat as he read it again. The salt stung his wounds.

He turned the page again. An ad for a sheep brothel, two letters from small children to their aged grandmothers which implied on the one hand that the child had unnatural desires for its grandparent, and on the other that the child knew of its grandfather's tainted blood but forgave all, the hockey ticket which he had found tucked in the pocket of a tan windbreaker with the odd set of words on its back:

S A T O R
A R E P O
T E N E T
O P E R A
R O T A S

And then the last one in the book, from just three days before, written tidily in Washable Blue ink in a student's hand:

tu modo nascenti puero, quo ferrea primum
desinet ac toto surget gens aurea mundo

There was no normal message on the reverse, no message at all. Just this brief scrap of Latin, pinned neatly to a bundle of clean swaddling clothes, blue blankets, and baby booties.

Albert unfolded the new book list, but lacking the strength to get up for paste or transparent tape, he merely placed the battered note between the pages with his own working book list, closed the scrapbook, laid it on the floor beside the bed without looking, and drifted off, his reading light still on, still propped up on his goose-down pillows, warm in the winter, untroubled by dreams, weary of bone and flesh, drifted off to sleep until gray dawn should wake him to the world again.

> *At some future time, possibly*
> *when you are my guest in China . . .*
> *I shall discuss with you some*
> *lesser-known properties of this*
> *species. . . .*
>
> —Fu-Manchu

Immediately the single lamp in the room was switched on by young Quiz-Brightling, and we all stood in a wavering circle around that smaller, fixed and yellow circle of light cast by the hooded table lamp.

"Now," said Quiz-Brightling, "I am going to open the safe, reveal its contents to you, and then, replacing those contents, close the safe, and give its combination in a sealed envelope to Sir Hugh Fitz-Hyffen, so that he and I will be the only men in the world in possession of that information."

Sir Hugh nodded a thoughtful assent.

"Then," young Anthony went on, "I am going to leave for London by aeroplane, carrying a packet of the appropriate size, hoping thereby to lure whoever is interested in the safe's contents after me on what I must be so bold as to call a 'wild goose chase.' Sir Hugh will, then, open the envelope and then the safe tomorrow in the presence of the P.M., giving to him the documents which will, in his hands and his hands alone, change the future of the entire world, West and Mysterious East alike."

The room was absolutely silent as Quiz-Brightling, shielding the dial with his body, spun the tumblers and opened the massive safe. He swung the door out, leaned into its dark interior, and then returned to the illuminated desk, carrying two items. He placed them on the gleaming desk top—one, a chamois pouch, smooth and yellowish tan, containing an object somewhat larger than but similar in shape to a hen's egg; the other, a robin's-egg blue envelope, stuffed full to the point of a frankly obese bulge.

We all leaned over to the light, the eyeglasses of Sir Hugh, Octavius Guy, and Constable Walker all catching the light and sending it dancing in small dim circles around the dark room and over our assembled faces, a dizzying but exhilarating effect, an aesthetic wonder!

Quiz-Brightling fumbled the pouch mouth open, inserted his fingers, still warm and sticky from the tea, into the smooth lips of chamois, spreading his fingers gently, working them in slowly and surely, and then moving them suddenly all the way in, writhing them about for a moment, driving his hand up and down, and then suddenly, with an ecstatic moan, he withdrew them, an enormous yellow gleaming gemstone clutched in them, catching the light from the lamp and the reflected light from the as suddenly focused spectacles and returning that concentration of light, light and light, multiplied and magnified, to the entire room, making it glare for a moment as if the sun had surely changed its course and come up startlingly again over the dark world, narrowing our pupils to eager points, blinding us to everything but its own magnificence.

"The Moonstone!" I could hear the voice of Octavius Guy blurting into the silence, his tone enlivened and enriched by a full chord of overtones of awe.

"The Moonstone, indeed," Quiz-Brightling replied, suddenly popping the massive diamond back into its snug pouch and drawing the strings tightly to, a conjurer's cruel act, an ecdysiast's tempting and feathery surprise.

The first sight which met my restored vision after a moment's healing passage was the face of Sir Hugh Fitz-Hyffen, his glasses gleaming once again in the dim lamplight, his features drawn into an absolutely frightening expression, which I had never seen there before and hope never to see again, a mixture of hunger, surprise, and grim determination. I blinked, and the expression was gone, as sudden and illusory in its coming and going as the fantastic appearance and disappearance of the stone itself, and his usual expression of bored incomprehension, with which he concealed his enormous interest in every small detail of the passing day, had replaced its confusing predecessor with such thoroughness that once again I was forced to doubt the very evidence of my accurate eyes.

"The envelope," Quiz-Brightling interposed, "must remain sealed, but it does, I assure you, contain perhaps the most singularly important documents you or I or anyone living today has ever been in the presence of."

Again that disquieting silence filled the dark atmosphere of the room.

"Inspector Guy," said Quiz-Brightling, breaking the ominous silence, "and Constable Walker will be responsible for seeking out and foiling any who might be attempting to purloin the Moonstone and thereby endangering the documents, and Sir Hugh Fitz-Hyffen will, as I have said, be responsible for the safe delivery of the documents themselves to the Prime Minister. We have allowed the two cases to overlap because of circumstances out of our control, but also happily because we are convinced that you gentlemen," a shy shuffling of feet around the desk, "together are more than capable of handling anything that might possibly go wrong and bringing it round aright."

"You may be assured," replied Sir Hugh, his thin voice rich with emotion, "that neither the stone nor the documents will be allowed to fall into strange hands." Anthony Quiz-Brightling gave an audible sigh of relief.

Shortly after, young Anthony having departed in the rear cockpit of the new Armstrong-Whitworth FK 3 on his ill-fated night flight to London, the decoy package which Sir Hugh had handed him tucked under his legs, and Guy and Walker having gone their way on the trail, no doubt, of Ali Aliynfri and his mysterious Hindoo companions, Sir Hugh and I made our way through the dark streets of Sheffield to a small fish-and-chips restaurant known oddly as the Plaice Place.

My recollections of that dinner are dim, my memory as muddled now as my emotions were at the time, but I do remember one moment as vividly as I do any moment of my modestly eventful life, a moment when the nape of my neck bristled like an excited terrier and the blood in my warm veins ran as chill as the icy waters of the nearby North Sea. Sir Hugh, his mouth for a moment empty of fish or chips, his breath tense and vinegary, leaned across the small table toward me, his eyes like diamond chips behind his glistening glasses, and said, "You realize, of course, that the brain which will be behind tomorrow's events is no ordinary brain," I nodded, "but is rather the most potent and potentially dangerous brain active in the entire civilized world today."

"You don't mean . . ." I managed to reply, having been caught in mid-chew and more-than-mid-swallow.

"No, I don't," he said quietly, "no, I don't at all."

I could only blush and force another piece of fish in with its crowded companions between my embarrassed lips. He said no more.

As we were leaving the restaurant, a large fat dark individual, wearing curious shoes that seemed almost to be of yellow silk and which curled up at the toes into something approximating an actual loop, pushed past us at the door. He was accompanied by three other dark gentlemen, each of whom wore a white turban and each of whom sported a fiercely bristling beard. Foreigners obviously, and I thought how small our island was becoming, how small and how large, but I soon dismissed the subject from my mind and replaced it with the larger matters (or matters as large) which were even more immediately at hand. Sir Hugh, his eyes still ablaze, seemed to notice the rude quartet not at all.

Outside, we stood in the blustery November night air, breathing deeply for our respective health's sakes and enjoying the warm briny glow that welled outward to our outermost extremities from our sea-and-soil-filled depths. We didn't, I suppose, knowing full well that I certainly didn't, even notice the large black closed touring car that stood halfway up the short block, its motor idling, its running lights dimmed, its windows curtained, its silvery and blunt nose pointed ominously in our direction. Nor did we, or, again, at least I, until it was pointed out later, notice the two muffled figures poised in a doorway across the street, the collars of their greatcoats turned up, their broad-brimmed hats turned down, until there seemed to be only two dimly luminous pairs of eyeglasses glowing like animal eyes from the firkins formed by the joining brims and collars. We did notice, however, both of us, that the auto was beginning to move down the street toward us, silently like some phantom, a portent of the gathering fog that was rolling over the town as silently as deadly gas or the approaching car.

The enormous machine paused with its passenger door directly before us, the door opening mysteriously then as if it were behaving of its own volition, for it was operated by no visible hand or lever, and a musically sibilant voice slid out to us in the gathering yellow fog, "Sir Hugh, you will please to enter my automobile."

I snorted, a sudden burst of derisive laughter twisting my still greasy lips, and replied, "Same to you, I'm sure," but again I was to be surprised by my companion, for he clapped his hand over my mouth, as suddenly withdrew it, wiped it on his handkerchief, and then pushed me into the dark interior of the car and followed himself. I did notice, as I was entering the door, that a figure, hauntingly familiar, a silhouette in the fog, flat, two-dimensional as if he were merely an illustration on the cover of some pulpy magazine, paused on a bicycle at the corner, his shoulders heaving as though he were exhausted, possibly some wanderer from a local bicycle race, but familiar nonetheless.

The door closed behind us, and the car began to move on its silent and indeterminate course. As our eyes adjusted to the darkness of the veiled interior, I saw that that darkness was not so total as I had at first believed, that it was in fact illuminated faintly and pungently by a joss stick smoldering before some hideous idol perched in the rear, curtained window and filling the air with the odor of burning mimosa. A woman sat indolently in the opposite corner of the vast seat upon which Sir Hugh now sat (I was hunched quite uncomfortably on a jump seat of sorts extending out not far enough from the rear of the partition separating this compartment from that of the invisible driver of the vehicle). She was Oriental, Chinese I would guess, but a most unusual and striking figure; her skin was of a particularly soft and engaging yellow, but even more striking was her bright and beautifully coiffed yellow hair, even her eyebrows were yellow; she was dressed in a yellow silk gown, and her long fingernails were tinted an elegant golden yellow; on her feet were yellow satin slippers, and her eyes were like flecks of yellow gold floating on the Yellow Sea; she was perilously striking, a figure encompassing all of the allure and danger of the Orient and the waning East.

"I wish to show you something, Sir Hugh," she said, "but, first . . ."

"But, first," Sir Hugh rejoined, his voice impatient and remarkably and unusually impolite, "I suspect that we had better make ourselves clear, Madame Fang-Loos," a long pause, "or should I better say, Fah Lo Suee?"

"Fah Lo Suee!" the mysterious lady replied, her voice losing its gentle sibilance and rising into an Occidental shrillness. "Fah Lo Suee!" Her eyes widened to become molten gold pools. "Fah Lo Suee! So that is what you take me for. Fool, have you not eyes to see? Fah Lo Suee, indeed!"

She thrust her hand out toward Sir Hugh, holding in it some sort of ormolu image, a small bird, enameled black-crested head, blue-greenish back, bright yellow below with a white patch on hind neck, but my attention was attracted elsewhere, for her silken gown slipped open as her arm extended, revealing a small and absolutely stunning right breast, round and yellow with a rich and darkly golden pap, pendulous and perfect, soft-seeming as the silk behind it, yellow on yellow. I fear my eyes must have bulged noticeably as I wondered at the ways of the East and was astonished that I did not look away as I certainly would have had the object of my vision been that of a young English lady (I blush even now at the very thought).

I heard Sir Hugh's voice then and realized that he, too, was struck oddly and forced into unnatural actions, for he said only the three startling words, "The Yellow Tit!"

"Yes, Sir Hugh," she said, her voice again calm and liquid, "and now that you know who I am, I trust you will Fah Lo Suee me no more Fah Lo Suees."

Much to my continuing surprise, Sir Hugh assented, and the yellow lady reclined back into the corner of the seat again, hiding from my very disappointed gaze that hypnotic yellow globe. As I was later to learn, that mysterious lady was indeed Madame Fang-Loos, but she was not the infamous Fah Lo Suee, was rather her enormously successful rival, possibly the finest secret agent the Orient has ever produced, the bearer of the inscrutable (until I saw what I now had seen) name by which Sir Hugh had just addressed her.

"I beg your pardon," he said, "but my mind has been somewhat occupied all evening. I should have realized."

"That is perfectly fine, Sir Hugh," Madame Fang-Loos replied, "but now that we know who we are, may I proceed to advise you of something."

"There is, I am sure, no need," he replied, "but I assure you," patting the pocket into which I had earlier seen him place the sealed letter with the safe's combination, "that your efforts will be quite in vain."

"We shall see what we shall see," Madame Fang-Loos said.

"We certainly shall," said Sir Hugh, and then he continued, "there are a number of things which I should like to discuss with you, if I may."

"Alone," she said, glancing my way.

I started to remonstrate, but Sir Hugh replied, his glasses reflecting the joss stick like burning match points, "Alone."

Madame Fang-Loos touched a small button at her elbow, and the automobile stopped. The door by which we entered opened again with a foggy swirl of night air, and I realized that we were drawn up at the curb before our own hotel. I was, frankly, astonished, but, at Sir Hugh's behest, I climbed out.

"I'll be along as soon as I've learned a few things," said Sir Hugh's oddly muffled voice from the interior of the black car. "Just run along to bed and don't worry about a thing."

I leaned back into the car, eager to complain and to suggest that I should quite possibly be given charge of the envelope, but the door was already silently closing, and I caught only a quick glimpse, so phantasmagoric that I can scarcely credit my senses, of Sir Hugh's back, two golden satin slippers waving over his shoulders, Madame Fang-Loos' head sunk back in her golden silk pillows, and that glowing orb, yellow and gold, caught up this time in what seemed like four astonishingly long, bony, and dead-white fingers, but then the door was closed and the car was gone in a whisper of gassy fumes, and I was standing, bent over foolishly, on an empty curb, staring only at the fog.

Then, just as I straightened up, a bicycle hissed by, its rider puffing furiously, and disappeared into the foggy dark in the direction Madame Fang-Loos' car had taken.

I turned to go into the hotel when a large dark man wrapped in a thick overcoat bumped in to me, and I could have sworn that fingers were suddenly in all my pockets and as suddenly gone, but the man apologized profusely, bowing and beaming, gave me his card, and left in the company of three other dark men in turbans. As they walked away, chattering incomprehensibly, I thought I saw two shadowy portions of the hotel's columnar façade detach and follow them into the night, but finally I decided that too much had happened to me that day and that my senses were no more to be trusted.

I followed Sir Hugh's good advice and went upstairs to bed and was soon in a deep and dreamless sleep.

The movie was already under way, the theater dark as the night edging toward dawn outside, empty of all but a few slumped figures, as Pudd sat in a seat in the middle of the back row, its springs worn and loose, sagging under the weight which his muscles released to it entirely. He looked up at the screen; the picture was black and white, mostly black, night or some dark place, and it was in a language he could neither understand nor place, spoken in voices which he could not distinguish as male or female. In front of him, three rows and to the left, the round form of a head, large, the head of a fat man slouched low enough to be that of a dwarf, snored uneasily, an irregular counterpoint to the guttural sounds issuing from the screen. A face flashed by on the screen, only a brief glimpse, wearing a half mask shielding the eyes and forehead, revealing a thin nose and a small jaw, a mouth so tight that it lacked shape, was only a line, a scar. The voices continued, niether rising nor falling in pitch or pace.

The woman filled Pudd's mind, the woman and the heaviness of his worn flesh. Not the prisoner, although the stump of her neck and the hard cold breasts lingered in his eyes and hands, the cold that still chilled him from his shoulders to his knees, not her but her mirrored double, her dark reflection who found him at the bus stop, who called him by name and caused him to miss the first bus.

"I know you're Pudd, and I know what you did tonight." Her eyes were dark, brown or black he could not tell in the flickering light of the red neon sign for Schwartz Carl's Hot Bar, her hair short in tight curls, small, breasts like avocados under a red blouse, nylon and tight, no brassiere, but the same nose, the same mouth, a shadow, a dangerous double, an image of anti-atoms cast from the same ylem, parallel, but living on beyond the hacked-off end of her life. "I was there, you see. And I have my sources. Newspaper. We have ways of knowing what we shouldn't. And, of course, we do." She laughed.

Pudd watched her eyes. They, too, never moved, never left his gaze, but they were out of focus, seemed to see beyond him, to be watching another pair of eyes an inch or two behind his, but never blinking, never wandering away. He heard the bus behind, heard the hisses and grunts, the rumble of its departure, but he stayed on, caught by her eyes, listening to her throaty voice.

"I won't mention your name, of course. I know that's a deep dark secret. I can write it up so you'll be protected, but I must talk to you. I really need the interview. I mean, my big break's due, and this could be it. You see, since it's her, I'll get big feature space. Oh, not tomorrow, but the follow-ups, juicy, I can taste them." Not looking away, her hands digging in her purse, brown leather with a brass device of some strange kind, too dark to see, then a small notebook in her hand, Blue Bear, Silver Horse, flipping it open, not pausing, then finally, looking away as she squinted in the wavering light, reading aloud. "Finally, my enemies have attained their end, which has been all along to put me to death: I do not pardon them the less for it than I pardon all those who have attempted anything against me. After my death, its authors will be known. But I die without accusing anyone, for fear the Lord should hear and avenge me." A pause, a pencil in her hand, squeezing the purse under an arm while she held the little notebook in her left hand, continuing, "That was her last statement. How does her pardon affect you? Do you fear the Lord's vengeance? I'll need to know the answers to those and . . ."

But now he was free, slipped loose of her eyes and stepping back, a bus stopped behind, which one he neither knew nor cared, and as he turned and stepped up and into it, her voice, "But, Pudd, I'll make it worth your while, really I will, the lobby of the Emstrand Hotel at noon," and the door closed. The bus pulled out, and Pudd did not look back.

But she was in his mind, her eyes, of course, and her teeth, rounded, not a smooth line but the tops separate one from the other, sharp, and the red blouse, the green promise of her breasts. He shifted in his seat, squelching an uneasy erection under the heel of his hand, sore and tired. The film was still dark, some sort of chapel, the light entered in dusty slants, an organ played an oppressive tune, deathly slow, and a voice, the priest's, the minister's, echoed among the stone pillars and pilastered walls until even the syllables of its strange tongue overlapped each other and became unclear. The snoring continued in the darkness, and Pudd's head slumped over onto his left shoulder, his eyes lidded heavily down, closing as the minister's mouth filled the screen, opening and closing, disconnected from the babel of sounds tumbling from behind the screen.

Pudd slept, and he dreamed. In his dream, he was sitting in the last row of a large and very old movie theater. In the darkness he could see baroque moldings and gilt columns, painted domes and dusty hangings. He was nearly alone in the darkness. Someone was snoring near him. The picture on the screen looked familiar, black and white, a woman's face, black hair, an evil face, Gloria Holden, no, it was Gale Sondergaard in a picture he had seen years ago as a much younger man, *The Spider Woman Strikes Back*, or perhaps something else. Her face filled the screen as she spoke on and on, a language of scarcely veiled threats, innuendoes of disaster; the scene never shifted from her face, her eyes. There was a book in his hands, a ratty paperback, Lenore Glen Offord's *The Glass Mask*. It was flaking cellophane and very heavy. He tried to see through the glass, to distinguish the face, to learn whose head was behind the mask. The glass was too thick. He held it up in his hands, a sphere, a bubble, and shook it, trying to shake the head out, to bounce it on the floor. Gale Sondergaard looked over his shoulder as he grew too tired to hold the mask, her teeth round and sharp. He dropped it, and it smashed on the floor. He looked into the darkness, searching for the fragments of broken glass, but his eyelids were too heavy. They slid shut as he leaned over into the next seat and off to sleep.

He was sitting stiffly in the last row of a movie theater; by leaning his head sharply back he could rest it uncomfortably on the artificial stone wall. Someone was asleep and breathing heavily nearby. In the picture, someone was running down a long corridor; it was brightly lit but apparently endless. The camera whizzed along, the walls blurring past, the sound a clatter of racing footsteps, on and on. Pudd held the letter he had found in his mailbox when he had come home after the execution. The execution, the woman reporter, and the letter had driven him, sleepless, out into the night, perhaps to see a movie. He looked at the letter. "Sir," it began, but blurred. He looked at the letter, "Sir," it began. He looked at the letter.

Sir:

My patience is at an absolute end. I have had it. I have written to you as politely as I know how, and you have chosen to ignore me. Well, two can play at that game, I remind you. I have the canceled check and it is stamped "Pudd" in bright red ink. The Better Business Bureau will like that, won't they?

Don't bother to send me any magazines. It is too late. I may weigh only ninety-seven pounds (morning weight—at night I can weigh up to 98 and once even 99 after spaghetti and lots of beer, although I normally don't drink), but I am no weakling. At least I can promise you this: if I ever do get a copy of your wretched magazine, I promise you I will ball it up and wipe my ass with it.

Yours faithfully,

Otto Otto

O. N. Otto
1001 Sator Drive
Sonoma, Cal.

)NO/ono

Someone to show it to would laugh along with the old letter still in his jersey safe against his stomach show her round spaced teeth her breasts jiggling up and down holding her blouse in a hand up and down. The end of the corridor was near; it grew larger and larger. The screen was panting now in the scramble of feet. A window was in the wall approaching; there were no turn-offs. The window filled the screen as the footsteps stopped and the window smashed through into glassy bits.

Pudd shouted, felt himself shout but heard no sound, only the roar, the pounding, whirring roar of the great press, the hundreds of spinning wheels, the paper lashing through, speeding blankly through a dizzy speckle of letters, words, columns, and blurred patches of photographs, shiny paper that gleamed sleek and white on the feeding rolls, spinning and winding out into the massive machine. He could see but could not move, waited stiffly, bound, waited, felt, was sure, knew, to be fed in, to be printed and split into pages, waited and tried to scream.

And then he awoke. Suddenly, to his own shout. The picture moved and shimmered at the other end of the dark theater. Someone near him groaned and said, "Keep it down, will you?" He was half onto the floor, wedged down into and off his seat. He squeezed all the way down onto his hands and knees and crawled to the end of the empty row and out into the aisle. His hands were dirty with dust and chewing gum. Something scrambled across his feet and under the

107

seats of the next row. He stood up, pulling on the armrests and backs of seats and walked out of the auditorium, into and across the lobby, through the swinging door, and out onto the noisy street.

The sunlight pressed the pupils of his eyes to pinpoints.

> *Its coming is sudden;*
> *It flames up, dies down, is thrown*
> *away.*
>
> —Hsiang Chuan

The sudden morning sunlight, flashing into my cracked eyes from the drawn drapes, absolutely blinded me, and so I did not see Sir Hugh, the drawer of the drapes and bringer of the day, until he took me by the shoulder and turned me around, away from the window, until I faced the rest of the room. And there he stood, immaculately attired, as if for a wedding or formal garden party, weary about the face, but with his eyes blazing with anticipation.

"You," I managed to say, despite my usual morning malaise, and added, "Madame Fang-Loos."

"O yes," he replied, his face now an impassive mask, "very interesting, quite. We discussed the *Dee Goong An* well into the night; she managed to take some very interesting and unusual positions on the subject. Pressed one to the extreme, I must admit."

"But, the documents, the safe."

"Oh, I wouldn't worry about that," Sir Hugh jauntily replied. "I can assure you that Madame Fang-Loos will never be a problem so far as that little problem is concerned."

I felt a chill run down my spine, both because Sir Hugh had playfully flipped the back of my nightgown up over my head, no doubt as an encouragement to me to rise and shine, as it were, and because I sensed something deeply inexplicable and dangerous behind and beneath his jauntiness, something that hovered like a wavering pilot flame deep at the heart of all these, to me, inexplicable events. But Sir Hugh's urgings caused me to put aside these doubts and turn promptly and refreshingly to my morning toilet.

After breakfast, we hurried over to the headquarters of the police, not wishing to be even a moment late for our essential assignation. But, even with all our haste, the room was well occupied upon our arrival. Octavius Guy was in the same seat by the window which he had held the day before with Constable Walker poised identically opposite him, the two of them swaying gently on their swivels as though blown by a wayward and wandering wind, mild but persistent; both appeared to be asleep, their lips puckering rhythmically under their sharp noses and round eyeglasses. A strange, but oddly familiar, young man stood over by the safe, yawning, his trousers distorted at the shin by what I was later to learn were bicycle clips. Two anonymous constables stood, one on each side of the room under the pictures on the walls, and, blustery and nervous, leaning on the desk top, stood the Prime Minister, his eyes flashing eagerly at us, his hands clenching and unclenching as in continual self reappraisal and reintroduction.

"Gentlemen," said Sir Hugh, doffing his hat, shedding his coat, tossing them both to me, and stepping across the room to the safe, "I trust I should get about it and settle the whole affair as soon as possible, eh?"

Before anyone could properly respond, he was at the safe, nudging the strangely familiar young man aside, flipping open the sealed envelope Anthony Quiz-Brightling had given him with a pointed fingernail, pulling out the enclosed sheet of paper with its Foreign Office seal, reading the combination, popping the paper absentmindedly into his mouth, chewing and swallowing it as he spun the dials and then swung the heavy door out into the room. The opening door mashed the unfortunate young man against the wall, and as the two constables rushed to his assistance, I could see Sir Hugh lean into the safe, his arms moving quickly, his coat twisting as though he were scratching an itch on his side, and then, just as the constables had finished rescuing the hapless stranger, Sir Hugh turned back, his features aflame with excitement and the morning sun, revealing to us all an empty safe, a safe devoid of blue envelope or chamois pouch!

"Gone," said Sir Hugh, "the documents and the Moonstone are gone!" The Prime Minister fainted dead away, and Octavius Guy and Constable Walker snorted simultaneously awake and both stared down at his crumpled form, lying so evenly and utterly between their feet.

"What," cried out Octavius Guy, his manner that of a man snatched out of a delightful dream into the careening course of a nightmare, "has happened?"

"More importantly," replied Sir Hugh, his voice oddly clipped and hasty, "who is this stranger in our midst, and what is he doing here?" I looked immediately at the stranger, who had regained much of his composure after being stood on his feet and brushed off by the solicitous constables, and my glance was soon followed by that of every eye in the room, bespectacled or bare, save, of course, for those of the Prime Minister, which were still rolled up into a rigid gaze at some vision of horror within his own skull.

"I," said the stranger, with an assurance that suddenly made me realize where I had seen him before, repeatedly on every railway news-stand in England, luridly drawn with his features carefully strengthened, a gun usually in both hands, printed cheaply and vividly on the covers of those pulpy magazine tales by Felix Clovelly, so that I almost was able to finish his sentence aloud with him, "am Gridley Quayle."

Sir Hugh's face, although I suspect it was more a trick of the morning light than physiological fact, suddenly blanched even whiter than its usual anemic pallor, but any fears which might have risen in me concerning his health were dispelled before they could even arise as Sir Hugh stepped forward, took Quayle by the shoulder,

Quayle wincing from the pain caused doubtlessly by his recent collision with the safe door, and said, "Good man, glad to have you with us."

"What," repeated Octavius Guy, "has happened?"

"I wish," said Sir Hugh, "I could be sure, but I can say that one of two things has occurred, and perhaps we can arrive at a sensible decision regarding the choice. Either," a pause while everyone in the room, save the still recumbent Prime Minister, leaned forward, "the Moonstone has been stolen along with the secret documents, or," another significant pause, "the secret documents have been stolen along with the Moonstone."

I must admit that I was stunned by the incision of Sir Hugh's penetrating summary of the situation.

But he was as stunned as I by my sudden perception: "Sir Hugh," I cried, tugging the now crumpled card given to me the night before by the large dark man out of my coat pocket, "the Hindoos, the the Moonstone, the fat man."

Sir Hugh seemed to frown at me, but Octavius Guy interrupted any aural results of his visible displeasure by asking me the contents of the card. I read it carefully aloud:

> "ALI ALIYNFRI
> ALL ITEMS LOST ARE FOUND
> KARACHI BASED, WORLD BOUND
> ENGLISH SPOKEN FLUIDLY"

"As I suspected," said Octavius Guy, "I believe that I have considerable light to shed on Sir Hugh's problem and on that card."

Sir Hugh examined the old detective's face carefully and, apparently satisfied with what he saw, said, "Do explain yourself."

"Walker and I," Guy began, "have not been what you might exactly call asleep," Walker nodded, "for, knowing that Aliynfri and the Hindoo trio were in town, we set about finding them, found them just as they entered the Plaice Place," I looked up in surprise, "followed them as they re-emerged immediately, offended no doubt by the animal fat in which the chips were asimmer, and followed them the rest of the evening."

"And," said Sir Hugh, "did they . . . ?"

"They did not."

"Then," said Sir Hugh, "they . . ."

"Precisely," responded Octavius Guy, "they returned to their hotel suite, or, rather, they attempted to return, but got hopelessly lost in the fog, so that Walker and I finally had to introduce ourselves and guide them there personally. It was on," he continued, staring at me, "those peregrinations that our friends met your friend," I blushed, "and," he paused as if thinking for the right word, "discovered," he at last continued, "that his pockets were empty of any, shall we say, gemstones."

"How the devil," I blustered, but to no avail, for Guy continued grandly on, "So, Walker and I challenged them to a friendly game of Parcheesi, which," and here he glared inexplicably at his dear friend the Constable, "lasted until only an hour ago."

"I blocked 'em," Walker added, in what I can only describe as a chortle, "blocked 'em for six and a half hours," followed by a laugh of indescribable glee.

Then, quicker than I could have dreamed his being able to move, Octavius Guy gritted his teeth and dealt Constable Walker a resounding smack on the nose. Walker's glasses buckled at the bridge even as his knees buckled beneath him, and he slumped down into an awkward heap beside the still slumbering Prime Minister.

"Forgive me," mumbled Guy, breathing heavily, his eyes dim and watery behind his spectacles, his teeth gritted in ebbing rage.

"Of course, my good fellow," said Sir Hugh soothingly, "I'm sure we all approve."

Guy began then to weep, but he did manage to choke out that there was no possibility of either Aliynfri's or the Hindoos' managing to enter Police Headquarters and make off with the missing articles before his own arrival in the room.

"Then," I ejaculated, waving my hands in consternation, "Madame Fang-Loos did . . ."

"No," said a voice which was as tough-sounding as a salted cod. I turned to see that Gridley Quayle had spoken.

"No," he continued, "she didn't."

"And, how," said Sir Hugh, superiority etched on his features and his voice, "would you know that?"

"I know more than you think," replied Quayle, his eyes steely and harsh, Sir Hugh's now weak as dying embers, "I followed her and her car all last night on my bicycle," he suddenly seemed exhausted, as though the very words had reminded his body of something, "need I say more?"

"Enough," said Sir Hugh, his voice rushing, vaulting over itself.

"And," continued Quayle, unheeding, "after she let a certain party out of the car at a certain hotel at a certain hour this morning not so long ago," Sir Hugh seemed to find something out the window and across the street enormously interesting, "her car proceeded to Emergency Hospital," Sir Hugh looked around, interested again, "where her driver, a big chink about seven feet tall, carried her out of the car, limp as a dishrag, and into the hospital."

"What was the matter?" I asked, remembering her extraordinary vitality, her almost pneumatic good health.

"Well, from the look of her," Quayle answered, "I'd guess it was yellow jaundice, but her big boy told the hospital people something that I don't quite understand, but it wasn't jaundice."

Again, I could not restrain myself and practically shouted, "Well, what was the matter? What did he say?"

"He said," said Quayle, "only three words, as best as I could make out, and they were, 'Arr sclew out.'"

I would swear that Sir Hugh blushed had I not known him better. He did seem taller and more confident than I had seen him for some time when he turned from the window and said, "They could have fooled you."

"That woman had something wrong with her," said Quayle, "and besides, there's no way they could have gotten here from the hospital without my knowing it."

"Then," said Sir Hugh, "our problem remains unsolved. With these suspects out of the way, who, then, remains? Let us see if there is a clue in the safe."

He reached back into the safe, exclaimed, "Ah, ha!" and turned back around with a scrap of paper in his hand. Several words were written on it in the finest imitation of Sir Hugh's hand that I have ever seen. Had I not known better, I would have instantly sworn that he had written it himself.

"Let me see that," said Quayle, rudely but typically, snatching the paper from Sir Hugh's fingers, and reading it aloud: "Kaiser Wilhelm über Alles! Otto."

"Huns!" I shouted. "Of course, Huns!" Sir Hugh beamed on me, and I remembered, basking in the glow of his warmth, a grinning face, a revolving body, those astonishing eyes, and I shouted again, "Of course, Otto the Acrobatic German Dwarf!"

"Quickly," said Octavius Guy with the authority of years of authority to the two constables, "find out where the dwarf is playing." The two startled constables bolted from the room, and Sir Hugh, Guy, Gridley Quayle, and I followed after them, leaving the Prime Minister and Constable Walker wrapped in their respective slumbers, blissfully unaware of the furious motion about them.

We thundered down the stairs, leaving a wake of surprised and wondering faces in all the office doors along our path, and secured the information that the German dwarf's acrobatic show had settled, gaudy caravan and all, in an open field between Mexborough and Denaby Main, an easy hour and a half's drive by fast car from our present location. Under Octavius Guy's command, we commandeered the motorcar commandeered from the Flying Squad of the C.I.D. by the Prime Minister's command, and, guided by Guy, set forth immediately for the field.

Guy chose not to go by way of Conisbrough with its hilltop castle familiar to careful readers of Sir Walter Scott, but chose instead to go by way of Swinton with its quaint colliers' homes. I can still remember the narrow streets of Swinton, the long row of narrow adjoining gray houses, white carnations placed in every front window, and busy Mexborough, but mostly I remember the tension in the car, Sir Hugh's hands busily clutching and unclutching some small object about the size of a large hen's egg in his pocket (I looked away, confused and embarrassed), Gridley Quayle's jaw jutting forth like the ramming prow of a quinquereme of Nineveh from distant Ophir, Octavius Guy snoring quietly in the corner of the back seat.

The dwarf's caravan was drawn up in a flat field by the railway line, the trampoline stretched on its roof, and the, by now, familiar figure of the bouncing Otto circling in tiny spirals over roof and trampoline. As we approached the caravan, the dwarf continued to bounce, grinning down at us as he did so, his flat yellow teeth gleaming in the sunlight.

"Come down from there," cried Sir Hugh, "the jig is up!"

"O nein," the dwarf replied, grinning and bouncing. A heavy freight train chuffed into view, and I could hear no more of the exchange between Sir Hugh and the dwarf, but, just as Gridley Quayle, who had crawled up the rear of the caravan on its scarlet ladder, reached out for Otto, the tiny German bounded higher than ever into the Yorkshire air, wrapped himself into a tiny ball, and sailed quite over Quayle's head and outstretched hands, over the narrow fence by the railway track, finally to land on his twisted feet on the top of the last car of the passing freight train.

As the train dwindled into the distance, its smoke mingling with the layer of permanent smoke which hung overhead, the stunted figure dancing on its roof, Sir Hugh spoke to the disappointed Quayle, luring him down from his dejected, if springy, perch, assuring him that the blame was not his, that if blame must be placed, it must be laid directly at the door of Anthony Quiz-Brightling.

"Think of it this way," he added, his fingers curiously crossed, I noticed, behind his back, "at least we solved one problem. We know that the Moonstone was stolen only because it was with the secret documents."

I didn't hear Quayle's reply, for suddenly the air was full of explosions, and the shadow of a wandering zeppelin slid over us like a bad dream. We could even see the grinning faces peering out of its gondola, and we barely missed being skewered by the foot-long steel dart which one of those gleeful Huns tossed out at us and which stuck instead right in the head of the peacefully slumbering Octavius Guy, after passing, of course, through the roof of the motorcar.

"What a pity," said Sir Hugh, as we looked in at the departed detective. "Who could have foreseen such luck? There," now speaking to Quayle, who had climbed down and joined us, as well as to me, "lies the only man alive today who might possibly have recovered the Moonstone and the purloined papers." We stood there, then, stiff as that unwavering steel dart, tears starting unwanted in our eyes, Sir Hugh's eyes, especially, burning with deep feeling.

We did not remain in town long enough to hear what the Prime Minister had to say about the whole business, Sir Hugh pleading urgent affairs in London. Instead we rushed back to our hotel, packed, and prepared to leave for the South immediately. I remember the scene well. I had just commented that we most likely would not be called on again for confidential government service and would probably not even be paid our expenses for this ill-starred adventure.

"Oh, I shouldn't worry about expenses," said Sir Hugh, patting with embarrassing affection the oval lump which still remained in his trousers pocket. "I'll be making a little visit to Septimus Luker's Sons tomorrow, which should solve our financial difficulties for some time."

He then removed a thick blue envelope from his pocket and held it musingly in his hand. It looked startlingly familiar. No doubt it was some decoy he had prepared to foil the thief, but which he had had no opportunity to press into service, for, after meditating over it for some time, he placed it in a large glass ash receptacle and, sadly, I thought, touched the flame of a freshly struck match to it.

As the black, greasy smoke coiled up from the burning paper into the room, filling it with an odor that could only be compared to that of burning flesh, I mumbled, half to myself but to Sir Hugh as well, "Some trifle, I suppose."

"Oh, I wouldn't say that," replied Sir Hugh, a little dreamily, a little (I'm sure of it this time) sadly, and, then, quoting, appropriately enough, the famous Sergeant Cuff, he added, "In all my experience along the dirtiest ways of this dirty little world, I have never met with such a thing as a trifle yet."

And on the street named Life after the investigation of the curious behavior of Miss Shirley Ease by the Our Own Block Home Improvement League and Environmental Protection Association acting as a Committee of the Whole, new events continued to occur, strange happenings of a nature entirely new and unexpected to that quiet community devoted to order and respect for the law. An examination of certain extracts from the journal of Mrs. Olivia Limpy offers an adequate summary of many of those events:

Monday the Tenth

A day that is very special to me, a day blessed to Saint Olivia. I always hang my Mexican white dove, the one with the body made of a blown dove's egg which I have always found so unbelievably ingenious, anyway I always hang the dove in my kitchen window to honor her, although Harold despised Catholics and called my interest in the saints "papist pap," which is not at all like the Harold I hold in my memory, so calm and dignified. The paperboy does look half starved now that you look at him. I offered him fresh crullers, but he said, as polite as you please, "No thanks, ma'am, I don't want to spoil my supper." The darling thoughtful boy, but he looked and looked at those crullers; I wish I'd been more persistent. Truly the seed from which he sprang was "sown on good ground." (Mark 4:26)

Tuesday the Eleventh

Saint Adelaide's day, poor thing, leprous and blind. I have worn smoked glasses (I smoked an old pair of Harold's and burned my thumb doing so) and mustard plasters all day to help me think of her terrible torments. The glasses made me crack my shin on that chair by the dining-room door at least three times today, and how I have missed the bright sun on this hot summer day. But, how she must have suffered! Auranthe came by to console me. Could Miss Ease be right about the paperboy, I wonder? Auranthe told me how he was smiling today when he was leaving Miss Ease's house. Could she have been telling the truth?

Wednesday the Twelfth

Saint Placidus. So I had a placid day, sitting in my chaise longue and sipping lemonade through a straw and taking the sun. It hasn't been cloudy for days and days. It is almost getting to be too hot. The mustard plasters left some blisters; it is so difficult making the transitions from saint to saint.

Thursday the Thirteenth

I knew I should have heeded the warning of thirteen and stood in bed today. And it is Saint Peregrinus's day, too. He was drowned. But anyway, under cover of a dark and heavy sky which sprang up out of nowhere, I got up my courage and slipped up to Miss Ease's parlor window. I was scared stiff! And there she was big as life. Prancing all around the room in nothing but that bra and those panties. No robe at all. And, of course, wouldn't you know the rain came, and it was a hard rain, and I couldn't very well leave without seeing things through. Harold always said, "Olivia, if you don't do anything else right, at least see things through." I was soaked to the bone (I am writing this now, dear Diary, covered with Vicks-Vap-O-Rub with my feet soaking in steaming hot water), and all she ever did was hop around and show herself off in her underwear. But he did smile so.

Wednesday the Nineteenth

I have been sick in bed for days. Couldn't tell anybody how I happened to get caught outside for so long in the rain. Nurse even had to pay the paperboy. It is sweltering hot. I am a martyr now like Saint Gervasius. I did it all for the boy's good.

Thursday the Twentieth

Saint Innocentius. The irony of it. Mr. Hoover has been caught looking in Miss Ease's window. The scandal! I dare not defend him, although I know why he was there. Fortunately he is not married and it will probably just be passed off to "sowing wild oats." (Gal. 6:7)

Friday the Twenty-first

Saint Aloysius Gonzaga, how we could use your stern and moral presence on this street today! Auranthe brought me some fish chowder today. She is so thoughtful. And the news, of course. The things that have been going on! The Riminis, a young couple down the block, newly wed, new to the neighborhood—both of them are dancing for the paperboy!!! They wear only something known as "The Bare Pair." What is called "Bikini" underwear. At first only Francie, the wife, did it, but then both of them started doing it together. The boy seemed delighted. So Miss Ease is not alone now. I do not know what to think. And Auranthe acted so odd that she was no help. If only Harold were here.

Saturday the Twenty-second

I have been reading poetry today (Mrs. Hemans) in honor of Saint Paulinus of Nola. I also played "Nola" on the piano, but my fingers seem so much stiffer than they used to be that I sounded like I had two left hands. Could I have arthritis? The paperboy collected today! I offered him some Apple-Cherry-Berry Juice for the heat, but he politely refused. He seemed disappointed nevertheless. He still smiled, but he seemed to expect something more of me that I did not offer. Do you think he expects . . . ? Of me????

121

Sunday the Twenty-third

Saint Audrey, and my cold is all gone now, but I still didn't feel quite up to church. Auranthe and I are determined to follow him on his rounds to see just how many are involved. He stops now and goes in almost every house. Maggie Peters of 2101 met him at the door this morning when he was delivering the Sunday paper, pulled up her pretty little skirts, and revealed her cotton underpants! She cried out so loudly that I could hear her all the way over here by cupping my hand behind my ear, "Took your picture!"

My random Bible selection from Harold's Bible for this week is: "For after this manner in the old time the holy women also, who trusted in God, adorned themselves, being in subjection unto their own husbands:" (I Peter 3:5)

I wonder . . .

I have always tried to be faithful to Harold's memory. It is so difficult to be in dutiful subjection when you don't know what your husband wants of you. I try, Harold. I really do.

Tomorrow I go to Rose's for a week. Even Diary must stay home.

Monday the First

Saint Thibaut welcomed me home again with his day. I wonder if his ulcers hurt as much as Harold's did. I blame Charles Evans Hughes for those. But I must not be bitter on such a bright day nor allow the past to intrude. My week was wonderful. Rose is such a dear, always introducing me as "my sister Olivia, the beauty of the family." Flattery, flattery, but I did steal Alvin Talbot away from her when she was sixteen and I was already eighteen and "over the hill." That Fenimore treats her dreadfully. He sits around in his undershirt and will never take out the garbage, and he belches dreadfully so you can't even leave the room to avoid the sound. Harold was a saint.

Tuesday the Second

Saint Otto, the apostle of Pomerania, was knocked down and dragged in the mud, and so was I, figuratively speaking, this very day. Auranthe came over to hear about my trip and to tell me about the things that have been going on while my back was turned. I was truly shocked, not that I ever believed that the League members were ever really sincere, but I am puzzled I'll admit. The paperboy whistled nearly all the way up the block today, a tune I've never heard before.

Here is the list that Auranthe made and left with me:

2100 — Ease — white bra and panties with garter straps, pink robe (?), struts

2102 — Franconia — Auranthe left herself and Conrad out

2104 — Limpy — Auranthe needless to say left me out

2106 — Harding — long red wool underwear, man & wife; child in something called "Eskimo Snuggies"

2108 — Hoover — stiffly starched boxer shorts and sleeveless undershirt; wears his collar and tie throughout

2110 — Rimini — the "Bare Pair"—both dance to Negro music

2112 — Marx — the three brothers wear "mod" underwear, different color combinations each day

2114 — Wilde — mauve siren suit for sleepwear, yellow-flowered

2116 — Leslie Ford and David Frome — the two twins in identical boxer shorts; Leslie in a "Navy" T-shirt; David in one marked "Scotland Yard" which is bright pink

2118 — Michael Venning and Daphne Sanders — he, in tiny swimsuit; she, in tinier pink nylon underwear; only one of them sees the boy at a time

2120 — Omega — does not subscribe to paper

That is our side of the street. In a week's time, everything has been lost, all rules of decent behavior have been lost; o why did I leave at such a crucial time?

The other side of the street has been infected as well. "These have one mind, and shall give their power and strength unto the beast." (Rev. 17:13)

2101 — Peters — man in Norwegian net underwear; Maggie lifts her skirt at the door [my addition]

2103 — Andrews — wife in orange sun suit; husband shows bandages around chest for broken ribs; allows boy to sign cast on knee

2105 — Z. B. D. James — a "skirt" made of covers of his paperback Western novels; his wife in a similar outfit with halter and skirt composed of reviews in small-town Nevada and Arizona newspapers

2107 — John — his dentist's smock, tiny blue sanitary face mask and boxer shorts, chases wife in blue panties and bra with bright red molars on them around room with novacaine needle

2109 — Philips — Tarzan striped briefs, no top; wife in nylon striped Sheena bra and bikini panties; both climb ropes in garage gym

2111 — Bartholomew — His and Hers Japanese "Open Door" silk undersuits

2113 — Thomas — in doubt

2115 — Matthews — man in one-piece fishing waders; wife in fish-scale nighty; infants in diapers

2117 — Alfred James — orange athletic supporter; lifts weights

2119 — Thaddeus — jockey briefs and T-shirt; wife in black bra and panties; he plays ukelele and they sing:

> "I'm not wearing anything
> Underneath my underwear;
> I'm not wearing anything
> At all. Poop-poop-pe-doop."

2121 — Simons — plastic "sweat" suits, semi-transparent!

I find myself very tired and depressed. I know that not everyone on our street is of the same class of people as the Franconias and myself, Harold always predicted that the level of the neighborhood was going to go down, but they all seemed to be such *normal* people, and now to behave in such a way. I just don't know. . . .

Wednesday the Third

Saint Anatolius of Laodicea and Saint Anatolius of Constantinople, their day but I don't know anything about them. How can I honor them? I have been near hysteria all day. The heat is unbearable. I hate everyone on the block. Auranthe went by carrying a box today, a bright purple box. I called out to her, but she pretended not to hear me, she just covered up the store name on the box with her hand and practically ran by. Is no one free from taint? I've been crying and crying. My head is splitting. "And they shall turn away *their* ears from the truth, and shall be turned unto fables." (II Tim. 4:4)

Thursday the Fourth

I am always so pleased that today is Saint Bertha's, but since Harold's death, there is no one to lock me in my bedroom closet and let me out at sunset. So I began the day by reading the Declaration of Independence aloud as Harold always used to do. But it only increased my confusion. He was whistling loudly when he came out of Auranthe's door. Her husband is in Cleveland with the Retailers Convention. Then he stopped at my walk, but he did not turn in. He threw the paper up on the stoop as gracefully and accurately as ever, but I knew his heart wasn't in it. He looked me right in the eye, and I knew what he was thinking. Could it really be? He is such a sweet child. His eyes are innocent as a puppy's. I must get up in the attic, but it is so very hot I would smother. They are exploding firecrackers up and down the block. My head is swimming.

Friday the Fifth

Saint Zoe was hung from a tree and a fire lit under her feet. Could anyone suffer more? I held my feet in the oven for a few minutes, but my day is confusion. My head hurt all morning, and then around noon a rain came. A cooling rain, laying the dust and washing everything clean. I was up in the attic by two. And then in late afternoon when everything was cool and damp, a mist blowing in the wind, I slipped to Auranthe's house, bringing her a silk scarf I found in the attic that I thought she might like. But the paperboy was just going in her door. I peeped in her window to see. . . . I will admit it. . . . To see what they were doing, but it was too dark in there. All I could see were two glowing bluish shapes moving about, one over the other. Once I thought I saw his smiling face in the glow. Auranthe wouldn't answer my knock, even after he was gone. He whistled and did a little step on the walk. The cool air has given me an inner clarity. Surrounded as I am, I know now what I must do. I think I shall sleep well for the first night in days. "For sin shall not have dominion over you: for ye are not under the law, but under grace." (Romans 6:14)

Saturday the Sixth

A nervous and exciting day. I sorted out the things I found in the trunks in the attic in the afternoon. I shook them out and washed some of them to get out the smell of dust and moth balls. Even an old pair of bloomers from my girlhood with lace around the bottoms of the legs. I am still slim enough to get into them easily. Quite pretty when I hike up my skirt. Makes me remember. The paperboy came and collected today. Oh, Harold, forgive me!

Albert Longinus had a rough day. He managed to convince his boss that he had nothing to do with the garage break-in and vandalism and the disappearance of the night watchman, but he still had to take blame for leaving his truck by the loading platform and not in its proper place and for not getting his laundry in on time.

"How did you get so scratched up?" the boss had said.

"My girl," he had answered, "she's a real harpy."

It satisfied the boss but not Albert. He worried the whole day through while he drove through the grime and stale air of Newark, an assault on all senses, for nothing was adding up for him. Every detail seemed at once to belong with all of the other details and at the same time to have nothing to do with them at all. Was the Albert who woke up in the grim morning the same Albert who had gone to bed the night before, or was it an entirely new Albert supplied with a set of memories as patently false as the notes and lists which he found in the laundry? Did even Newark, as physical and awfully factual a place as there could possibly be, exist only when he was looking at it and become only a hollow spot in blank space when he turned his back? Who was Miss Parker really? And the mysterious author of those notes, why didn't he ever show his face or tip his hand? He was sick of portents and mysteries, just as sick as he was of that interminable song, "We're Gonna Wash That Crud Right Outta Your Wash," over and over, block after block, day after day, year after year, or was that an illusion, too, someone's idea of a joke?

He collected the wash, sorted the bundles, delivered the clean clothes in their rattling paper wrappers and plastic inner seals. It all seemed real, as real as the grit gathering under his nails and the grime penciling in the lines of his aging skin. He wondered, and he determined to keep on wondering, bag after bag, bundle after bundle, until sooner or later it would all come together like the diagram of a Gallic campaign and make sense at last.

He found only one of the notes that day, a sharply creased note tucked in with an old jersey, some trousers, and a bundle of very stained underwear. He noticed that it had a letter on the back, so he tucked it in his pocket for a close perusal once he got home and had the time. Nothing else.

He checked in at the laundry on time, pulled in under the open door and up to the loading dock, parked in his assigned row and slot, walked over by the boss's office to punch the time clock.

The boss leaned out of his door, still in his swivel chair, and said, "Hey, Longinus, some dame left you a package," and then rolled back to his desk and its stack of laundry slips with no further comment.

The package was lying by the time clock, wrapped in brown paper which on closer inspection proved to be an opened-out grocery bag from the Knight Owl Grocery Chain with its familiar mailed bird, lance in wing, in green ink on the side. It felt like a large volume of some kind, about the size of his album but heavier, so he tucked it awkwardly under his left arm and set out for home. Night was thick as smoke around him, and on the way he thought mainly of light, heat, and food, and scarcely at all of his new, mysterious acquisitions.

After a dinner of classical simplicity, sausage and bacon and eggs, Albert settled down in his armchair, worn to his shape, pulled the chain that turned on his reading lamp, a fringed floor lamp with an attached ashtray and cigar lighter, a tinted scene from ancient Pompeii on its yellowed shade, and hefted the heavy package to his lap. He sliced the twine wrappings away with his letter opener, a small and not very sturdy replica of the Roman gladius, which he kept sheathed and leaning ready in the ashtray.

With paper and twine wreathed around his feet like the disorderly nest of some careless bird of prey, Albert examined his find, a large book, leather-bound and flaking, very old obviously, a Bible, King James version, a family Bible complete with pages filled with brown and spidery handwriting in its front. These pages seemed legitimate enough, a chronicle of births and deaths, Vuelphs and Roderbergs, Keatses and Shelleys, Kittos and Hamiltons, nothing of interest to Albert, nothing that even seemed to tie in with his collection or his life.

He leafed on through the Bible, heading leisurely toward the back pages in search of further writing, but nearly at the end, his eye caught sight of something wrong, a page that bent outward from the rest, creased and askew. It turned out to have a small square of print cut from one of its columns, something missing in the Book of Revelations. This curious absence caught Albert's attention, for it seemed to promise perhaps the mystery he was seeking in its pages. He laid the book carefully on the floor, got up, stepping carefully over the open volume, and fetched his own childhood copy of the Bible, also the King James version, but with no leather binding, only a tattered cloth one, the copy which had been given to him by a visiting missionary who had come to his school when he was in the third grade when he had correctly been able to recite the shortest verse in the New Testament after everyone else in the class had failed.

Back in his chair with both books now balanced, one atop the other in his lap, he compared passages and found that one of two passages had been cut out (the other having come along solely because of its being on the other side). He copied the two passages out into his spiral notebook so that, if he deemed it proper, he could

transfer one or both of them easily into his giant scrapbook.
The first read:

> gnawed their tongues for pain,
> 11 And blasphemed the God of heaven
> because of their pains and their sores,
> and repented not of their deeds.
> 12 And the sixth angel poured out his

Certainly the sentiments expressed in this passage would easily belong with his collection, but the fragmentary structure caused him to turn his attention to the other alternative:

> 5 And upon her forehead *was* a name written, MYSTERY, BABYLON THE GREAT, THE MOTHER OF HAR-LOTS AND ABOMINATIONS OF THE EARTH.

This one, too, would certainly seem to belong, but it was, in its wholeness, as puzzling and unsatisfactory as the other passage with its fragments. Albert peered closely at the mutilated page with his narrow eyes, his lips pursed in anxiety and frustration. He sighed and leafed on, reaching almost immediately another handwritten passage, this one in a very modern hand, rounded *o*'s and looping *l*'s and *d*'s, written in apparent haste with a balky pen, for it was a tissue of splotches and splatters.
Albert read it through:

> No question of it, we were betrayed, the bastard sold us out for cash, may it scald his hand. So I fell into their hands, my God the word haunts me, so write it, write again, hand, hand, hand. They tied me and carried me to him, I grabbed him about the knees and begged, they loosened my hold, carried me to the bench, and, say it, say, he cut off my hand and sealed the deed with a hot poker, and he carried off the hand to do with it what I can't even imagine, may it

choke him dead. And Matilda they raped, all of them, she stopped screaming and just lay there I hear after a while, and left her for dead. I found her and we got away, they didn't care anyway, what could I do handless and she heavy with child. He was born and we named him Albert, so I am entering his name here even though there is no way we can keep him, only half ours and God only knows the seedy mix that is his father. So, here—Albert Long In Us and soon gone.

It stopped suddenly, as did Albert, but Albert went back and read it again and then again. His head was spinning and was beginning to hurt; the sausage and bacon and egg fought their polyglot way back up his throat. He threw the large book from him; it banged onto the floor and slid under the sagging sofa.

Albert was mumbling to himself as he quickly unfolded the note he had found in the laundry. He stared at it, seeing nothing, for a good while, then forced his hot eyes into focus, stared at it, and finally read:

Dear Sir:

Enclosed please find a check for $15.00 (fifteen dollars). Please sign me up for a two-year subscription to your magazine and two extra copies for enclosing cash.

I am a great fan of your magazine, small in stature but big on guts, and I am eagerly looking forward to getting my first copy (in a plain brown wrapper).

Thank you.

Yours eagerly,

O. N. Otto

O. N. Otto
1001 Rotas Lane
Sonoma, California

)N)/ono

No sense. No sense at all. A fake, or, really, no fake at all. A trifle. He balled it up to throw it away, but just as he prepared to pitch it toward the wastebasket in the corner, he noticed a line in different ink from either the letter or the laundry note, a line in bright purple. He uncrumpled the note and read:

Come see me, see me, see me. 666 Ugly. Hot dog. Midnight. Miss Parkkr.

It made no sense. No sense at all, but he smoothed out the paper, folded it neatly, and pressed it in his wallet, and then turned his chair around so that he was facing the wall.

Hard-eyed, lynx-eyed, the perfect private eye, I see only what is there, and what is there is there.

Mallory Quayle is the name, a name given to me by my famous father, the English dick, missing in action since 1916 but still famed and fabled in better than two hundred volumes of the "British Pluck Library" (monthly), those gaudy little volumes that found their way irresistibly to the bedside table of every insomniac in the empire. Which is the main reason I am now in America, the U.S. of A., where as Mal Quayle, Private Investigator, I don't have to worry about having to compete with the stern jaw and fists of steel of my daring dad.

So, I get by. I make a living. I photograph cheerless adulteries over hotel transoms; I repossess still-new Fords and Chevrolets from hot-eyed families; I track down seedy little guys who have fled town with the bank's treasured deposits. I've tangled in a few murders, the kind where some whacky dame does in the husband and the kids with an iron while they're asleep; nothing fancy, but I've seen it all, all the tricks, all the turns. If it's there, I'll find it; if I don't, it's not. No mystery to it, just hard work and knowing where to look, how to look, and what to look for. No surprises, just a job, and I do it and do it well.

So I wasn't surprised or especially interested when she came in my office on Wednesday. She didn't knock, but nobody does any more. A knock, it seems to me, isn't too much to ask. But I don't ask, and I don't knock myself so much these days. I just went on examining the point on my Dixon Ticonderoga No. 2 pencil. The sun had just finished wringing its last light out on the edge of my office window, and I had just finished sharpening my pencils again. I had ground one down to the metal flange around the eraser just a few minutes before, and sparks had jumped out of the sharpener and singed my green desk blotter. It had been that kind of day, a dull winter's day, no colder than it ought to be and certainly no better.

But when I finally did look up, I admit I got more interested. She had bottle blond hair, but it was a good bottle. She was wearing a severely cut tweed suit, but the figure it did no service to was far from severe, long and limber with good legs. Her eyes looked like chips of marble, polished and speckled. I told her to have a seat, which she did, pulling her skirt tightly around her legs but giving me a good glimpse of her knees just the same, and I asked her what she wanted and who she was.

"Silver," she said, in a voice like used motor oil, smooth and thick and dirty. "Clarissa Silver."

I nodded and waited for her to go on. She did.

"Mr. Mallory, I have a job for you, an easy job but one that I can't do alone. It won't take more than an hour, but I'll pay you a full day's fee."

I tried to show some enthusiasm, but I must not have succeeded, for she added, "I promise, I'll make it worth your while." And that did it, that deep voice, those legs, the unspoken promise which I read in the spoken one. So I agreed and asked for details.

It amounted to this: that I accompany her to the Greyhound bus depot, that I meet the New York Express with her, that I help her pick up a suitcase (a brown and white speckled one, cardboard, cheap) which the driver of the bus, an old acquaintance, would be bringing to her, and that I make sure that nothing unexpected or untoward happened during the whole transaction.

When I pressed for more details, I got none. Normally I would have been more wary, but a promise is a promise, and the job seemed easy enough. And if I saw trouble I would recognize it and know what to do about it. When she smiled, she showed her good teeth and no expanse of gum above it. I was satisfied.

So we worked out a fee, twenty-five bucks, which would keep me in Rittenhouse rye and copies of *Dime Detective* for a couple of days, and we left for the bus depot.

The sun was edging itself along behind the buildings across the street as we walked down the few blocks to the depot, so that only Miss Silver's loose hair seemed to cast any light in the shadowy street along the way.

The building was practically empty when we arrived, but, aside from glancing at the girl behind the magazine counter who was doing her nails in bright red polish and humming "I Don't Want to Set the World on Fire," I didn't have time to check the place out thoroughly, because the New York Express had just pulled into the loading tunnel. We walked out through the swinging door into the tunnel, past some incoming passengers carrying their bags and looking worn and harried, and into the stale, gassy air.

By the time we got to the bus, there was no one in sight, just the empty bus with its luggage doors hanging open along its flanks, not a suitcase in sight, only a single wooden crate with some kind of dog in it that was yapping at us like we were the ones responsible for weaning it.

I followed Miss Silver through the door and up the steps to where the driver was sitting. He was a fat man, his hair a yellow white, his skin red and splotched, his fat gut tucked in under the wheel, his stubby arms spread out over the wheel, and his short legs stretched out to the pedals. He was leaning back in the seat with his head thrown back as if he were staring at some message on the roof of the bus. When Miss Silver spoke to him, he didn't even twitch.

There was a featherless arrow, a crossbow bolt, stuck right through his neck, and he was just about as dead as he could be.

Miss Silver drew in her breath sharply and grabbed my arm just about as sharply, but I didn't have time either to feel manly and protective or to complain, because the corpse sat up suddenly, lowered his head, stared blankly at us for a minute, and then gasped, "Hands . . . Foot . . . Toe . . . The . . . ," before a gush of blood filled his mouth and he tumbled over onto the floor, his feet still stretching for the pedals.

Miss Silver was dead white, but she managed to say, "The suitcase," so we searched the bus racks and under the driver's seat, even his pockets, and, aside from blood, we found nothing.

So, we left, Miss Silver down through the tunnel and out onto the street while I went back through the lobby, past the rows of lockers and the magazine counter where the girl was still at her nails, although she was now humming the Hut Sut song. Except for some kid or maybe a midget, innocently empty-handed, who was just heading out of the door, there was nothing else, no one else, in sight. So I eased my way past the counter and out the door to the sidewalk where Miss Silver was waiting.

When she saw that I was empty-handed, her face darkened with a look of what Felix Clovelly would doubtless have called grim determination. She was staring right at me, so I felt called upon to make some kind of statement, so I asked her, "What did he mean with all that stuff about hands and feet and toes?"

She didn't seem even to hear, but when I started to go on, she said, "Do you know of a place run by a one-eyed man named Hands?"

"What kind of place?"

"I don't know," she said, "maybe a bar or a restaurant. Or a club."

I thought about it, but couldn't come with an answer. I'd run into plenty of guys with missing eyes and arms and hands and legs and whatever. If it can be missing, I've probably met somebody who is missing it. But I couldn't think of anybody named Hands offhand.

We walked down the street until we came to a phone booth, and it occurred to me that if this guy Hands was pleased enough with his name, he might have named the place after himself and that, if he did, it might be in the Yellow Pages. So we looked, and the best we could come up with was a place named Hänselnplatz, which advertised itself as an unusual spot for eating and drinking. So, lacking any better leads, we decided to go there for dinner and maybe for something more.

The Hänselnplatz turned out to be located in a rough part of town on a street filled with bars and clubs catering mainly to sailors and soldiers from the nearby military bases. At my suggestion, we got out of the cab, which we had called from the phone booth, a couple of doors away from the restaurant. If anything funny was going to happen in the Hänselnplatz, I wanted to know the lay of the land outside before it started happening.

We passed three bars, the usual dull places, dim lights and loud laughter, and one club before we reached the Hänselnplatz. The doors of the club were open, and we could see a Mexican magician, complete with a brocaded sombrero, up on a low stage squeezing eggs out of his nose with an expression on his face like he had bad sinus trouble. The buildings on the other side were much the same in character; there was one strip joint farther on down, but it was too far down, unfortunately, to warrant checking out. We strolled back and forth before the heavy-looking doors of the Hänselnplatz for a couple of minutes, then, giving the rough-hewn wood of the doors a good shove, we went in.

The place was as dimly lit as the bars had been. There were ten or twelve round tables with red-and-white-checked tablecloths. A jukebox in the rear corner was changing colors as it played "Three Little Fishies," and the bar was over on the left. Behind it, wiping it with a damp cloth, back and forth, back and forth, was a big guy with a red beard, muscles in his arms like you usually only see on wrestlers and weightlifters, a bright shirt and gray leather trousers with straps over the shoulders, Lederhosen I assumed, and one sharp, roving eye, the other one covered with a gray leather patch.

So we were in business. Well enough.

I steered Miss Silver to a corner table on the side of the room farthest from the bar, making no comment about the bartender until we were seated. Then, insisting that she not make any show of it, I asked her to look him over and see if she knew him. She did, and she didn't.

The waiter, a skinny blond guy also in Lederhosen, took our order, and just as he was about to leave, I called him back.

"I hate to bother you," I said, "but the bartender looks familiar to me. What's his name?"

"That's quite all right," he said, as if he were used to the question, "it happens all the time. He is the owner, the great wrestler Mr. Bogenschiesser."

"Bogenschiesser?" I said. "I don't think I know the name."

He laughed, a laugh as phony as his Bavarian outfit. I was about to get a little mad, when he added, "One-eyed Hans. He wrestled under the name One-eyed Hans."

Miss Silver went pale and looked more than a little woozy, so I thanked the waiter, saying "Of course, of course" a few times, and sent him on his way. Then I turned back to her.

"Is that the man?"

She nodded. "I think so, it must be."

So I figured the suitcase would be around here somewhere, but I wasn't sure just how to get at it. I looked around the room, checking out the crowd, spotting the doors, listening to the jukebox, which seemed to be stuck on Kay Kyser.

The crowd looked pretty ordinary, sailors, soldiers, some dames you wouldn't look at more than twice. Except for the table right next to ours. There were two little old men at it, a thin one with little round glasses and a nose so veined and red that it could have passed for the taillight of a Model T, and a plump one, so nondescript that you had to concentrate to be sure that he was really there. They were both ancient and looked like they belonged in the place about as much as the *Queen Mary*.

I was staring at them, trying to fit them into the picture I was forming of the place, when the plump one caught my eye. I tried to glance away, but I was too late. He leaned over toward us and said, "Itty bitty poo?"

"Itty bitty poo?" I said.

"Itty bitty poo," he said, and I thought, here I am in the middle of a case in the company of a beautiful woman in the lair of my opponent, and I have to meet up with two old faggots who have nothing better to do than to say "Itty bitty poo" to me.

"Just what do you want, mac?" I growled, and suddenly they were sitting at our table, mumbling in very English accents about how pleased they were to join us, and the one with the glasses seemed to be trying to hypnotize Miss Silver, he was sitting so close to her and staring into her eyes so hard.

The waiter came back with a little tray with a couple of drinks on it, rye for me, a gin fizz for Miss Silver. The two old fruits had brought their own drinks with them from their table, straight gin would be my guess, so we raised our glasses to our mutual good health, and I took mine at one belt.

The old pair chattered on, especially the plump one, about this and mostly that, while Miss Silver seemed to be entranced. I kept on trying to size up the place, but the room seemed to be getting subtly dimmer. The jukebox had finally switched to another tune, "Why Don't We Do This More Often?" but it seemed a long way away. Miss Silver's hair and eyes seemed to be glowing, and then she and the old guys started a slow turn around me, swinging the table with them.

The jukebox seemed to get brighter and to spin around and and around like a record. I was lying on the floor and then, before I could get up, on the ceiling. I heard the plump faggot cry out in seeming genuine alarm, "Sir . . . You . . . What's happening?" And then the lights went out. I kicked out as hard as I could, and my foot connected with something brittle that snapped like a loud twig. Something smashed me in the back of the head then, and everything went silent and black.

It seemed to me like a long time had passed when I finally came to, and even then I wasn't so sure that I was awake. It was pitch dark.

I held my eyelids open with my fingers to make sure that they were open, and gradually my eyes adjusted to the darkness. I could see tables and chairs around me in the dark. I was propped up against the wall with something heavy lying across my lap.

I sat there, waiting for my head to clear for some time, and then I began to inspect the object in my lap. It felt like a rifle, for it was long and had a stock, but I soon realized that it had a bow attached to what should have been the barrel.

A crossbow. The realization crossed me like a cold breeze, and I just sat there staring at the thing in the dark.

Then something that had been in the back of my mind for some time came to the fore. A police siren, far away at first but getting closer. I tried to get up but fell back with the crossbow still across my lap. As I was trying again, I heard the siren, loud now, right outside, and a squeal of tires. Just as I heard car doors slamming and the siren dying down just outside the door, a lot of things came together, and a lot of things made a whole lot of sense.

Life on the street called Life had given itself over to open competition. No one, save perhaps the aloof and mysterious Alfred Omega, who did not even subscribe to the paper, was immune. Meetings of the Our Own Block Home Improvement League and Environmental Protection Association became as tense and careful and as openly and painfully polite as any meeting of a truce commission or even the Security Council of the United Nations. Even the Hardings were appealed to for succor and support, and Nan found herself invited to tea up and down the block as mutual pacts formed and dissolved like oil patterns on a rain puddle in the street.

Miss Shirley Ease, still isolated by her League member neighbors despite (and, of course, because of) her role as prime mover of events, was hurt by a lessening of attention which she sensed in her small friend, the paperboy, so she brought about, however unwittingly, an escalation of tensions by making an effort to restore his attention. She bought a copy of *Fotoromance*, with a cover article about what Mrs. O told O about J, R, and E, in the pharmacy in the building in which she worked. In the pages of that magazine of the stars she found an advertisement from which she ordered an array of intriguing and inventive undergarments, this in utter disregard of Dr. Omwake's warning that such items were likely to be shoddily made and disappointing, else there would be photographs in the ad rather than those startling and implausible drawings.

Late in sultry July, on an afternoon when water arched and sprayed from green plastic hoses onto wet, green lawns all along the block, she appeared to the boy in her new Signor Federico's Uplift Peekaboo-Tip Black Lace Bra and her equally new and eye-opening Tru-Passion Scanty Bikini-Plus Panties, also black lace. The paperboy was as stunned as he had been the first day when she had been sick. She was so thrilled by her success that for hours after his hesitant and faltering departure her nipples remained firm, red, and goosy.

After this opening blow, a steady increase of arcane undergarmentry followed up and down the block. Rubberwear and elastic bandages, trusses, false and extraordinarily large "bottoms," leather girdles, spiked heels and small whips, earmuffs and embroidered ties, even innocent hair ribbons not so innocently placed, all were substituted for normal underwear. The Z. B. D. Jameses wore sagging gunbelts and even strips of wampum. Debates broke out in the aisles of the supermarket over the best and most strategic use of band-aids and vaccination cups.

And there were equally startling reversals: men began to appear in women's briefs and padded bras; women, in men's baggy boxers. Mr. Bartholomew appeared in the skimpy garb of a Japanese girl pearl diver, while his wife made an even more intriguing appearance in the abbreviated costume of a Sumo wrestler. Mrs. Peters made her debut in a catcher's chest protector and protective aluminum cup.

Those who were more conservative vied in the brightness of colors, the whiteness of whites. The clotheslines of the neighborhood blossomed into a shining array, unmatched certainly by any in the city, perhaps none in the state, few in the world. On Monday afternoons, the housewives marched up and down the street as their laundry flapped in the breeze, examining each other's wash and taking careful notes.

And, too, methods of presentation became more elaborate. The Riminis danced to more elaborate music, utilizing even Moondog and Yoko Ono Apple efforts. The Philipses climbed higher ropes strung in their back yard and essayed simple gymnastic stunts. The brothers Marx worked out an elaborate routine in which by careful turnings and weavings they were able to cover themselves with a small hand fan and a single borrowed burlesque pasty. Alvah and Thelma Thaddeus taught themselves guitar and kazoo to accompany their song. Conrad Franconia hired a local electrician to rig an involved system of colored lights and infrared devices in the Franconia parlor, while Auranthe enrolled in a tap and acrobatic dance class.

And those who were less athletic developed other methods of holding the boy's attention and adding stimulus and interest to his days. Some showed home movies of visits to the beach; the Peterses were able to present a complete twelve-part slide-and-film show of Maggie's development from pink blanket and bare skin to pink skin and pinker pinafore of the blushing present. Leslie Ford and David Frome, less mixed and modern in their choice of media, sat the boy down on afternoon after afternoon and, dressed in their now familiar attire, recounted to him their curious history, how their mother, convinced that her twin sons, though identical to the eye, were in fact the sons of two different fathers, had insisted upon naming them accordingly and sent baby David off to England to be raised by the puzzled Fromes and kept baby Leslie in Annapolis to be raised by herself and her husband, the long-suffering but understanding Mr. Brown, and finally how the two brothers had found each other after years of detective work, had solved the mystery of their identity (no small feat), and had settled down together to spend their waning years in autumnal communion on the street called Life.

A climax of sorts was reached on a Saturday morning in August when Mrs. Olivia Limpy received a package C.O.D., wrapped in a plain brown wrapper. It was a small package, but it aroused considerable interest in Mrs. Limpy and no little curiosity in the homes of her neighbors.

"I opened the package eagerly," her journal for that Saint Mamas day reads. "I had no idea what I would find, for I had just circled a number in the coupon without looking at the terrible ad itself. All those bosoms like missiles!! I found only a tiny bit of stiff black lace and nothing else tucked in wadded-up pages from the *National Enquirer* with which the box was stuffed. Then I realized that they were little pants. That gave me such a tremor. They were so very tiny! I held them up to the light for a closer inspection, and at first I thought that they had been damaged in shipment. Then I blushed as red as ever I did on our wedding night when Harold jumped out of the closet, and I even exclaimed aloud, 'They have no bottom!'"

Another climax of sorts was also reached in August, this one by Mr. Herbert Hoover. After his unfortunate run-in with the police in June, Mr. Hoover had become very much a recluse. Still, driven by the need for some human contact and by a still vivid vision of a certain item fluttering on a certain washline, he did make his way, usually under cover of the darkness of the summer night, up the street to the door of the young couple, Mike Venning and Daphne Sanders. Their door, although it was sometimes slow to open to his hesitant knock, always did open, and the young people seemed to welcome Mr. Hoover's visits, although always separately. Mr. Hoover worried a good deal about this. Some evenings Mike would open the door, and the two men would have a beer and talk about mannish things—football, politics, the prospect of good things ahead just around the corner. And on other evenings, Daphne would welcome him in, and they would discuss menus and nature and the necessity for women's liberation. But never, not even once, were both Mike and Daphne at home when Mr. Hoover called.

Finally, on a very late August evening, Mr. Hoover could stand it no more. His curiosity forced him to overlook the lessons he thought he had learned from his experience at Miss Ease's window, and besides, as he told himself, lightning simply does not strike the same spot twice. So he slipped down the dark street, but when he reached the tidy front yard of 2118, instead of walking up the curving walk, he slipped across the grass between the house and the dark neighboring house of early-retiring Mr. Omega and took up a position beneath a leafy lilac which afforded him a clear view through the clean window into the bedroom of Michael Venning and Daphne Sanders.

The room was empty, but Mr. Hoover's curiosity was of an intensity which made his patience long. And his patience was at last rewarded, though not exactly with what he came to see, which is most often the case.

Mike came into the room, yawning and stretching, dressed in blue jeans, faded with darker blue patches, and a blue work shirt, no shoes or socks. He pulled off his shirt, revealing his bare chest, then tugged off his belt, tossing it over onto a cluttered dresser top, and unbuttoned his jeans. Mr. Hoover gulped and glanced around him in the dark. To be caught now would be so much worse than his being caught before in similar but so very different circumstances. The night was still and empty of movement, only the sweet smell of flowering plants drifting on the still air.

When he looked back, Mike was naked but, fortunately for Mr. Hoover's remaining dignity, facing away from the window, a normal naked young man of the kind he had seen in gym locker rooms for most of his educational life, nothing unusual and certainly nothing to get this excited about. But just then everything changed. The naked Mike had walked over to the other dresser, taken that potent and familiar pair of small pink panties trimmed in white out of one of its drawers, and was now pulling them on, up his legs.

Mr. Hoover was horribly embarrassed. To have glimpsed another human being's totally private quirks was more than he could stand, for this was no innocent satisfying of curiosity but a sinful espying into the very depths of another person's privacy, the very integrity of his identity. But, driven by impulses too often more powerful than dignity or thought, Mr. Hoover stared on.

The figure in the pink panties turned around, naturally and gracefully, her small breasts exposed to the room and to Mr. Hoover's secret gaze, her skin as soft as a baby's, stretching her arms to pull on the familiar red-and-white-striped cotton knit top which she wore so often when they spent their pleasant evenings of conversation together, Daphne Sanders without a doubt.

Mr. Hoover, for the second time in that eventful summer, fainted dead away.

Through all of this striving and confusion, the little paperboy grinned and went his cheerful and winning way. He watched politely and interestedly in each and every home, accepting what each person offered to show. He was quite impartial, although occasionally he was startled into delighted applause. But he would never pause long, for he insisted on trudging home before dark each shortening day.

Red-eyed, bleary-eyed, I sat at my desk, nursed my hurt head, and tried to read the newspaper. Nothing in it much but maneuverings and mutters of war. Even Dick Tracy had a fatal ring to it, at least for the Mole, what with their dumping snow from the blizzard on the boiler entrance to his hideout, but the elements seem to have a way of helping Tracy out like they did my fictional dad that the rest of us dicks can't quite count on. It was cold and gray outside the office, and maybe not so cold but just as gray inside. The kind of day on which things don't happen, but this day they'd better.

Oh, sure, I got out of the Hänselnplatz place just as the police were coming in, and they didn't see me. There was some luck in that, but more of being able to do what you have to do when you have to do it. So I got up and out, dragging the crossbow with me, made it across town with it, and stuck it in a locker at the bus depot before coming up here to the office, where I figured to sleep it off. I did sleep, but it was still with me when I woke up—a head with a lump on it like a pigeon egg (the choice of bird is intentional), a stomach that felt like it had just finished hosting a convention of jitterbuggers, and a refreshened insight into the ways and wiles of women.

So, seeing no way to act but to wait, I waited. Somebody was bound to get interested in the whereabouts of that crossbow, or maybe just in the whereabouts of me. And it wouldn't take them long to get around to looking here.

I was just turning back to the sports pages for the third time when there came a knock at the door—a knock, a genuinely polite tap-tap. So I tossed the paper toward the waste can and sang out, "Come in."

She was the first one in, Miss Clarissa Silver herself, looking a little the worse for wear but still sharp enough to hook my eye, followed by the two English faggolas, the thin one with the glasses now swinging rather limply on a pair of new crutches and the plump one bobbing around in his wake, shutting the door behind them. It was some parade, and if they'd managed to be carrying a flag, I surely would have stood up and given them a salute—any flag would have done.

So, suddenly the office was crowded. They took all the chairs in the room, being pretty careful not to say anything until they were all tucked in and tidy, so I didn't say anything either, just watched.

Finally, when the fat fruit had stopped hovering over the skinny one and had sat down himself, Miss Silver opened the conversation.

"I suppose," she said, in that same old viscous voice, "that you probably feel we owe you an explanation."

"In a pig's valise," I countered. "Now what have you got to explain to me that I might want to hear? I can't imagine. Now why should I want to hear why you suckered me to some dump where you could get me mickey-finned and knocked out, both at the same time, so I could be set up for a murder rap that you know good and well you're the only witness who could prove me innocent? Now why would I want to know that?"

"Your bitterness is quite understandable," said the thin old guy, his fluttery voice suddenly edged with something like carborundum, hard and edgy and cutting, "but I suspect you should hear Miss Miller out."

"I'd be glad to," I answered, not willing yet to give any quarter, "if you'd tell me who the hell Miss Miller is and, for that matter, who the hell you are."

"Very well," he answered, absolutely sure of himself, not even glancing at Miss Silver or at his bunk buddy, "I'd hoped earlier that it wouldn't come to this, but it has, and so I have no other recourse. I am, shall we say, an old acquaintance of your father's."

I let my eyebrows raise a bit, since that seemed to be what he required to go on.

"My name is Sir Hugh Fitz-Hyffen," he said, "a name which you may have heard, but which I hope you have not remembered. I last saw your father some twenty-six years ago, not long before he entered the army, haven't, in fact, been back to England in that time. Like the present Duke of Windsor, I'm afraid I'm not awfully welcome there these days." He paused, but when I didn't comment, he continued, "But, as you seem to have found out quite by yourself, there are other places. Yes, despite what they say or the wind says, there are other places."

His voice trailed off, but Miss Silver took up where he left off.

"Sir Hugh and his compatriot," she said, not noticing that Fitz-Hyffen winced at the word, "have been following me for some time. Longer than I had any idea."

She stopped and stared at me for a long time, her eyes weary but somehow warm. As she spoke, I felt a stirring of old and foolish feelings, which I found that I could not suppress but which I could at least not allow to show.

"I don't know why I'm telling you this or why I'm even here," she said, then, looking at Fitz-Hyffen, "but all last night, that is, well, Sir Hugh has some very persuasive methods. Look, what I mean is, my name is not Clarissa Silver. It's Mary Miller, and I'm a thief."

This time I didn't let my eyebrows go up. I just sat still like a bunny or a Buddha.

"I'm Mary Miller," she went on, "and I've been working with three men to steal and get away with stealing the silver hands. We got them."

"Their names?" I said.

"The hands?" she said, nervous now.

"The men," I answered.

"Well, one of them you know, two of them really. The driver of the bus, Karl Kutscher; the wrestler, Hans Bogenschiesser, the strong arm of the team; and Otto Wolf, the brains."

"The hands," said Fitz-Hyffen, as if from a long way off, "are said to have been those of another Otto, a legendary Otto, favorite of the Holy Roman Emperor. His hand was severed as a child. The emperor ordered a silver replacement fashioned. Then, as the boy grew, another, and another, then, for the man, a last other."

"They were in the museum," the revealed Miss Miller interjected, "the graduated hands arranged under glass, in Nürnberg. We managed to remove them during the Nazi Party Rally in 1934 at the exact moment, according to Otto's plan, that Chancellor Hitler was receiving the crown, orb, and scepter of Charlemagne. If you look closely for us in *Die Triumph des Willens*, you'll see us in a crowd cheering Hitler's passage through town; Otto is disguised as a child, while Hans and I were his mother and father, and Karl is there in the uniform of a member of the Labor Service Corps.

"We were able to succeed because of Otto's sharing his name with the prominent financier, and we got the hands out of Germany and into Austria by the same means. They have been traveling across Europe and the ocean for the past seven years, and they are somewhere in town today."

"And you want me to get them for you," I said.

"No," said Fitz-Hyffen, his voice regaining its strength, its compelling edge, "we want you to help us recover them and, naturally enough, share in the reward offered by the German government."

"The rest of the story . . ." Miss Miller tried to say.

"The rest of the story," I interrupted, "I know. You were double-crossed. Your friend One-eyed Hans shot the bus driver, and he tried to pack the blame on me. And now he and your pal Otto have the hands, and you're very angry.

"Oh, I see it all. Hands, Hans. Foot, toe, Otto. Oh, it's all clear. I'm not and I won't be anyone's patsy. Not even yours.

"But," I went on, "I don't see how I can help you and your new little friends at all."

"But," said Fitz-Hyffen, "you don't see. Otto Wolf will be here any moment."

"How do you know that?"

"Sir Hugh," said the fat one, whom I had completely forgotten, "has his ways."

And, of course, as sure as a scene in a Charlie Chan movie, the door opened, and in walked a forty-year-old midget.

"Otto," said Fitz-Hyffen, as calm as if he'd known the midget all his life.

"Sir Hugh," said Otto. "Fräulein Miller. Herr Quayle." He, too, was as calm as you please. Only Miss Miller was less than cool, and the flush that spread over her cheeks made her eyes gleam, and I was glad, frankly, that I was sitting down behind my desk.

"I am quite sure," the midget continued, still standing, his little hands hanging by their thumbs from the pockets of his vest, his face stubbly and unkempt in contrast to the rest of his tidy attire, "that I have no idea why you requested my presence here."

Fitz-Hyffen pulled a folded piece of paper from his pocket then and handed it to his buddy. The old fellow unfolded the paper and peered at it closely.

"French poetry," he said, surprised.

"Yes," said Fitz-Hyffen, "and would you mind giving us a free rendering of it in English?"

"But, I . . ."

"Do, go on."

The old man stared at the paper some more and then began:

> "My aim is an Amazon queen
> Who comes like a moist cathedral. . . ."

I cleared my throat, and Miss Miller looked down at her feet, the color of her face becoming an even richer and rosier red.

"May I," Fitz-Hyffen said, "be so bold as to offer some emendations to that excellent attempt? Especially to the first line."

Why we were sitting there listening to two old fairies argue about French poetry was, for the moment, beyond me. And, from what I could tell from the midget's face, it was beyond Wolf, too. But we were both due to be enlightened shortly.

"The first line," Fitz-Hyffen continued, "should be rendered, 'My aim is an amazing key,' yes," as he was raising a crutch in a declamatory manner, "a key." And suddenly he slammed the crutch into the back of the midget's head, knocking him flat, and, as quickly, he jumped onto the floor, favoring his right leg, rifled Wolf's pockets, and settled back on the floor holding a small key aloft. The key, I recognized instantly, was to a bus or train-station locker!

I stepped over the recumbent Mr. Wolf, took the key from Fitz-Hyffen, stuck it in my coat pocket, and said, "I think we should probably get moving, and, by the way, Fitz-Hyffen, when it comes to quick reflexes, your cylinders are hitting all the way around."

"Well, *Mister* Quayle," he replied, wincing as he swung himself up on his crutches, his right leg stiff and obviously painful, "I have had some proof of the quickness of yours as well."

I didn't follow him up on that, but, giving Wolf a quick shake to see if he was as out as he appeared, I suggested instead that we try the lockers in the nearby bus depot. So we did.

At the bus depot, things were pretty much as they were the day before. The same girl was behind the magazine counter, still humming, still painting her nails; only the song was different—this time it was "The White Cliffs of Dover." She kept up, did that girl. There were a few passengers dozing on the benches, propped on their suitcases and stuffed shopping bags. A couple of porters loafed by the door into the loading tunnel. But, on the whole, the place was the same. With one difference. This time I had the key to things.

I pulled the locker key out of my pocket, read the number on it, and led the way down an aisle of lockers to number 1002, a box on the bottom row. I knelt down, haunted by a sense of *déjà vu*, turned the key in the lock, and opened the door to reveal the crossbow!

So I had mixed up the keys. It could happen to anyone, but someone didn't seem to know that, for I heard a thump behind me and a voice saying, "Just give me the suitcase and no one will get hurt."

I knew that voice even though I had never heard it before, not while I was conscious anyway, so I grabbed the crossbow with both hands and swung it back and up as hard as I could right into the startled face of the bartender Hans with a smack that was so hard that it would have crossed his eyes if he'd had two of them to cross. As it was it knocked him cold, and he keeled over on the body of the plump old guy, who was already lying at Hans's feet.

"Very nimble," said Fitz-Hyffen.

"Just returning something I borrowed," I said.

I got out the other key, opened the next locker, 1001, and pulled out a battered cardboard suitcase. I swung it flat out onto the floor and snapped open the latches. Inside were four worn and smooth silver hands, strikingly lifelike, snug as bugs in a velvet-covered board with appropriate indentations.

"It is they," breathed Miss Miller, like a low, warm southern breeze. I felt the hairs on the back of my neck turning in it.

"Then let us be off," said Fitz-Hyffen, poking his buddy idly with his crutch.

And off we were, in more ways than one in my opinion, leaving One-eyed Hans sprawled in the corner rear of the aisle of lockers, with me carrying Fitz-Hyffen's chum over my shoulder. "Shouldn't ever take a drink," I said to the counter girl, but she didn't even look up, figuring I was just offering her some unneeded advice, I guess.

We went back to my office, found no Wolf behind the door, tipped the police off anonymously as to where to find a murderer and a murder weapon in close proximity, and, suitcase in hand (my hand, since Miss Miller had almost broken her back carrying the thing to the office, and since the pudgy Englishman was now afoot again), we went off to the German Consulate, where the bald consul thanked (and paid) us profusely and promised that the silver hands would be placed under the personal protection of the Führer himself.

And so the caper was closed.

We had dinner that evening at a little German restaurant, chosen by Miss Miller with a strong sense of appropriate irony, and, warmed by Wienerschnitzel and Rhine wine and candles and Miss Miller's close presence, I even developed a certain affection for the two old men. They were pretty harmless old things for all that.

So, relaxed and happy, I asked Miss Miller what caused her to get involved with those three krauts.

"It was Otto," she said. "There's more to that guy than shows." And she added, with a wink at Fitz-Hyffen, "And that's more true than not most of the time."

So I dropped the subject, but when we finally got around to splitting up the reward, I have to admit I got another little surprise.

"It's all yours," said Fitz-Hyffen. "I haven't needed any money for some years," and he got that odd look in his eyes again, "no, not for some years, so it's all yours, my boy, all yours, the least I can do for a son of your father, for you, for you."

So I took it. I had always wanted to see the Pacific, and now I had the chance. I looked dreamily across the table at Miss Miller, thinking, embargo or no embargo, baby, stick with me and it's silk all the way. I could see us lying on the beach, splashing in the ocean, dancing to ukelele music, electric guitars, grass skirts, the whole thing.

I guess I must have been dreaming on for quite a while, because quite soon, it seemed at the time, Fitz-Hyffen took my hand and said farewell. And as sentimental as I had gotten, I wasn't unhappy to see him go.

"Good luck," I said. "Nice knowing you."

But then he and the plump guy got up to leave, and Miss Miller got up with them.

"No need for you to go," I said, "besides I've got things to say to you."

"I'm sorry," she said, low and smooth, "don't think badly of me, but . . ."

"But, what?" I said.

"But, I'm going with Sir Hugh. There's so much he's taught me already, secrets he's shown me. I've got to have more, so much more." She kissed me lightly on the forehead then, a brush like an angel's wing, and off they went, Fitz-Hyffen on his crutches, Miss Miller hovering over him, touching him lightly with her fingertips, the little plump guy trotting along behind like a nervous lap dog.

"Dames," I said, "women, broads. There's no telling, none at all."

But the candle is still lit, there is still wine in the bottle, and the reward is still snug in my pocket. Well, I say to myself, the world is so full of a number of things, more than one anyway, and that's for sure.

I can get a ticket on a Clipper in the morning and take off. Just lock the office door behind me. Be in Honolulu by Saturday night, on the beach the next morning.

Things are turning out okay. When the world is this bright and clear, not much can happen to change it very quickly. That I know and know for sure.

So now I am settled and happy and dreaming.

Winter in Waikiki, December on Diamond Head, Sunday in the sand. I can see it now.

Thursday Noon
PUDD KEEPS A DATE

The Emstrand had been completed and formally opened in 1938, its architecture futuristic, all the corners rounded, a spire with rainbow-shaped and colored aluminum at its base, illuminated at night in its early days before the war. It was dirty now, in the part of town where trolley tracks still dissected the brick streets, uncovered and rusty with long disuse, now only warping tires and tossing cars erratically into each other's flanks.

Pudd stood on the sidewalk under the marquee watching the lunch crowds from the factories and the dingy offices on the second floors of the bars and pawnshops all along the street push their way by each other and through the noonday sun. His hands were in his jersey pocket, one at each end of the tube, fingering the envelopes there, the one frayed and worn soft, the other crisp and new, together in the pocket where the iron key had been the day before; he was sweating, his head ached, and the muscles of his arms and back, the backs of his legs and balls of his feet, all hurt, all flamed as he hunched his back, turned to the shabby doors and the ancient doorman, sitting on a stool, making no effort to rise or even be alert to when he should arise, and went into the dim lobby of the hotel.

He stood for a moment, waiting for his vision to clear, and then for another moment as his eyes wandered from the desk and its stern cross-eyed clerk, his thin white hair combed vainly and in vain across his balding head, to the racks of travel folders, airline and bus timetables, a black felt board with white plastic letters announcing that Dr. Thomas Wise, Ph.D., would be addressing the Ladies' Poetry Society at 2:30 in the Whittier Room Annex, a rack of postcards with colorful and comic animals, views of the arena, the museum, the prison, cartoons and gaudy slogans, DONTBEAN ORZIZZAS, two shelves of paperback books, murder mysteries, Z. B. D. James westerns, and titles promising throbbing and unremitting lust, the plush and dusty chairs, the smooth tile floor, the six marble pillars, round as the curving corners of the walls, the aluminum trim, dust gathering in furry tribes along the edges of the walls, the three elevators, dormant, their doors open but uninviting, and the open double door and red neon sign of the restaurant and coffeeshop.

The doorway was formed, top and sides, by panels of mirrored glass, two feet wide, framing the door so that reflected lobby and restaurant met and joined along the inner edges, the movement in and out of one customer's approach transformed in a blur of activity, a stream of entrance and egress. Pudd was at first whole and then split as he moved forward and stopped again, his trunk cut in half, one arm, one leg, the faded blue jeans, the blue jersey, half of each, one scuffed shoe, the hand tucked away in the jersey pocket, and half a head, red eye, red nose, splotched cheeks, the pale red hair of head and eye, the eye open, wide, staring, for the other half of his body in the door was hers, the black curled hair springing from his red, her small face, eye squinting, peering back at him, red cotton blouse, one pear of a breast, black skirt, one cocked hip, leg, no stocking, and patent-leather shoe, the two halves matching along the glassy seam, Tiresias, the "morphodike" of every boy's carnival dreams, the split made whole, the severed joined, the blissful end of Platonic Aristophanes' dream, full circle, whole egg, broken when Pudd stepped on by the mirror, through the door to stop before the young reporter's narrow gaze.

158

"Oh, Pudd!" She gasped and blushed. "You came. I'm sorry, my eyes, I've lost my glasses, you see. Please come in, I've reserved a table," leading him by the arm, not even letting him get a hand out of his pocket, pulling out a chair for him and pushing him into it, and around the table, sitting herself, and leaning across to stare again an inch through and behind his eyes. Pudd escaped those eyes this time, pulled his hands out of his pocket and onto the table and his gaze down onto the hands, the blunt nails, the red hair coiled sparsely on the white and mottled flesh, the fingers a mosaic of warts, Byzantine in their complexity but mutable as no golden bird. And on the table, two drinks, Manhattans, the cherries red and gleaming in the glasses. Pudd tasted his, sweet and thick, as the reporter drank hers down, her eyes closed so that Pudd dared watch her throat.

"Oh, this day," she said, opening her notebook, poising her pencil over a clean new page, "and what is your background? I won't use it, you know, really, but it will help me. That's why I picked this place, the Emstrand, I had reasons for moving our interview here, there's no darker place, no one comes here, the kind of place where you sleep with one eye open. We'll be secure from prying here. And what do you feel about being, I mean, your profession? How did you get into it? Won't you say anything?"

And Pudd, speaking, his voice slow and Southern, a faint touch of Irish in some words, slurred and rolled, looking at the blank paper and her pencil, beginning to move, dots lines and curves, illegible and in no tongue known to Pudd, "My life is like," the pencil darting and hopping, catching it all, "the autumn leaf that trembles in the moon's pale ray; its hold is frail, its date is brief, restless, soon to pass away," the pencil faltering, her head turning up away from the page, "yet when that leaf shall fall and fade, the parent tree will mourn," the pencil stopping altogether, her eyes fixed on his forehead, his eyes still down on the page, "its shade, the wind bewail the leafless tree, but none shall breathe a sigh for me."

His red and watery eyes leaped up, his voice rising and secure, his eyes meeting hers, diving into those unfocused deeps, plunging up, up down and in, "My life I've spent in wandering, born by the bay

Espíritu Santo, I have fought sharks, ridden the tall ship and wrestled the creaking sails of José Gaspar, and walked the air thick with mosquitoes on Davis' isle," the pencil still motionless, lying then down on the paper, her fingers frozen at the edge of the table, his voice deeper and richer, soft as summer air combing Spanish moss, hints of a double moon low over and in green water, "I became a man in tropic climes, but found a future around the globe," the voice suddenly different, still rich but more clipped and nasal, a touch of autumn in it, "sailed from Gloucester aboard the *We're Here*, gaffed halibut and cod, sliced bait and rode a broken spar in storm to port," and now it was flat and cold, accentless and bare, "lived beyond the Yukon in high mountains and higher risk, stalked moose and elk with iron-barbed arrows, broke my bow and killed by hand," then sweet and low, deep and faintly French, late April outside of Paris in the rippling fields, "I can show you pleasures unmentionable, give you the in and out and in of unspeakable delight, halve you with one steady stroke, touch your ears and eyes with truth beyond hope, with love beyond love," standing now, his drink empty, holding her hand, lifting her, his voice Southern and slow again, the sorrow of defeat, the emptiness of loss, the nostalgia of regret, her eyes deep in his, following him, moving with him out of the room, the lobby, the hotel, into the sunny and empty street:

> "My life is like the print, which feet
>   Have left on TAMPA's desert strand.
> Soon as the rising tide shall beat,
>   Their track will vanish from the sand:
> Yet, as if grieving to efface
> All vestige of the human race,
> On that lone shore loud moans the sea,
> But none shall thus lament for me!"

The sun, the heat, the long bus ride, her purse now hanging from his hand, leading her, touching her on the bus, in public, where she had never been touched before, through the screen door, down the narrow hall and into the room, hot and damp, the dust balls rolling on the floor, the closed windows and unmade bed.

She sat on the bed, prim and proper, knees touching lightly, hands folded in her lap, saw her purse laid on a table, saw a black wad of nylon lifted from behind her and tossed through the open closet door, a mirror reflecting part of the bed, exposed mattress and hanging sheet, felt her sling pumps being pulled off, and lay back on the bed, alone in a dark, hot, and dirty room.

Pudd closed the bathroom door and stood before the mirror, his face a spatter of color through the orange smears that slashed it up and down. He held his fingers under his nose and breathed deeply, an acrid smell. He smiled and pissed long and hard, speaking aloud to the steady splatter, his voice rotund and orotund, a wink caught and returned in the blades in the window:

> "Was ever woman in this humor wooed?
> Was ever woman in this humor won?
> I'll have her, but I will not keep her long."

Flushed, out, back down the short hall and into the bedroom, Pudd sat on the bed beside her. She was lying back, the red rubber band around her thumb, staring at the ceiling. She raised a leg, her skirt pulling up on the strained thigh, and he put his hand where it had been before, no underpants, bristling, damp. Then the black skirt off and on the floor, the red blouse, the breasts very small, the nipples soft as the rubber membrane trembling over the switch of an electric motor, flat against her chest as she lay back again, naked, bare, no make-up, the eyes open and empty, the black curly hair, short and tidy. Pudd reached to muss it, to tangle it, and it slid on her head, her mouth popping open, her eyes, came off in his hand, black nylon, a wig, and her hair, mouse brown, long and tangled, fell over her shoulders, over her breasts as she sat up.

"Pudd," she said softly, reaching for his belt as he got up, walked to the closet and back carrying a black cardboard suitcase, "you must know," as he sat again, opening the suitcase on the floor, her hands rubbing the hump of his trousers, "what I know," as he removed and placed in a tidy row by the bed, her hands falling away, her eyes squinting at the row: a length of electric wire with a male plug at one end, a stale grapefruit, two jars of cold cream, a chipped superball, a pair of handcuffs, a jar of dirt alive with worms, two silver spoons, a knife, three artgum erasers, a corked and double-pointed etching tool, two copies of the *National Geographic*, and a tinned ham.

"Pudd," she said louder, doubt in her voice and on her face, as he smiled, pulled off his jersey over his head, "Pudd," as he pushed her onto her back, "Pudd," as he leaned over her, seeing in the closet mirror for a second, her body, his, both hot and headless, and as he snapped off the light, "Pudd, what are you?"

The note, if you chose to believe it, and Albert Longinus, so confused now by event and false event that he felt an ebbing of the drive even to separate the two, much less understand them and their joinings and partings, did so choose, was clear enough. Miss Parkkr was, by either the erroneous workings of chance or of Newarkkian cause, Miss Parker, his missing partner of what now seemed months, years ago. An examination of his city map revealed a street named Ugly far off his laundry beat, but near enough. Midnight, though puzzling in one sense, was temporally clear enough. And the hot dog in question was, he felt sure, unquestionable.

Unsure of the past now as well as the present, Albert decided to set out in quest of the future, to seek freshets of meaning there that the arid plain of his daily dealings had so far denied him. He dressed in his best suit, knotted his wide red tie, gave his shining shoes a last rub on the backs of his trouser legs, slammed the door to behind him, and walked out into the night.

The first trial to face him was the simple question of transportation. The laundry truck was safely stowed away in the large garage under the watchful eyes of a new night watchman. Albert did not own a car. No bus line ran nearby, and the city lacked a genuine subway. Shank's mare had long been his steed, and she must do him this night as well.

But it didn't hurt to try other means, so Albert thrust out his thumb at each passing car or truck, pausing in his brisk hike long enough for the vehicle of the moment to sweep by, only occasionally accompanied by a jeer or noisy suggestion. Finally an old wagon creaked down the street, pulled by two old nags in tandem, heading, however slowly, in the right direction, moving so slowly that Albert didn't even bother to stick out his thumb but simply spoke out to the old man driving it.

SPENSER FEBRUARY * LIGHT HAULING AND REHAULING read the sign painted on the old wagon's weathered side, so Albert said, "Excuse me, Mr. February," and then when the old man looked his way, "Are you going my way?"

"That depends, sonny," the old man said, wiping his wet nose on the incredibly frayed sleeve of his gray overcoat, his voice as frayed and frankly dirty as the sleeve, "on which way you're going."

"I'm heading toward the street called Ugly," Albert replied.

The old man winked a rheumy eye, laughed, and said, "I see," in such a way that Albert suddenly knew that the old man did see a great deal more than he did, and then added, "Where else do you think I'd be heading?"

Taking that as an invitation, correctly as it turned out, Albert stepped out into the street and swung himself up and onto the slowly moving wagon. He could have walked the distance faster, he knew, but this way he would arrive rested and ready for whatever might follow.

"Up, Cod!" the old man shouted, flapping his reins over the backs of the two old horses, no doubt feeling the need of expressing his good will that way. "Up, Ecod!" When the two ancient beasts continued their steady and unchanging plod, the old man seemed satisfied and turned his attention directly to Albert.

"Beastly weather," said nervous Albert, who had faced too many stares the last few days to be at ease, his eyes seeming to squeeze even closer to his narrow nose as if seeking shelter from the old man's watery gaze.

"It's always the same," old February replied. "Hot some days, cold some days, dry some days, wet some days, always the same."

Albert started to respond, but the old man, like so many old men, too aware of time's rush and their own slow pace, spoke on, riding over even the first stammer of Albert's planned response, "Listen to me, sonny, everything changes, changes all the time, nothing stays the same, listen to me."

Again Albert clenched to speak but then settled back to listen.

"It's like I told you. The street named Ugly is a long, long street. I'm on it most of my life, and if you learn anything, it's that nothing changes, everything stays the same. You scheme and calculate, calculate and scheme, and the sun still comes up in one place and sets in another, comes up in another place and sets in another. You listen to an old man." He smacked the two old horses again, again to no avail.

"No speeding up, no slowing down," he went on, "you speed up, you slow down. Everything that moves delights in change. Everything that moves wants to settle down. It's all clear as the day, clear as the day." He waved his hand at the night. Albert nodded. This old man, he thought, is a sage. This old man, he thought, makes sense.

"Oh, I've seen it all," the old man said, "fires, floods, almost lost those two horses in a flood but they slid before it and swum away, landslides, the lot. Take that stink in the air that everyone's talking about, you take that." He smacked the horses again.

They turned onto the street named Ugly as Albert, scarcely daring to breathe lest he interrupt the old man's thoughts, his sayings, failed to notice.

"One more thing," the old man said, "and you remember it and remember it well."

"I will," said Albert, choking it out of his tight throat.

"You take a look, sonny," he said, Spenser February, pulling the horses back as if trying to stop them or slow them down, failing to vary their pace in the least, "and you can be sure you'll see what you see. You remember that, and here's where you get off."

He poked Albert with his elbow. It punched like a dagger into his ribs, and Albert almost fell off the wagon, caught himself, and swung over the side into the street.

"You look," the old man said, the garish neon light catching his face in such a way that he had only one leaking eye, "and you'll see." And then the wagon was gone, and Albert Longinus was standing, silent and alone, on the street named Ugly, looking down its flickering length after the old man's wagon but seeing it not at all.

The neighborhood proved to be the worst in Newark, darker, dingier, and more dangerous than any other, and the street named Ugly was at its bleak heart, lit only by the glare of neon tubing and the flash of silenced pistol fire.

The street numbers were hidden in a maze of bar signs and strip-joint posters.

FLESH. FLESH. FLESH. FLESH. FLESH. FLESH. FLESH.

"She strips as naked as the day," said a barker bundled in sealskin and furs like an eskimo, waving his untipped cane at Albert's elbow. "Lies on her back and kicks her heels. Wiggles and squirms like an eel. You see it all. No other show like it anywhere. Look!" He flashed the door open and shut. A black woman in a gold fishnet with sparkling sequins in her wet hair was walking rhythmically along a platform behind a bar and its yawning bartender.

"Ishtar the Fish Queen," the barker continued, "naked as she came from the sea."

Desperate for some sign of his location on the block, Albert spoke to the barker when he caught his breath for a second.

"Which way is 666?"

"That's your problem, buddy," the barker replied, "but if you hurry in here, you'll be just in time to catch Ishtar the Fish Queen hunching on the wily angler's line. Must be seen to be believed."

"I'm looking," said Albert, "for 666. Is this it?"

"This is it if it's hot and humid female flesh you're after," the

166

barker replied, raising his voice over Albert toward a group of recently teen-aged boys cowering on the curb.

Albert walked on down the ugly street, his eyes wavering in the flickering red light. Prostitutes in tight and high slit dresses moved alongside him like wary sharks.

"Hey, mister," one said, dyed blond, red lips, wounded eyes, "you look just like President Nixon."

Albert hurried on down the street. The neon flickered all around him, the occasional streetlight's steady beam lost in the chaos of names and slogans. EL PUSSYGATO. THE GROTTO with its light, blue and wavering. THE SLOT. THE GOLDEN HIND. The difficult-to-find QUARK. He passed by clubs named QUIM and QUIFF with noisy barkers dressed like arctic explorers, waving their canes, offering hyperborean delights, as the red light streamed past them like scoriac rivers of lava down Yaanek in the ultimate climes of the Pole. The names and bodies of strippers, fluorescent and neon, glowed on every side. BLACK BOTTOM. HOLLY COST. TRICIA VIXEN. MISS HURRY CANE. OTTAVIA RIMA. CLARISSA SILVER. The doors winked open and closed as he passed like hot red eyes, revealing an arm, a bare leg, a fringed behind, hot and red-eyed customers leaning forward, their drinks sweating in their tight hands, the eyes of demons, the eyes of the lost or the too late found.

One bar, THE SMART SET, catered exclusively to patrons of the small movie theater next door to it, a dusty niche in the wall which played the same two films year in and year out, *Frankenstein Meets the Space Monster* and *The Mole People*, the favorite movies of the jaded sophisticates and the burnt-out-case Mull freaks, former junkies and heads whose nerves could find stimulus only in the occasional appearances of the Mull monster on the speckled and cracked screen. In the bar, two strippers worked on the raised platform behind the bartender in shifts designed to alternate with the two movies, Mulla in her hairy costume and bangles of bear claws, Molanna the Nubbly Nubian in her bare and bumpy skin and little else.

Albert pressed on down the street, actually turning his head the other way in uneasy embarrassment as he passed the QUIRKY BAR with its male strippers moving among the customers sitting around the room on squeaky throw pillows.

But, wait. Albert saw a familiar face, a familiar figure on one of those posters he had just passed. He retraced his steps, re-examining each one in its turn. And there she was! By the light of the hissing and sputtering yellow neon spelling out YE QUEYNTE INN, Miss Parker. Painted bright pink and green, bare as a babe, and labeled Ginger Snap of the Loose and Easy Three, but Miss Parker it was.

"See the Loose and Easy Three," the hooded barker was shouting, rapping his cold cane on the poster right in front of Albert's nose. "See them take it off each other. See six tits and only one pasty. Guaranteed. A spectacle unlike no other."

"666?" asked Albert of him.

"Sex. Sex. Sex. You got it, pal. It's all laid out right before your very eyes," the barker responded at top volume.

"No," said blushing Albert, glancing nervously around his nose at the momentarily empty street behind him, "I mean the address. 666."

"You a process server?" the barker asked out of the side of his mouth.

"No," said Albert, "I just want to see Ginger Snap."

"Snap she does," said the barker, "twists like a pretzel. Real acrobatics. Back and over." He flicked the door open to a burst of music, a glimpse of intricate dance, a sense of flesh, and, before Albert could see or say anything more, pushed him down and into the red and smoky interior.

It was nearly noon on a bright August Saturday when the small paperboy finally got up the courage to walk up the curving flagstone walk to the forbidding front door of 2120 Life Street, the home of Alfred Omega, the only non-subscriber to the newspaper on the block. He had seen a great deal over the last few weeks and was both an older and a wiser boy for it, and a braver one. Knowing what he knew, he wished to make one last attempt to include Mr. Omega on his list. And besides there was the bicycle which he had an outside chance of winning in the paper's new subscription drive, the bicycle which his grandparents could scarcely afford to buy him.

So the boy went up the walk, climbed the steps up onto the stoop, and paused before reaching out to ring the bell. In the quiet afternoon, with only the distant buzz of a lawnmower to offer any distraction, the boy could hear clearly the sounds which were issuing from around the door, as baffling as those which so long ago he heard at Miss Ease's home, far more frightening. Still as the air, his breath easing in and ebbing out like the slow tide of time, the boy stood and listened.

There was, first of all, the sound of a large voice, laughing—laughing and laughing, enjoying itself immensely, not a warm laughter but not evil either. Then there was, under and through the laughter, an unpleasant growling, as of a dog, a cur, or perhaps something as large as a wolf, the laughter and the growling forming a curious and unsettling counterpoint, as if they were directly related but opposed, as if the laughter caused the growling or the growling gave rise to the laughter. And last, spoken by the same voice as that which made the laughter but impossibly simultaneous, a set of sounds, words, syllables, unknown and possibly unknowable, certainly to the small boy, or so it seemed to him:

"AR-O-GO-GO-RU-ABRAO . . . growl . . . laugh . . . SOTOU . . . MUDORIO . . . growl . . . laugh . . . PhALARThAO . . . OOO . . . growl . . . laugh . . . OTTTO . . . growl . . . laugh . . . AEPE . . . BABALON-BAL-BIN-ABAFT."

The laughter rose then, strong and strong, and the growling increased also. The boy wondered why the whole neighborhood did not come running, but the day was as silent and peaceful as before. And, then, much to his surprise, his hand reached out and his thumb pressed the doorbell, a sudden bing-bong in the midst of the inexplicable nexus of sound within.

Suddenly there was a snap, a flash of light as if he had flicked a wall switch and the ceiling lamp had popped into suicidal light, a snap of light and sound and the smell of a match popped quickly on the nail of a thumb. And the door opened.

It opened into darkness, or, at least, into a room so dim that it seemed completely dark to the boy's sun-trimmed eyes. He could barely make out what appeared to be the figure of an enormously fat man dressed in some sort of bathrobe, blue with silver stars and moons, his head totally bald and gleaming faintly from what little light there was in the room. The head seemed almost like a huge staring eye and not a head at all, but, just as the boy almost turned to run, the large voice he had heard from behind the door said, "Come in." The boy instantly obeyed.

The giant man closed the door behind him, so that he was standing in the relatively total darkness of the room with no contrasting sunlight to which to turn at all. As his eyes adjusted to the new environment, he turned to his left and peered into the room opening before him. It was a large room, smoky and strange, filled with dark large objects. An owl, stuffed or possibly real and alive, perched on the back of one of the objects, unblinking and unmoving, looking directly at the boy. As his eyes continued to widen and adjust, he saw some sort of picture over the mantel across the room. No, not a picture, a set of words; he could just make them out:

```
S A T O R
A R E P O
T E N E T
O P E R A
R O T A S
```

They made no more sense to him than the words he had earlier heard on the stoop. And right before him, gigantic and imposing, the looming figure of the man, his face blurred and glowing, frightening and very hard to see, or to look at.

"Who are you?" the boy said, his voice as small as an egg.

"I am," the huge voice replied but from over his shoulder, "I am Alfred Omega," and the man suddenly yanked open the blinds of a large window, saying, "Why it's no wonder that you didn't know. In this light it would be a smart child indeed who knew his own dad!"

The boy blinked in the new bright light, his eyes squeezing back into shape for the day, and suddenly he realized that he had not been looking into the room at all, but into a large mirror on the wall a few inches from his nose.

He was so surprised that he continued to stare into the glass for a moment, long enough anyway for the mysterious words on the wall to resolve themselves in the bright light into a portrait of a lady, dressed in a very old-fashioned way, carrying a bouquet of roses in her right hand, and under her was the word AMAM. A picture of Mr. Omega's mother, the name reversed by the mirror.

The boy turned around, and sure enough the roses were in her left hand now, but the legend under the picture read ISIS. He started to turn back around, but the bird on the perch caught his eye, a big white pigeon, cooing and thrusting its head busily in and out of the space under its wing. But before he could examine the room for more strange changes, Mr. Omega spoke again.

"I'm sorry you find me at apparently so awkward a time, but what can I do for you?"

"Well, sir," the boy began, "I was just wondering, that is, would you like, you see . . ."

"Just ask," Mr. Omega said.

"Would you please subscribe to the paper? I'm the paperboy."

"I know who you are," said Mr. Omega, "and I'm happy to subscribe. No one ever asked me before."

They were both smiling widely now, the small boy and the fat bald old man in his dressing gown. The smell of burnt matches had almost completely faded from the air of the room, and the sunlight was washing through the wide window.

"Just what do I owe you?" said Alfred Omega.

"O nothing, sir," the boy answered, quickly. "I can't take pay in advance. A paperboy collects from week to week."

"But you must want some token of good faith."

"O no," said the little boy, "your word is fine with me."

The large man frowned and then insisted that he would give the boy something, a reminder, a token, a pledge. He rummaged around in the drawer of a secretary standing by the window and finally found a small round object which caught the sun's rays as he held it up and broke them into the colors of the rainbow, a dazzling display which passed in an instant.

"Here," he said. "Take this, just an old coin, something to look at. When this you see, as the albums all say, remember me."

The boy, hesitant but obliging, as always, took the coin. It was round and flat and brassy. He could tell from experiences he had had with coded rings and badges he had ordered from cereal-box backs that it would turn his fingers green if he handled it very much. But, for now, he held it in his hand as he thanked the old man and allowed himself to be ushered out the door by a beaming Alfred Omega.

Once he was outside on the stoop, the door closed firmly behind him, and the boy paused to examine the coin more closely. It, too, held a kind of code, or, at least, a design. He squinted at it in the sunlight:

He turned the coin over in his fingers. The other side was very smooth and shiny, almost as if it were composed of another metal entirely. He looked carefully into its bright surface but could only see his own round blue eye looking carefully back.

As he was studying the coin, he heard Mr. Omega's laugh behind him through the door, and he felt a sudden chill, physically inexplicable on such a warm day but recognizable even to so young a boy as a certain symptom of fear.

He put the coin in his jeans pocket and walked quickly off the stoop and across the flat green lawn, a shiver still tingling over his skin, away from the house and into the sharp noon day, a landscape completely without shadows.

We do have an unusual city.

—Richard J. Daley

Sir Hugh, bundled and steaming (seldom now at ninety-six pipeless, indoors and out, burning Four Square tobacco, an ancient exile's nostalgic choice, that we carried with us aromatically packed in the small leather bag, the leather flaking and peeling to take on the texture of Sir Hugh's own face, the mottled backs of his thin (but still, I assure you, exceedingly graceful) hands, along in that bag with the Eno's Fruit Salts, the Phensics, the Benzedrex inhalers (all essential items which Sir Hugh dared not be without, but which he feared unobtainable in the middle wilds of far America), and, of course, his well-thumbed (and tellingly annotated, I may add without betraying a confidence) copies of *Uncensored Recollections* and, in mint dust jacket, that veiled author's other volume, and, along with those, his favorite single piece of writing, the chapter torn hurriedly out of a first edition (the concluding chapter, "One Way In," having caused Sir Hugh undue embarrassment when it was idly perused by young Dolly, the hope of his youthful ardor and amour, when visiting his rooms one day in late autumn while he was still residing in George Nympton and had invited lush Dolly down for a weekend's tumble on the tufted turf of Exmoor and perhaps (I can

now tell, for time has put those light days as far away as another
country, and besides dear Dolly is long dead) even on the dusty
plush of his sitting-room sofa (soft as a brush, she was, my eyes as
well as Sir Hugh's, I may as well confess, lingering longingly on her
lithe ankles, the capricious curve of her wrists, hair like bright coiled
fish, the smile, the wicked gray of her eyes, dear Dolly, the past mists
my gaze, I must sort you out and file you away (our joke, if you could
only remember, dear departed, "File this," and the laughter it
caused, Sir Hugh's face wrinkling like one of the prunes he was always nibbling in those days before patented relief, my own redden-
ing (as I could feel, if not observe, although I occasionally could see,
if we happened to be at Dolly's, in one of her endless mirrors, reflected wet red face to wet red neck and on and on over my shoulder
and behind my back, down a long curving corridor of mirth), Dolly's,
dimpling, pink as a baby, pinker) and return, as I must, to this confusing time, the present, escaping under my pen like ink, farewell),
"The Curate's Bump," which, even though it is but one chapter,
Sir Hugh reads and rereads with the regularity he strives for and has
striven for all his life, occasionally with a lost and far lorn look as he
wanders down some crystal corridor of his labyrinthine mind (which,
much to my endless delight and wonder, has lost none of the quick-
silver quality it had when I first met Sir Hugh, both of us pacing
separately the dockside, impatient during the Great Dock Strike,
Sir Hugh only eighteen and I almost as young, both of us waiting
for, as it turned out, identical small parcels located unpleasantly in
the musty hold of the S.S. *Kuhlfrigan*, a Frisian frigate freighted
low in the murky Thames with bright possibilities from the Mediterranean and points east from whence she had just returned, the two
of us recognizing by some way, which I do not remember now and
did not really understand then, that we were, in truth, after the same
thing and striking up on the spot the friendship which has lasted,
lo, these many years), as often with a light in his eye which as often
as not leads us on another chase, a new scent as dangerous as it is
exciting, as we have together done so many times in the past, lost
land), bundled and steaming like a Christmas pudding off on a hur-

176

ried journey across the garden to the neighbor's door on a dim holiday morning, before the sun has yet begun to do more than peep shyly over the assembled chimney pots or rural hedges, Sir Hugh Fitz-Hyffen, secure in his years but far from resting on his accumulated laurels, maintaining the drained vitality of the (as I have noted elsewhere) unnaturally long line of Fitz-Hyffens in his frail form, cold even in his hairy car robe, almost half as old as Sir Hugh himself, purchased in untoward Ontario on a cold day during our search for the fabled Fabergé "pearl ice" mounted in platinum and beyond the grasp of the Mounted Police (not ours), still sturdy and snug, cold even though the day simmered under an August sun and the pavements and street grates of State Street shimmered their own radiance into the blinding day and the curious bustle of the Chicago afternoon, yawned.

The taxi stopped.

As we emerged onto the pavement and into the important events of the day, although occupied thoroughly with disengaging Sir Hugh from his robe and his kit from the car, I noted a policeman, bright blue from toe to helmet, at the end of the block talking animatedly with a smaller figure which seemed to have an enormous head far out of proportion to its body and which was bearing a banner with a strange device, gold star, face, or seal, bobbed in my view by the large (dare I say, a freak's) round head.

Sir Hugh's small glasses winked once in the sun as he followed my gaze, but no more, for he was lightly across the walk and up the steps to the door, already opening, of the stone building before which we stood, Sir Hugh stepping eagerly to the dark interior and I, muffled in fur and leather, leaning into the door of the cab to ascertain the fee. When I finished that task and turned, myself, to the now closed door, the policeman and his odd companion had both disappeared. I could, however, hear a distant sound of chanting, tum-pause-tum-pause-tum-tum-tum, which I ascribed to the surf of Lake Michigan pounding into the city shore.

Inside, unencumbered, sitting across the room from Sir Hugh, drifting in a swirl of disconnected conversation among the three or four athletic but worried-looking young men in the room, a pastiche of unfamiliar or only faintly familiar names—Bobby, Lynn, Don, Ted, Humbert, Jean—all this while Sir Hugh talked privately with the short stout man behind the wide desk that dominated the room with its dark bulk, its flat glass top covering a veritable acre of press clippings (my eye musing across their reversed faces, catching a WE LOVE OUR WAVER or an occasionally bold WINS REFLECTION BID), the mayor or his assistant, perhaps a District Attorney, I forget (how difficult to remember the details of yesterday when uncountable yesterdays pile eagerly behind it, wriggling for attention, the rough pat of affectionate memory), a stout man with a bright face, earnest, talking to Sir Hugh, who remained impassive, an impassivity which I had long since learned masked his raw appetite for fact, for action.

Sir Hugh was, as everyone should by now know, a detective, not a vulgar professional, Sam, Mal, or Phil, soiling the mind's quick workings with the lure of the buck, the need for the bottle, but the real thing, modern as only the mind itself, puzzling out the secrets of each slight moment for their own value alone.

Of course, the city had offered a considerable sum for Sir Hugh's kind services which he did not turn down, despite the comfortable fortune he had come into so suddenly so many years ago, for fear, as he told me, of offending the raw sentiments of the Americans, young in their vigor, unbred, honest as they are uncouth, easily hurt by even the slightest of slights, the most trifling of misunderstandings. I understood and questioned him no further.

It was, as Sir Hugh was to explain to me as we sped to the large hotel in which we were to be ensconced and which was to be the center of our future activities, a murder—the murder of a prominent man in the life of the city, a murder which pointed with however unlikely a finger to a serial murderer, for despite apparent disconnections, some evidence did point to a pattern in several murders of the preceding months. Despite Sir Hugh's early "failure" with Jack the Ripper, the truth of which I hope Sir Hugh will someday tell the unsuspecting world, we were to solve it, both because the police, for some reason or the other, professed to be too busy to work further on the case this week, and because they had been forced to admit that they were baffled by the crime and its implications. The murder had been committed on Sunday, three days before; several suspects had been gathered in, and now it was up to Sir Hugh to clear away the confusion, to smooth out this tortured texture of blurred event, to focus his small eyes (keen as the creases on his shining trousers) on coy truth in her clever disguise.

The taxi stopped beside a large white van with a black eye painted on its side, and, as I stooped to pay the driver as Sir Hugh staggered out of his robe and into the gutter, I noticed a young and unkempt man carrying a large placard with an intent and clean young man on it staring at a small fire in his fingertips and the slogan DUCK THE DRAFT, a warm sentiment of which I knew chill Sir Hugh would approve. He, Sir Hugh, was just climbing to his feet, mumbling some words I could not quite catch, as, bundled again in hot fur and peeling leather, I turned to go into the hotel. It seems that a shard of heavy glass, apparently a carafe or ashtray, bearing the words (or initials or fragments of words) LEAN WITH GE had become wedged into the tight crevice between his shoulder blades, and his ill humor rose rapidly. I dropped my burdens into the street to Sir Hugh's further displeasure in order to dislodge the glass from his back. He did look at it, once proffered, even in his rage, but then tossed it aside. A flashbulb winked in our faces at that precise moment, and Sir Hugh growled, loud enough only for me to hear, "Clever, our opponent, his traps are well laid," then laying a finger aside his sharp nose, he bounded through the large glass doors of the hotel, laughing a wild laugh of the chase, as I stooped to the furry mass at my feet.

"The room," he said later, as we were having late tea in our room, "was locked, the key in the victim's stomach (assuredly there, X-ray proof, autopsy, without vital peristalsis no other way it could have gotten there), this key, acid eaten, acid of the victim's stomach, you see, you see," eating then another Cream-Filled Zinger, a curiously modern confection to which Sir Hugh had developed an attachment during our brief American stay, chewing, removing and rinsing his teeth in the water glass, putting them firmly back into place, reaching for another Zinger, "very confusing, apparently clear at first, for beside the body with the murder gun in hand, a man, a public official or, at least, a public figure, named Charles," another Zinger, the chewing, rinsing, replacing, and reaching for another, a routine I knew, the familiar rhythm of our conversations for some years, ever since Sir Hugh had acquired his new teeth from a grateful dentist who had insisted on removing all of Sir Hugh's apparently sound teeth and replacing them in gratitude for our effective extraction of the reluctant and impacted truth from a muddled mystery in Moose Jaw, Wyoming, in 1947, "McCarthy." I gasped.

"But, Sir Hugh . . ." I said.

"Yes, amnesia, no recollection, possibly drugged, but," continuing, staring reflectively at the Zinger bending slowly over in his fingertips like a wilting plant, "another person, his inseparable companion, his man, also present, also without memory, both amnesiacs, both drugged, we must reflect."

He was asleep, I realized, his mind continuing to kick over for a moment like an automobile engine encrusted with corrosive carbon. I removed the limp and staling pastry from his fingers, draped the car rug and a bright HILTON blanket over his slumped figure, and retired to the toilet for a nap myself.

It was after six when the knock on the door aroused us, and I opened the door to a small bellboy, bright crimson in uniform and face (I am ashamed to say that in the confusion of the moment I had forgotten to cover the disarray of my sleep properly, and my shame was revealed more than only in that bright face), who said finally, looking then down the hall as he spoke, "Sir Fitz-Hyffen is to be in Room 732 at 7:15."

"The murder room," said Sir Hugh behind me ominously. I turned to him for a brief glance (he was fully clothed, eagerness in the very tilt of his wandering eye, his glasses being polished in his nervous hands even as I looked), and when I turned back to the boy, he was gone.

"Shall I?"—this to Sir Hugh.

"No need, no need," he said, "I'll get to the bottom of that boy eventually, need your help here more."

I dressed hurriedly as he spoke on, more to himself than to me, more to the muttering night beyond the window than to us both. "The zodiac holds the answer, that ancient animal ring. The first murder was in May in the cancer ward of a Des Moines hospital, a patient needled fatally in the heart, a note attached to the needle, 'No Cancer here: To lie is to die.' At first they were baffled. The patient did have cancer, a terminal case; the autopsy concurred. The note was as mad as its mad writer; the heart had filled with air and popped like a pimple.

"No one could see the truth, until in the Chicago Zoo in late June a lion choked on the copper claw of a Chinese back scratcher immersed in its meat, and a message was scrawled in chalk on the walk before its open-air cage, 'No Leo here: The wart hog survives.' Curious. You agree. Still no sense to it. If the lion isn't Leo, then cancer isn't cancer. A clue. A connection. But still no sense.

"Then the clinching clue, the last link, in late July a lady lashed to death in a mysterious establishment on Michigan Avenue in this city, a message, 'No Virgo here, agreed: All clear, proceed.' Needless to say, the lady was scarcely virginal, but," glittering now with Sir Hugh's excitement, his eyeglasses were looped over his perked ears and before his tiny eyes, "she was born in November! It is all quite clear; the cancer patient born in October; the lion born in March; the wart hog in early July; the man found upstairs in this hotel, Albert S. Corpio, needless to say, born in January, a note tubed tidily through the plastic 'Lucrezia' ring by means of which he was drugged before he was shot, 'No Scorpio here: The coast is clear for a family affair.'

"Corpio was a 'hitler,' as I believe they say, a hired hood for an important group of Italo-Americans known as the Family. They are upset, and rightly so, this group; the police are upset; I am as calm as this August night. The answer lies in the zodiac. Libra is clearly next. Neither of us is a Libran, but we have seen an L today, haven't we?"

A nod from me, now in bib and tucker, fit for the evening ahead. "Be prepared," he touched my forearm with his hand, lightly but seriously, "avoid GE."

And suddenly I felt as cold as Sir Hugh always does, shivering involuntarily until I saw his eyes, magnified to a normal size by his glasses, both of them now firmly fixed on the one remaining Zinger on the tray, and I knew then that all was well, that this day would hold no further violence. Sir Hugh had seen the light.

The room was as like ours as one of Sir Hugh's eyes the other, identical except for size, the direction the room faced, other minor details. In it were ourselves, both eager for the climax, and four other men, all worthy of description: Charles McCarthy, a dapper dandy who peered often through a beribboned monocle, who had been alone, save for his man Edgar when we arrived, who had given Sir Hugh a fat envelope and smiled a wooden smile at Sir Hugh's evident appreciation of the contents; the aforementioned Edgar, a loose-lipped bulky man who kept his own counsel; the manager of the hotel, Gerald Abbey, small, rubescent, bright-eyed, twitchy, his eyes constantly darting to the window or the door at each strange sound from without; Sergeant William Clubb, who had an arm in a cast and was, as it came to mind from long acquaintance with the military, no doubt "excused duty" for the important business of the night of which we had heard so much and so little.

I had noted in my notebook the facts so far ascertained and, at Sir Hugh's request, read them out to the assembly:

"1. The door was locked.

"2. The door could only be locked from without and with a key.

"3. The door key (the only one, due to a quaint hotel policy forbidding a pass key which could fit the door to this 'family' room and an unfortunate series of thefts and mail delays in the weeks preceding the crime) was in the victim's stomach. Does this mean that he locked the door from without only to die within?"

"Does this mean," asked Sergeant Clubb belligerently (I thought), "that you believe that Corpio locked the door outside, swallowed the key, and then came in to his death?"

"Sergeant," chided Sir Hugh, "I'm surprised."

"I see," I said.

The apparently mollified Clubb only grunted.

"4." I went on, "McCarthy and his man Edgar remember nothing of the entire day."

"I have a plan," said Sir Hugh, "to flush out the murderer."

Everyone leaned forward. A mingled shouting from without filled the silence. Someone seemed to be calling a pig over and over, "Pig . . . Pig . . . Mucking Pig," but that seemed to be scarcely likely on a busy and bustling Chicago street, far from the stock pens, especially at night.

"The French," said Sir Hugh, his voice crackling a bit with excitement, muffled by a tight nose. "My bag," he said to me, as if he were reading this as yet unwritten account of the night's events. I handed it, open, to him, and he extracted a Benzedrex inhaler, unboxed and uncapped it, and inhaled from it deeply, the disturbing tip wedged deep in his narrow nostril and then in the other. I noticed in the bag an unfamiliar parcel labeled IOCKSMITN or something equally unintelligible, reached for it to ask Sir Hugh if it could be something dangerous, only to have him snatch it from my hand, mutter something to do with while I was asleep, and pocket the package quickly. Then, as his nostrils cleared and his voice revived, he declaimed:

> "Factory windows are always broken.
> Something or other is going wrong.
> Something is rotten—I think, in Denmark.
> Something, something, something song."

He smiled. His favorite Chicago poet.

"The French," he continued, his voice restored to its old familiar and frail fullness, his nose wrinkled now only with distaste, "deplorable as they may otherwise be," a wry smile, "have developed an interesting method," he winked at McCarthy and I thought I could actually hear distant voices shouting "McCarthy" as he did so, "of re-creating the scene of the crime. I shall, for once, use their method." Nods around the room. "You," to the manager, "may be the corpse, would you mind lying just there face down," pointing to the chalk marks near the manager's toe.

With reluctance and concern etched on his rosy features, the man lay where Sir Hugh indicated. Outside, objects of some sort flew down past the window, fortunately, I thought, beyond the manager's floor-bound gaze.

"Now," Sir Hugh said, his voice as tight and lively as I could recall hearing it in years, "you," taking me by the arm, his grip as tight as my stiff collar, "and the Sergeant will please look out the window, and, mind you, do not turn around for any reason."

The Sergeant and I did as he said. Some sort of gathering seemed to be going on far below—lights were flashing, fog was drifting up on the night air, a great deal of running about perhaps, movement anyway. Clubb peered down at it, cupping his good hand against the glass to shield against the room's glare.

I could see the dim reflections of figures in the room moving about behind us: Sir Hugh with something in his hands; McCarthy, taking something from his inside coat pocket. A rattling of paper from over my shoulders mingled with the muffled voices filtering through the window. I felt something tug at my left-hand coat pocket, and I could see from the corner of my eye a familiar hand placing something small in the distracted Sergeant Clubb's pocket as that gentleman continued to peer down at the busy night.

"Now," said Sir Hugh's voice, "the surprises will commence."

We turned around to find the room as it was, except that the manager was getting up from his knees.

"What," he said anxiously, "is going on out there?" A heavy crash came down from the floor above, followed by a series of thumps and bangs, muffled shouts.

"Be still, man," Sir Hugh ordered. "We are at a crisis."

I started to feel my pocket to see just what had been placed there.

"Please," said Sir Hugh just at that moment, "be so kind as to empty your left-hand coat pockets on the bed."

Each of us did as he said, Sergeant Clubb grumbling and saying, "Everything?" and Sir Hugh insisting.

McCarthy dropped a single item, a brass key. Edgar also dropped what appeared to be an identical, if brighter, key. Then the manager dropped a small tube of wafers marked TUMS which appeared to have been savagely torn open, another marked ROLLAIDS, and another brass key. Sergeant Clubb dropped two wooden matches, what appeared to be a gold or brass coin with a soldier in a classical helmet on it, and another brass key. I hastily tugged out a small object from my otherwise empty pocket and found it to be yet another brass key. Sir Hugh casually tossed still another key onto the bed.

"What's with this?" said the Sergeant, and the manager added a nervous echo.

"I didn't have no key in that pocket," continued the Sergeant.

An enormous thump came from the ceiling as he spoke, and the manager, his red features wild with anguish, shrieked, ran to the door, wrenched it open, and ran out of the room.

"Yet there they are," said Sir Hugh, unflustered, "six keys, and I suggest that they all fit this," pointing to the now open door through which a great din rushed, "door."

"Bull," said the Sergeant, suddenly pulling a fat envelope similar to one I had seen earlier in the day out of his right pocket, "and what the hell is this?"

I regret having to repeat the Sergeant's intemperate words, but extremely obscene language was a contributing factor to the violence described in this report, and its frequency and intensity were such that to omit it would inevitably underestimate the effect it had.

In any case, the irate Clubb tore the fat familiar envelope open with a quick green flash, looked in, riffled something with his thumb, tucked the envelope back in his pocket, his face filling with an entirely new shade of red, and he added, quietly, "Well, I guess I did have that key after all."

"Good man," said Sir Hugh, clapping him on the shoulder, apparently jouncing his cast in its sling, for a wince crossed the policeman's face, "and now, I'm bound to proceed." He gathered the six keys up from the bed and walked to the door. "I shall lock the door from without and open it with one after the other of these keys. It will, I assure you, all come out." He exited, slamming the door after him, locking it immediately after that with a click of anonymous key.

A sudden clamor burst through the sealed door, a clattering and screaming, thick thuds, shouts, again the name "McCarthy," the inexplicable cry of "peas." Then a long silence.

Finally, a scratching came from the door and its important lock, a firmer sound, a click, and the door swung open revealing, not, to my surprise, Sir Hugh, but a dwarf, anyway a dwarfish cleaning woman, carrying the bucket and mop of her trade, her face a man's but her clothes revealing her true sex, clutching immediately for the key still in the lock with snarled fingers stained with vividly orange dust, grasping the key and retrieving it with quick, seemingly sly movements.

"O beg pardon, sirs," she said in a whining falsetto, ducking her crooked head on her crooked neck, "I thought this place was empty." She moved to leave, but the quick Sergeant Clubb caught her by the arm. The little woman looked up at him, her face now as bent and gnarled as her body, the chin speckled with the appearance of the bristling nubs of a poor shave.

"Please," said the Sergeant, releasing his hold on her arm, "lock the door after you, will you?"

She grinned what must be described as a hateful grin, dived through the door as the Sergeant slammed it, and we soon heard the lock click again.

Some hour and a half later, we heard another key scrape in the lock. The television set, with its convoluted colophon, round G and rounder E, having proved annoyingly inoperative, McCarthy had been sitting, indecently, to my eye, but the Sergeant did not seem to mind, slumped in Edgar's lap (more evidence, I feel quite certain, of the deterioration of the formerly chill American moral climate). Some sort of stinging air had been seeping through the cooling machine, and I was actually in tears when the door at last opened and Sir Hugh entered the room.

We all as one man leaped to our feet. Sir Hugh had a huge slab of gauze taped over his right eye, and he walked with a quaint sidelong motion. I feared the worst had occurred; my mind swam with zodiacs, archers and twins, insects and scales, bizarre deaths.

"What . . . ?" I shouted.

"I was," Sir Hugh whispered, "delayed unavoidably. The keys, all of the keys are fortunately lost." He fainted. I was aghast; that he had faltered even a nonce in his speech terrified me, to have said "fortunately" when he had so obviously meant its opposite was much more alarming to me than the loose and crumpled figure on the carpet.

"The case," said the Sergeant, looking ominously at McCarthy and bulky Edgar, "is closed."

The next day, as a smooth and fresh young lady strapped us into the comfortable seats of an Air France aircruiser, I felt finally confident enough of Sir Hugh's unimpaired faculties to ask him about the case. We had been seen off to the airport by several policemen in a large black American car (the name of which eludes me more quickly than ever did those early beauties, the Franklins, LaSalles, and Stars, the Brazzados), the policemen wearing a strange assortment of bandages and bruises, one of them presenting Sir Hugh with an official-appearing envelope and uttering simultaneously the mysterious word of approval that was so American, so suited for the lips of young and old alike, "Check." And now we were nearly air-borne.

"Do you remember the problem of the door?" I asked. "I have never been able to ascertain how the police got in the first time, when the murder occurred, without doing it some damage. And what about the mark in orange chalk that was on our hotel door when we returned to it last night," I sketched the mark in the air with a hesitant finger (⌂), "and what about the one question that really seems important to me, and which, I hate to say, still puzzles me: who *was* the murderer?"

Sir Hugh smiled in his seat, the morning paper on his lap open to a photograph of him and me, his rug crumpled at our feet, Sir Hugh tossing something bright aside, with its mystifying caption (GENET AND BURROUGHS AID FALLEN YOUTH AS GLASS FLIES), looking far off, not out the window which was above his head, but away, past me, past the smiling knees of the lovely young woman who had seated us, past the passengers across the way, the large lady with the crooked hat and the tin button with the blue broken ribbon on it and its indecipherable letters, the tiny crippled child grinning at us, his face so hideous that it seemed to have the ugly beginnings of a beard, although his clothing and his size indicated that he would be far too young, deformed even to the texture of his skin, past them, past the day, past the mechanically cold air in the airplane which caused his hands to tremble, his cold pipe, held lightly on the page, to rattle the paper ever so slightly, and his voice, lazy as an amblyopic eye, low as my spirits, saying, "Oddly enough one of my very first recollections of anything is connected with the late King Edward, and in a rather comic way," and I smiled, knowing that the present must give way, remembering oddly Dolly, the day I caught sight of her knee peeking perkily over the back of a silk sofa in those quaint rooms in Soho, and heard a low familiar laugh that could not have been hers (which I knew better than my own, hearing its melodies so much more often than my own heavy heaves) but could, I am sure, have been no man's, as I slipped cautiously away to the kitchen, where, not long after, she and Sir Hugh, both oddly breathless and flushed, appeared together, he no doubt having just come in silently from his walk, and, as I caught sight of the young lady's knee down the aisle, thinking of Dolly's graceful granddaughter, her home in precious Capri, her affection for those tiny bathing costumes named after some or the other exotic atoll, feeling an odd tremble of affection myself, always surprising, the first such surprise in many years, and surprised further, as I shifted awkwardly away in my seat from the strange sad and ugly child's hungry gaze (peering over some magazine his fat mother had doubtless given him, blazoned with blue stars and odd signs, the fanciful emblems and kilroys of some pulpy super-hero no doubt), by Sir Hugh's voice again, relaxed and relieved, as he patted his coat pocket where he had placed the policeman's envelope beside one I had seen earlier, "I see a warm winter," continuing, "a balmy bask among the Basques, or a caper on Capri, or perhaps a stroll on Stromboli," he was again asleep, but his voice did continue just long and loud enough for me to hear, "There are some things you shouldn't tell."

And he was, of course, right, and I haven't.

The show was going strong, but no Miss Parker was in sight. Instead the blindered young band was blaring out a noisy version of that old classic "I'm Umpa Bumping All the Way from Gumpa," while a woman, not so young, probably not from Gumpa, but certainly umpa bumping, was bathing herself in the intense red light, dressed only in a G-string and two flashing pasties.

After assuring himself that Miss Parker was nowhere in sight, Albert looked away from the spectacle on the small stage, feeling himself, in the words of Lucretius, which he had studied carefully not so very long ago, "invaded from without by images emanating from various bodies with tidings of an alluring face and a delightful complexion." Attempting to repel that invasion, he stepped back almost against the rear wall of the narrow club with its plaster colonial decor, painted into the semblance of wooden beams and knobs, and found himself facing a row of framed photographs with brass nameplates neatly engraved and screwed (or glued) to the plastic frames, again simulating wood. A close study of these, he decided, might well save him from the temptations on the stage.

But, he was soon to be disappointed. The pictures were of other ecdysiasts in full strip, poised and potent. But once begun, Albert could not now easily turn away, so he walked the length of the wall, examining each photograph in turn.

There were eight of them, the names hard to see in the lurid light, but the pictures clear and burning. The first was of a young woman stretching her long, lovely legs out before her, seated on a couch of furs, her eyes blazing and dark; the legend read, as best as he could make out, ANN CORPIO, with no further elucidation. The second offered more explanation but made less sense. It was of a lean, sharp-faced woman, her eyes the eyes of hawks, focused miles away, dressed in a long gray dress, the legend on the tiny brass plate reading, FELICITY CRAVEN, THE GORGEOUS GOVERNESS. Somehow to Albert she seemed out of place, scarcely lewd, but he supposed that her imposing presence, like the artifices of the decor, was designed to support the club's "queynte" name.

The third and fourth pictures were of very beautiful and elegant girls, delicate of feature and form, wearing startlingly little, fresh out of finishing school and, in their own way, as out of place as the lean lady before them; they were, the legends informed Albert, MARGIE HART and GYPSY ROSE LEE.

The fifth and sixth pictures were of two sisters, Albert supposed, although they certainly didn't look alike. The first was HELEN PEELER, THE BLIND BOMBSHELL, a nearly nude young woman with a guide dog, a white cane, and a very strategically poised cup. The second was a thin, attractive, but faintly soiled-looking young woman, with eyes that spoke of scandal and shame, named simply PRISTINE PEELER. Both seemed faintly familiar to Albert, and he feared for a horrible moment that this whole place was nothing more than an amplified version of his laundry notes, a three-dimensional and multi-sensual coded note.

But the next picture was of the favorite actress of his boyhood, GEORGIA SOTHERN, whom he had seen selling War Bonds and had fallen for, hopeless and in vain, on the spot. He was relieved and relaxed to see her familiar face here and pleased to see much more of the rest of her than he had ever dreamed possible. So pleased was he that he scarcely noticed the last picture. It was of HOT TONIA, THE MIDGET MARVEL, a small figure with a twisted and unpleasant face, its body as twisted, the entire image looking like an animate pretzel, almost as if the image had been distorted in the camera lens or in the later developing bath. Even the creature's chin seemed to be speckled with dust or hair.

Albert looked away with disgust, but he found that he could not resist reading the last lines of the unpleasant picture's brass legend. "A stunted runt," they said, "is a sprite, a sheer delight from top to toe." They were signed "Lucretius." Again the sweat of cold fear popped out on Albert's forehead and hands, and he felt water oozing in his kneecaps, but before he could follow his impulse to turn and flee back out into the night and onto the street named Ugly, the drums broke into a roll, the band broke as a whole into "Three Little Words," and there on the stage was Miss Parker, grinning in the red light, with two companions, three women completely naked save for the advertised pasty and a small paper fan which they passed back and forth among themselves in intricate patterns as they danced back and forth, around and around. Miss Parker was the center of the three, guiding the intricate weave as far as he could tell. The pictures and Albert's fearful speculations disappeared in the forceful presence of fact; he was here, and so was Miss Parker, and something, he was sure, would happen now.

She saw him. She winked at him on one of her turns his way. She gestured for him to go to her left toward the rear of the club. And so Albert made his way through the clustered whores and sailors, past the teen-age band, their eyes glazed in their blinders, sweating and obviously tired, until finally he passed through an open door and into a dark hallway. He thought he could hear breathing in the darkness around him, but he could see no one, feel nothing.

He groped his way down the Stygian hall, found a door, turned the knob, pushed, and suddenly found himself in a dimly lit, but lit, dressing room.

He was alone with one mirrored image of himself, a cluttered dressing table, and a narrow bed. Fearing fleas or worse, he did not

193

sit down, but waited, standing, fingering the edge of the single chair nervously, balancing himself with the uneasy delicacy of a man standing in a pirogue.

After not too long a time, the band stopped playing, and there was sporadic applause. He heard footsteps in the hall, and suddenly the Loose and Easy Three were upon him, one tossing the pasty onto the table, another pitching the fan onto the bed, and the third, Ginger Snap, naked and hot, in his arms, kissing his face all over, clawing his back, and hissing, "Al, Al, Al, Al."

Albert was embarrassed and again wanted to run, to hide. But Lucretius rose to his mind and offered his classical understanding to Albert's aid, his words sliding calmly through the choppy waters of Albert's fuddled thoughts: "Do not imagine that a woman is always sighing with feigned love when she clings to a man in close embrace, body to body, and prolongs his kisses by the tension of moist lips. Often she is acting from the heart and in longing for a shared delight tempts him to run love's race to the end."

So Albert stayed, embarrassed but assured. The room was nude. The three women surrounded him, pulled at his clothes, and off came coat and tie, shirt and trousers, socks and shoes, leaving Albert nervous in his underwear.

"Take them off," the three girls chanted in unison. "Take them off. Take them off. Take them off."

They wove around him an elaborate pattern. He was dizzy. Ginger Snap clutched at him and whispered, "Take them off."

Albert could not resist. He took them off, T-shirt and jockey shorts, and he was buck naked in a room of nude women. The Loose and Easy Three wove on around him, gave him the fan with which to hide his male parts, stuck the pasty in the center of his forehead, a bright red third eye, sequined and glittering and blind. They wove on around him.

Suddenly they stopped as if on signal.

Ginger Snap, Miss Parker, yelled, "Cut!"

The room exploded with white light, the multiple pop of flashbulbs.

194

Albert knew he had been had. That he was all washed up. He wished for Bacchic vines to wrap him up as they had the pirate ship, to hide him away. He was unable to see. The room smelled like a kennel and seemed full of people. He crouched down to the floor, felt around for his clothes, lost his balance, and fell over on his back.

He heard an unbelievably gruff voice, gruff as Cerberus. It said, "Hot dog."

He was awake. Of that much he was sure, but of very little more. He could not see even to verify that, could not see at all. Only a dull brown light, a surface of air hard and stiff as brown paper, as cardboard. Could not see, but could feel, felt, knew that he was changed, that everything was changed, but into what? His head hurt, and he was so stiff, rolled tight and straight out, that he could move neither to relax himself nor to rub his aching parts. The pain was harsh and general, headache and body, pain of limb and limb, all blurred into one long hurt, running over him from the sharp slice of his spine into a multifoliate agony.

The room around him rumbled and shook with an even, repetitive clatter. He could not remember where he was or why. There was a girl, a head, no head, hair red or blond or black or brown, skin always very white, and a very long night. Surprises. A dream, the same dream, another dream, the roar of presses, the clatter of machines, and always the pain. The scream, the shrill truth, the recognition: "I am a magazine. I am. I *am* a *magazine*. I *am*." Over and over, identical, a thousand copies, thousands.

He could not be sure, could never be sure, where it had ended.

This dark place sounded, felt like a train. Perhaps he was on a train, snug behind dark-green curtains, rocking his way to . . . But there again no answer, no end came. But an end must be coming, must be.

And muffled voices, laughing or sobbing, through the dark, the stiff and unyielding dark. And then a sway, a lurch, surely a train, only a train, and something very heavy fell on him. He still could not move, and the voices were clearer, male or female, old or young, near or far, but clear, clearer.

He could hear whole words, "mash" and "mailing," and later, "muscle boys" and "California," and then, not too clearly, not too distinctly, but no mistaking it, his own name, "Pudd," spoken firmly and confidently, "Pudd."

He relaxed, then, as best he could, hearing his own name, knew he was among friends, at least among those who knew him, knew where he was, spoke his name.

And a voice said, "Otto, erotic nonsense," and added, "The hell with it!" But another laughed and said, "No," and something changed. Pudd felt a weight gone even though he still could neither see nor move.

The air was stiff and brown and hard. He was awake. He was on a train, perhaps a train going to California, rolled up tight and clean and smooth, full of memories, images of himself, unsaid words and taut muscles, stepping westward where the sun would rise and set as it always had, out in the world, that long moment that slices future into past, finished and finally on his way, with nothing behind and the sure promise of something ahead.

One day in September, just after Labor Day and before the start of school, called into extraordinary session despite the tensions and rivalries that ran rampant on the street called Life, the Our Own Block Home Improvement League and Environmental Protection Association met again in the home of Mr. Oscar Wilde, this time with its new members, Miss Shirley Ease and the Warren Hardings, in attendance.

An air of importance and impending disaster hung over the room, dispelling all competitiveness and dissent, causing even Mr. Hoover's burning and mesmeric stare to wander from Miss Daphne Sanders and focus on the problem at hand.

The meeting proceeded in serious tones, for it had just been learned by one and all that the paperboy would be relinquishing his route in the next week to devote all of his afternoons to his school work, to the business of his growing life.

"We ought to," said Mrs. Limpy, "lay aside all our personal interests and feelings, and," she continued, "we ought to think of some communal activity with which to send him off."

"Ought to, ought to," said Mr. Thomas, "the time for such things is past. 'Ought to,' that has a nasty ring to it. The word is 'must,' even 'will,' yes, that's the word." Even Mrs. Limpy, hurt to the bone by his words, agreed, so important was the subject.

On the last Saturday, then, of his career, a bright blue and glowing day, the paperboy stopped at each house and was greeted with inventiveness and enthusiasm beyond anything he had yet experienced. Colors were brighter and more startling, shapes more amazing, tumbling and turning, leaping and spinning, all more involved and spectacular than ever before. The Riminis' ballet of the gas mask and World War I helmet to the strains of the *Secular Requiem* brought him to his feet, saluting. The flossing demonstration by Dr. John and his plump wife was both a farewell to the innocent pleasures of the summer and a preview of the education waiting in the approaching fall. By the time he reached the home of Alfred Omega, it was very late. The sun was a vast orange wall at the end of the street.

Mr. Omega met him on the stoop, wearing his familiar astronomical robe, apparently pleased to see the shining coin which the boy was wearing around his neck on a short chain. The huge man looked down the street as if expecting to see a signal, and when he didn't see what he was looking for, he began to talk to the boy, at him really.

"Certain things," he said, his voice round and shining, "you look at to see what is there; others, to see what may be there; others, simply to see." The boy nodded politely, tucking his black collection book into his belt for the last time.

"When you look," continued Mr. Omega, "never expect to see just what you expect. Expect only," raising his head as if in receipt of the signal for which he had been waiting, "to be changed by what you see, and always, always, to be surprised."

Then Mr. Omega, with a grand flourish, doffed his sparkling robe and stood clothed only in white underwear, sleeveless top and boxer bottom stretching over his bulging flesh. Simultaneously, there came all around the startled boy a shouting, a clamor of voices, old and young, male and female, all calling his name, all alive and lively.

It was all of the people on the block, out in their front lawns, in their underwear, all of it clean and white and pure in the late sunlight. Leslie Ford and David Frome, grinning and looking more identical than ever stripped down to basics, Z. B. D. James, the prancing Marx boys, all of them, the whole neighborhood, gathered and complete.

"We want to say goodbye," they cried in unison, a loving chorus.

"But I've got to go," the boy replied, "I'm all finished." Tears edged into the corners of his round blue eyes, one already streaking his freckled cheek. "I'll be late."

Little Maggie Peters, freshly bathed and in spotless cotton Carter's Spanky Pants and a bright Littlest Angel training bra, ran up the street from her house, pushing her new blue birthday bike, singing out with delight, "Take my bike. You can have it for keeps. I love you."

Blushing, the boy mounted the bike, a girl's model but a sturdy one, accepted Maggie's kiss on his wet cheek, and waved as the assembled multitude cheered, "Hooray!"

He pumped once, rose on the pedals, drifting, and turned to look back. The air was filled with white, a September snow of spotless underwear, and the lawns were filled with naked bodies, dancing out together into the street and waving their arms.

"Goodbye," they sang together. "Goodbye."

A laundryman from a green laundry truck parked on the side street by Miss Ease's house, its tuneful loudspeaker for once discreetly silent, began to walk among the naked, dancing people, picking up the white garments, touched lightly with green grass stain, and stuffing them into a single large white laundry bag. Mrs. Limpy and Miss Ease, Auranthe Franconia and Warren Harding, the mighty and wobbling bulk of Alfred Omega, the Bartholomews and the Riminis, around and around they danced, not looking at the balancing boy now, exposed, naked and free, as the laundryman walked and stooped among them, as little Maggie bawled at the wonder and romance of it all. Mike Venning and Daphne Sanders, naked as the dawn, spun each other in a happy and dizzy dance, while near them, on his back in the grass, fainted dead away, lay Mr. Herbert Hoover, his eyes closed, clad only in the beatific smile which wreathed his face.

The paperboy pushed off then for good, grinning and whistling a wild tune, pumping right and left, and right and left again, standing on the pedals, the coin gleaming like a startled animal's eye at his throat, tossing his curly head in the tumult, a huge and happy silhouette against the golden sun.

And then he was over the hill and gone.

H. G. WELLS: Certainly that boy is one of them. They don't see life as we see it. They can't think of it in our way. And they make us begin to doubt that we see it ourselves as we have always imagined we did.

* * * *

A snap, a flash of light as if you had flicked a wall switch and the ceiling lamp had popped into sudden and suicidal light, the orange filaments fading suddenly like a sunset or a cat's hooding eye.

The snow's slow sift under the door, crawling across the floor with the steadiness of glacial flow. Ice ages, the aging of ice, the rumble of eons. You know only that you are cold, are dizzy. Events have woven you into a cold corner. You are trapped in the dark. You dare not make a sound.

But memories cross your eye like caravans or Eskimos. The slow bounce and dizzy spin of a severed head, sprinkling blood out of its gashes like a summer lawn sprinkler until the entire scene is wet and moving, moving, moving like red snow across the silent floor. The snuffling of a dog, a wolf at the door, at your palm. Its need for the flesh of your hand, the munch of your bones. And a heavy laughter like lard. It fills the arteries of your pounding heart.

His face.

Her face.

The two old men, huddled in the stony corner and dark silence like china figurines, the comic yin and yang of some as yet untranslated cosmology, huddled and whispering, bound up in furs, their thin breathing sprinkled on the chill air like weak ghosts.

The magazine on the low rude table by the barren fireplace. Its cover and opening pages torn out, ragged and soiled, filled with reprinted prose and clumsy photography, muscles and muscles, a heavy man, his face startled and filled with something beyond even despair.

It is all too much. In at the end, you are aware only of something beginning, something that you do not understand.

You will.

* * * *

Saint Augustine: And yet we do measure time. But the times we measure are not those which do not yet exist, not those which no longer exist, not those which are without duration, not those which are without beginning and end. Therefore, what we measure is neither the future nor the past nor the present nor what is passing.

* * * *

Edmund Husserl: The phenomenological data are the apprehensions of time, the lived experiences in which the temporal in the Objective sense appears. Again, phenomenologically given are the moments of lived experience which specifically establish apprehensions of time as such, and, therefore, establish, if the occasion should arise, the specific temporal content (that which conventional nativism calls the primordially temporal). But nothing of this is Objective time. One cannot discover the least trace of Objective time through phenomenological analysis.

* * * *

The two Albanians, the first so swathed and swaddled in heavy coats and scarves and mufflers, a fur cap topping off the bundle, that only the cold tip of a pointed nose and the gleam of two deeply buried round circles of glass emerge as evidence of the inner man, and the second so loaded down with suitcases and briefcases that nothing at all is to be seen of his true features, are rising slowly and steadily up the last layer of escalators in the Notting Hill Gate underground station, fresh off the Central Line and hot on the chase.

Scooped off of the moving risers at the top like an egg by a careful spatula from its hot slick pan, the two figures make their way past the ticket stations and plaques of tidy commendation toward the sunny entrance, out the door and onto the sidewalk on this rare day, turning blindly to their right, crossing dangerous street after dangerous street, pausing finally, wobbling slightly in the gentle breeze, on the Bayswater Road by Kensington's bright Gardens, the first leading the second then like some shaggy prospector's pack mule across the road and into the relative security of Linden Gardens to the very door of the Lime Court Hotel.

A police cruiser and a black police van are pulled up at the curbing, and the two Albanian travelers, no longer so secure in their behavior, stumble one into the other, forming for a quickly passing moment a single indeterminate but clearly alien ball of fur in the center of the sunny street. Then the two part, fall back with a single muffled thump to the curbstone and sit in stunned and separate silence.

A fist, clenched white at the knuckles, is suddenly shaken out of a window of the building to the left of the Lime Court. The three policemen on the sidewalk under the window recoil and cluster. The whole scene has the look and feel of modern ballet; even the music of nearby Bayswater, the mechanical grindings and snortings of traffic, the shuffle of feet, the eager questions of tourists, form the appropriate music.

A voice cries from the window, a man's, angry and tight like the fist, "You'll not get me out here, you ruddy bastids, even with a bloody shoehorn."

"Here, here," a startled policeman answers, his face flushing, "I say now."

An angry woman in a dusty pink duster, appears in the doorway of the building, saying to the policemen, "Now get on with it, will you? I haven't got all day," her cheeks shaking like red warning flags in the breeze.

Two pale and clearly foreign faces appear in the window of the Lime Court tucked into the L formed by the juncture of the two buildings and nearest to the window of the fist, worried and interested—a lovely blond young woman and a young man who seems clearly to know more about things than he is saying. He stares especially hard at the two Albanians and mutters something to his companion that makes her smile. Neither of the two bundled travelers will dare look into his bright face, even when his voice floats down to them, clearly audible, or at least some words of what he is saying, "Annie" and "hyphen" and possibly "partridge."

But just then, two events occur simultaneously, both sudden and surprising: an extraordinarily handsome Russian, passing along the street opposite with his attractive companion Vera, turns to her and says a few words of apparent but foreign disapproval, and an eager-eyed young man, obviously English in his dress and manner, pops out of the green door of the Lime Court and almost skips up to the two tired and slumped Albanians.

"Fitz-Hyffen!" he says to the nearest furry form, his voice alive and loud with excitement. The figure spoken to rolls over onto its side, rocking slightly and slowly. A policeman leaves the blue and agitated clump under the window, offering his help, but is waved away by six hands, those of the young man and his two elderly and mysterious companions. As he turns away, the first hints of curiosity beginning to crease his calm face, that curiosity dies aborning, for a large red lamp, complete with a chartreuse shade and a trailing wire and plug, sails out the window, silent and sure, to land with a multiple pop and smash smack in the middle of his clustered comrades.

The noise increases. Two policemen, undamaged, rush up the front steps toward the impatient lady, her cheeks grown dangerously redder, and, as they rush through the open door into the building, the young Englishman and his two friends disappear from the scene entirely.

Actually, while all those backs are turned, they have gotten themselves assembled and erect again and have walked around the corner and back onto the Bayswater Road, where the young man successfully flags down a cab.

They load their bags and baggage into the cab's open front and climb themselves into the rear. The young man orders the cabby, a man whose whole face seems designed solely as a mount for his impressive squint, to stand his ground, engine idling, and await further instructions. He turns his concave features slowly over the three passengers, the two balls of flustered fur and the alert young man, pauses a moment for thought, and, for reasons left uncommunicated, agrees.

"Sir Hugh," says the young man, "you must try to pardon my brusqueness. I am, as you doubtless know, Party Quayle, but no time now for further introductions."

"Those men, the police," comes the frail reply, "I thought."

"Of course, of course," says the young man. "But, no, no."

"No?"

"No, only an evacuation, an eviction, something of the kind. No one, I repeat with emphasis, *No One* knows that you're here or even in the country."

"Yes," replies Sir Hugh Fitz-Hyffen, for it is he. "Yes. Your father . . . your grandfather . . . your mother . . . I ought to . . ."

"He's here," the young man interrupts.

"He?" the old man responds.

"Here, just around the corner. In a moment, he'll pull out of Linden Court in a sealed car. With the mask."

"The mask?"

"He has the mask. It entered the country concealed in a set of Spode—you see, that aroused suspicions, imported Spode, you see, deucedly odd—anyway, he picked it up. Made no bones about it. I'm sure he knew he was being watched. Your arrival comes at such an opportune moment."

"Moment?" Sir Hugh's voice an echo, curiously similar to the young man's but indescribably more ancient.

Just then a black Bentley with gold trim and flashing American "spinners" on its wheels pulls out of Lime Court and turns into the Bayswater Road. Young Quayle, performing the ritual to perfection, leans forward to the driver, his voice excited by the prospects of the chase and of the saying of the words themselves, "Follow that car."

And follow it they do, down Bayswater past the Marble Arch, then down Oxford Street and onto New Oxford Street and onto Holborn to Holborn Viaduct to Newgate Street, the cab driver wielding his vehicle steadily and surely, onto Cheapside, then Poultry and onto Cornhill and then onto Leadenhall Street.

At one point on the chase, a suitcase falls out of the cab, bursting its cardboard sides on the pavement, scattering a vast collection of tiny bottles and pasteboard packets and assorted sweets, a shattering and colorful rain, but, before the cab can slow, Sir Hugh, his voice sharpened by a genuine anguish but ringing true, cries out, "No matter, no matter, press on, press on," and the cab does.

From Leadenhall onto Aldgate, High Street, and Whitechapel High Street and finally onto Whitechapel Road, the driver never allowing himself to swerve from his course in the dizzying chase.

Once the occupants of the cab catch sight of someone in the

fleeing Bentley, a hooded figure, really just a black hood billowed out as if by the winds of passage, rising to a peak just above the dim back seat of the car.

And, then, to their complete wonder, the Bentley stops, directly before a small milk bar, its frontage fashioned into the figure of an enormous plastic cow, its flanks emblazoned with the name of the establishment, MOO COW, and then, as the cab driver's eyes widen into white and astonished saucers, a small figure, completely robed and hooded in black, a sudden medieval shadow, slips out of the stopped car, across the sidewalk, under the pink plastic udder, and into the building.

The Bentley pulls out slowly, so slowly that its driver seems not to care whether he is followed or not.

"Guv?" says the cab driver.

"Stay here," says Party Quayle.

"But," says the cab driver, his voice wavering with a righteous wonder.

"It's all right," says Quayle, flashing for a flickering instant the inner flap of his wallet, "M.I. 5."

The three passengers climb out of the cab, Sir Hugh, dizzy from the elaborate chase, wobbling for a moment on his feet. Then they move across the sidewalk, looking to passers-by like a young trainer and his two reluctant bears, and into the waiting Moo Cow.

The interior is dim after the bright sunlight, but they are able to see long rows of booths, shapely and scantily attired waitresses, fluorescent appliquéed cows brightening their backsides, stacks of gleaming Lanettaware behind the bar, the enormous plaster or plastic cow at the rear, and the foaming white fluid flowing in steady streams from its swollen dugs. Grinning young men and women are standing along the bar, flashing their white teeth, solid on their strong bones, their long hair flowing down over their shoulders.

Then young Quayle taps his companions on their respective padded shoulders and leads them down the room until they stand before a booth in which sits a single hooded figure, its head bowed so that its face is completely invisible.

Sir Hugh, with some difficulty, slides into the booth directly opposite the figure, and his friend follows. Quayle slips in beside the silent monk.

"So," begins Sir Hugh, his voice wrinkled and stiff like an old, hopelessly scuffed and completely useless shoe, "we meet again and in circumstances again not to your liking."

The dark figure says nothing, is motionless in the dim light.

"It's no wonder," says Sir Hugh, "that you have nothing to say, no, no wonder," laughing now like a parrot clearing its throat, feathery and brittle, "nothing at all to say now that we've caught you red-handed."

He reaches suddenly across the table, snatches one of the hooded figure's hands out of its long concealing sleeve, and it is far from red. Rather it is the pale cream color of old ivory, a delicate beautiful hand with long pointed nails and several gleaming dark rings.

Sir Hugh stops as suddenly as he began, holds the hand as if both he and it were frozen, were only a photograph in some long-closed album.

Then, stunned but not into inaction, Party Quayle snatches back the heavy hood, revealing the long black hair and beautiful ivory face of a young woman, Eurasian from the look of her, her dark almond eyes flecked with a familiar blue, staring, blankly but directly, into the icy blue eyes of Sir Hugh, all four of their eyes unblinking and wide open.

"Drugged," says Quayle. "The fiend, the fiend."

"The mask," says Fitz-Hyffen's companion.

"Not here. Gone. With him. The fiend."

And then Sir Hugh releases the young woman's hand, his face now naked and open, stunned and surprised. He looks down into his hand to see in it a coin, gold in the dim light of the Moo Cow. He drops it onto the center of the table, where it spins for a moment, then wobbles itself into flat stillness. He looks back into the girl's open eyes, but Quayle and Sir Hugh's ancient friend lean over and stare at the coin.

A waitress comes up to the booth, the hem of her red miniskirt resting lightly on the table's edge, her eyes sour and weary under the bright Moo Cow cap with its bobbed horns and imitation hide, her creamy order pad poised, and she looks down at this curious quartet, the dark-robed woman and the furred old man caught in each other's eyes, and the other old man and his young friend staring down at the table top as if in prayer.

"Well," she says, her voice weary and worldly wise, "I fought I'd seen everyfing."

But she hasn't. Not yet.

* * * *

CLASS NOTES: THE ELEMENTS OF FICTION (I)

In a work of verbal narrative art, we see that the impersonal *you* is the focal point of the point of view of the reader. In other words, the *you* becomes for the reader the reader's eye. Since the *you* is the reader's eye, he translates the *you* in his mind's eye to *I*, so that, for all intents and purposes, to the reader's eye the *you* is actually *I*.

* * * *

KALERGIS, DIMITRIOS (1803–1867), a Greek states-
man and military leader, born in Crete. After studying in
Russia and Austria, he returned to Greece to join the War
of Greek Independence. In 1825 he and Giacinto Provana
di Collegno were given command of New Navarino. Despite
his efforts the stronghold was taken by the army of Ibrahim
Pasha. He was not captured with New Navarino, but rather
escaped to join the army of Georgios Karaïskasis. In May
of 1827 he was captured at Phaleron. The Turks held him
for ransom, threatening his execution. He was freed after
some time and the payment of the ransom, and he became
aide-de-camp to Col. Baron Charles Fabvier. He later served
in that capacity under Count I. A. Kapodistrias. His relationship with King Otho, however, was, at best, strained. In
1843, as leader of the cavalry, he was a major force in the
removal of Otho's Bavarian entourage, the Baron Trutz-
Drachen and, unfortunately, with them a number of price-
less valuables, and also in the establishment of a constitu-
tion and ironically the salvation of the dynasty (see
GREECE: History; OTTOKAR, KING: Sceptre). He was
appointed military commander in Athens but was exiled
after the fall of the Mavrokordatos ministry in 1845. He
lived in London for a time, where he became intimate with
Louis Napoleon. He returned to Greece in 1848, hoping to
start a revolution, but was captured and held for a time.
In 1853 he was sent to Paris, but in 1854 he was recalled
to Greece and appointed a minister in the new Mavrokordatos cabinet. Despite pressure from his friends among the
western powers, he was forced to resign in October of 1855
by his longtime enemy, King Otho. In 1861, he was appointed minister plenipotentiary in Paris and was a moving
force in the accession of Prince George of Denmark to the
Greek throne in 1862. He died in Athens on January 24,
1867.

C. S.

Interesting and accurate, as far as it goes. One could speculate about a number of things. Kapodistrias' infamous grandson, perhaps, *da capo ad infinitum*. But only two corrections are essential. Not corrections, additions. The first garnered from family legend; the second, from even more obscure legend, unknown even to the family.

First:

When Kalergis was captured at Phaleron and held for ransom in 1827, the ransom note was accompanied by his left ear and the sure promise of more parts to follow. The ransom was soon paid.

Second:

Disturbed by the disfigurement, Kalergis had a gold mask fashioned during his later stay in London. The mask covered the top half of his face, a gold domino concealing both the good ear and the ghastly scar where the other had grown and gone. After Kalergis' death, the mask disappeared for a time, but in its absence, its legend grew. Its wearer, so legend said, would hold dominion over the earth, would be absolute monarch of all he chose to survey, would be able to cause the very heavens to sway to his command. But the mask has never reappeared, fortunately or unfortunately for mankind.

There have been rumors. One has it that the gold mask of the veiled prophet Al Mokanna was never actually rediscovered and that the mask which Dr. Fu-Manchu used in 1932 to instigate his abortive Arab revolt was in fact the mask of Dimitrios.

Another would have it that the ring of Judas used by the paper-hanger Shicklgruber to transform himself into the dictator Hitler was in fact no ring at all, but the gold mask.

The two rumors are, of course, mutually exclusive, but they do stand as evidence of the mask's power at least to stimulate discussion and speculation, even if it was, as is most likely the case, melted down and sold as part of an ingot which passed into the hands of the Vuelph family in the infamous gold-silver exchange of April 1, 1872.

* * * *

ALFRED NORTH WHITEHEAD: The production of a scheme is a major effort of the speculative Reason. It involves imagination far outrunning the direct observations.

* * * *

Tucked away in the dark corner of Mitre Square on a moonlit early Sunday morning, long before sunrise, young Hugh Fitz-Hyffen lies waiting, an eager and optimistic boy of sixteen on his first case. Young Hugh, secure in his new determination not to be a police inspector like his former hero, the indomitable Sergeant Cuff, but rather to be a consulting detective like his newly discovered hero, Mr. Sherlock Holmes, has decided that what better beginning is possible for his career than to bring in none other than the Whitechapel murderer, the man who but two days before had named himself "Jack the Ripper." And where else to catch him but in Whitechapel?

Young Hugh, thin and pale, dressed in dark clothes, his face painted in lampblack, even his round glasses blacked over save for the essential small circles in the center, has chosen Mitre Square to lie in lurk this first night out both because it is dark and secluded, a perfect spot for a Saturday-night murder and mutilation, and because it lies between the warehouses of Messrs. Kearley and Tonge, where he knew he could bask in the mingled scents of Ceylon and Foochow and Formosa, congous and oolongs, caffeine and tannin, teas, the headiest brews his palate has touched. And there, swimming in exotic smells, disappointed that Saturday has passed into Sunday without even a scent of violence, but delighted with his circumstances nonetheless, Hugh lies, a darker shade in the moon-cast shadow along the warehouse wall.

As he reclines there, alert and happy, he reviews the general shape and substance that the two murders have given to the shadowy ripper. He is a man, quick and sure of himself, strong and no doubt athletic, a skilled scientist or surgeon, a frequenter of prostitutes, possibly a hater of prostitutes, a master of disguise, a man recently associated with Americans, as his letter to the newspaper had revealed, an extraordinarily cunning and clever man, possibly a brilliant one. Surely, it will not be too difficult to find such a man; one with his attributes must stand out from his surroundings like the central figure of some heroic painting.

His musings are interrupted by approaching footsteps. A prostitute's? His body thrills at the very thought. The ripper? The small hairs at the nape of his neck stand erect. But, as it has been every fifteen minutes for the hours that Hugh has lain here, it is the constable on his beat, plodding through the romantic scene with mundane and dull stolidity.

Hugh lies still until he passes on his way, then twists to look at his pocket watch: 1:30. He will have to go home soon, for he doesn't want to be caught by the embarrassing sunrise in his black attire.

He replaces his watch and lies back, inhaling deeply. But then, there are more footsteps. His body tenses again with its accustomed regularity. This time, maybe, this time.

It is a man and a woman, leaning on each other and moving briskly along. In the strong moonlight, Hugh can see them both clearly.

The woman is wearing a black cloth jacket with imitation fur collar and three large metal buttons. Her dress appears to be of dark-green print, the pattern composed of Michaelmas daisies and golden lilies. She is wearing a bonnet of black straw, trimmed with black beads and velvet. She has some sort of white cloth and riband tied loosely around her neck. Her shoes are a man's laced boots.

The man looks to be in his early thirties. He seems to be about five feet nine inches tall, but he also appears to be stooping slightly. He is dressed darkly in something like navy serge with a red neckerchief around his throat, and he is wearing a deerstalker.

The two pause. The woman flings her arms around the man, and they turn slowly in the moonlight until her back is to young Hugh. Then she crumples suddenly like a dropped doll, and Hugh sees a long knife in the man's hand, already dark with blood, and quicker than his eyes can follow clearly, the man rolls the woman flat on her back, tosses up her skirts and underclothes, and sets to work with his blade.

Hugh is petrified, his eyes held through their tiny peepholes on the scene. A slice, and then the man pulls out a long string of wobbling pale intestine and drapes it over the woman's right shoulder. He is carving quickly and surely. He places a length of severed intestine between her left arm and body. He removes a bloody gobbet, pulls off the red neckerchief, wraps the meat in it, and tucks it in his coat pocket. Then, with extraordinary care and swiftness, he slices off the woman's lower eyelids, following that deft act with a sudden and furious attack on her face, slashing it to an indescribable mask of blood and horror.

Hugh is frozen, unable even to retch and certainly unable to move or cry out.

The man, finished with his task, stands up, straightens his clothing, and looks carefully around the square. The moon flashes on his fierce face as he seems to look directly at the concealed Hugh. The eyes are sharp and piercing, burning over his thin hawklike nose, the thin unreal mustache, and square, prominent chin. And then the whole face is lost in the shadow of the deerstalker's bill, and almost as suddenly the lean figure of the man is lost in the night, gone as silently as if he had never been there.

Only the woman remains, gutted and gone.

And Hugh, his face drawn in a terror so deep that he will never again look like a boy or even a young man. He has lost something this night that he will never find again, even glimpse again.

He glances at his watch: 1:42. The constable will be returning in three minutes.

He calls upon what is left of his strength, of his will, and climbs to his feet and runs out into the Aldgate and down the dark street. He calls upon everything in which he believes to keep him going, to keep him from crumpling into a black heap in the middle of the street.

"Holmes!" he cries out into the moonlight and shadow, his voice tinted with a darkness deeper than the lampblack on his twisted face. "He is Holmes!" And, then, one final time, he utters the name which he will never speak again in his life, which he will never allow spoken in his presence, ever, "Sherlock Holmes!"

* * * *

ROBERT FROST: If design govern in a thing so small.

* * * *

CLASS NOTES: INTRODUCTION TO LOGIC

The primary method of thought is that of reduction. The analytical and logical mental act is disjunctive and reductive. We sever and we reduce.

Let us examine the Cartesian proposition. I think therefore I am. The "I" of the proposition is strictly dependent upon the act of thought and the act of being. It may be discarded. I think therefore I am > think therefore am > think am > am Thus is the irresistible course of logic. The subjective self is reduced to the single logical fact, "am."

Let us apply this logical method and its factual consequence to the objective reality, the so-called other. He thinks therefore he is > thinks therefore is > thinks is > is Our second fact, the second atom of our understanding, "is."

We need really go no further. But, for those of a scientific inclination, we might note that this reductive method in the form of the close analysis of quantum mechanics has given us the understanding we enjoy today of a random and patternless universe.

And, for those of an aesthetic bent, dubious of the value of analytical method in regard to artistic production, we may point out that the aim of all art, like that of all thought, is reduction. A work of narrative art, a novel, say, may be defined accurately as the direct movement through described experience to its ultimate end, the final period of the final sentence on the final page.

* * * *

Otto is a reduction of everything, a perverse anagram of the whole.

*   *   *   *

Among the first sensations which one feels upon being enclosed in a "black room," a controlled environment of absolute visual and auditory sensual deprivation, is a steady humming sound, as if the entire body were an electrical machine, an elaborate electric clock keeping time, time, time, which, of course, it is.

*   *   *   *

The surrounding mountaintops, craggy and bare, are shivering with blown snow. It plumes off them, disappears and circles windily to other sharp peaks. And far below in the high winding pass, following a wavering, crooked, and stumpy trail of mingled footprints in the chill snow, is a party of humans, four bundled figures, and a huge hound tugging asthmatically at his stout leather leash.

The trailing party stops as the path they are following nears a narrow cleft in the mountain walls. They converge into a small circle, the dog crouched at the center, leaning their fur-rimmed hoods together over the dog, forming a cozy and breathy room for conversation, walled by fur and the four faces.

"We should be careful here. The pass narrows and is a perfect place for an ambush." The speaker is a young man, an Englishman.

"Quite right, young Party, but we have no choice. . . ."

"True, Sir Hugh."

"But . . ."

"Hush, there's no time for that now."

"Have we the strength?"

"That question is best answered by Miss Fang-Yugh."

Six eyes turn in the circle to focus in the dim furry light on the blue-flecked almond eyes of the fourth pale face.

"Do not worry about me."

"The question . . ."

"No question of it. . . ."

"Now?"

"Not now, I'm sure."

"We must . . ."

The large dog growls, and the party suddenly parts. The great beast, its hackles bristled and its eyes rolling, braces itself in the shifting snow, faced up the trail, and emits a huge and dangerously echoing bark. It then stands rigidly and silently while its four companions stand as still, as quiet, and watch the object of the dog's terrified attention.

A black figure, that of an enormous wolf, stands at the narrowest and highest point of the pass, its eyes red and burning, its fangs bared and gleaming like yellow icicles. It watches the silent party with the bristling, rigid dog for a moment, and then rises up onto its hind legs. Waving its forepaws in the air, it paces a few awkward steps in the snow, its tail wagging, marching like an addled grenadier too long in the sun. And then, suddenly and naturally, it begins to dance, its front legs and tail keeping time, its hind legs stepping out an elaborate pattern in the high mountain snow.

"Sir Hugh," one of the men says, his voice shrill and electric with excitement. "Sir Hugh."

"Hush," his companion replies.

The huge hound begins to growl, a low rumbling crescendo.

And then, with the suddenness of a dream, the great black wolf throws back its bobbing head and howls, a long, low, mournful sound, the pitch varying smoothly upward, laid over with a dozen harmonically related and chilling overtones, a howl joined and answered even as it ebbs by another cry, a long, piercing, gurgling, human shriek from somewhere behind the wolf.

The wolf disappears. The hound breaks into frustrated barking, dragging one of its masters after it on the straining leash and the other three on their own accord. They run up the slippery pass, leaving spinning puffs of freezing breath hanging in the cold air behind them.

They reach the site of the dance, observe the pattern of paw prints in the snow for a moment as if it were a puzzle capable of solution, and then, at the sound of another scream, they rush on over the crest of the pass, skidding down onto a long rocky slope, bounding along until they come to a sudden halt, dog and all, by the fallen figure of a man, heavily clothed in colorful peasant garb, his head thrown back, his arms and legs splayed out, and, under his full black beard, his throat draining blood from two puckering puncture wounds.

The hound begins to whimper, tucks its tail between its legs, and slinks behind its masters. They crouch around the recumbent figure of the dying man.

"Who did this thing to you?"

"Vă rog să-mi daţi rufele la spălat," he answers, his voice weak and wet, "Vă rog să dati pantalonii aceştia la călcat."

"Do you speak English?"

The man stares blankly.

"Chinese?" Even more blankly.

"Is there anything we can do for you?"

"Te rog să-mi aduci încă o pătură," he says, his voice fading and falling, "mi-a fost frig."

"An Inca, eh?" says Sir Hugh. "And far from home."

But as he is about to continue in his musings, the dying man begins to sing, his voice suddenly loud and strong, filled with a surprising warmth:

> "Fire, fire, trandafire,
> Dar tu ce te-ai zabovit . . ."

His voice sticks, clicks like a switch, and stops. His eyes are open like his mouth. The blood stops flowing from the two small wounds. He is as pale as the sifting snow, and he is dead.

Already he has frozen to the ground.

"I think we ought to . . ."

"There is no way, no way at all."

The tracks they have been following, fewer of them now, really only those of one person and the paw prints of a large dog or wolf, lead on down the pass, between the towering mountain walls, through the whistling snow, and toward the invisible but fast-approaching sunset.

* * * *

JOHN COWPER POWYS: My sequence of thought, in this matter of the soul's "creative" power, may thus be indicated. In the process of preparing the ground for those rare moments of illumination wherein we attain the eternal vision the soul is occupied, and the person attempting to think is occupied, with what I call "the difficult work of art" of concentrating its various energies and fusing them into one balanced point of rhythmic harmony. This effort of contemplative tension is a "creative effort" similar to that which all artists are compelled to make. In addition to this aspect of what I call "creation," there also remains the fact that the individual soul modifies and changes that first half-real something which I name the objective mystery, until it becomes all the colours, shapes, sounds and so forth, produced by the impression upon the soul of all the other personalities brought into contract with it by the omnipresent personality of the universal ether.

* * * *

CLASS NOTES: INTRODUCTION TO IMAGINATIVE THOUGHT

The primary method of imaginative thought is expansion. The imaginative and creative mental act is conjunctive and expansive. We combine and we expand.

The logical act of reduction requires expansion. Life itself tells us this. Think of Emerson's circles or Poe's universe pulsing like the Heart Divine. Think of the very shape of human mental development. Professor Robinson accurately describes it as a movement from sensation to reason to imagination.

If the "I" of the self must rationally and logically be reduced to the "is" of fact, then the cosmos itself, organic and unified as a thought, demands of us an additional expansion.

I $>$ is $<$ IS

It is the awareness of belonging and the freedom to follow this course of necessary reduction and expansion that Einstein has given to us. The shape of that journey, I might add, should then be the form of all meaningful and relevant narrative art.

* * * *

Let's take the story of the man,
Who, nibbling at a fingertip,
Became enamored of his flesh,
And thoroughly devoured himself.
His meal was slow, and after one last gulp
What then remained? The teeth,
Those yellow bones (no arms or hands
To brush them early on), a heart,
(He bit it last to die), a stomach,
No other guts, no eyes, no ears,
The bones all cracked and gone
For marrow. The helpful nurses
Cleared the bed, a sackful
For the grave, no smiling undertaker
Needed here, no, none at all.

* * * *

RALPH WALDO EMERSON: Then the new molecular philosophy shows astronomical interspaces betwixt atom and atom, shows that the world is all outside; it has no inside.

* * * *

COLIN WILSON: Consciousness isn't supposed to perceive meaning; it's supposed to perceive *objects*.

* * * *

THE NOVEL OF TODAY

It seems to me that a novel can be written that is genuinely post-Einsteinian in its essentials, one based on these four assumptions: that we must concern ourselves with events and not stable bodies, that time like physical matter is particulate, that time is capable of dilation (of moving at different speeds and directions at once), and that, for all its particularity and dilation, time is nevertheless organically unified in an experiential field which has vital form if not traditional structure.

A novel growing from these assumptions would be concerned with events rather than with characters in the usual sense, would be particulate (composed of small, apparently discrete particles or fragments), would be composed of a number of different but simultaneous time movements, and would finally reveal itself to be formally unified. A modern book of changes.

*　*　*　*

Schloss Varban. The name carved in Gothic stone and style above the heavy, rough wooden doors. The snow coiling in the dark around the feet of the weary travelers, the two old men, the young man, and the girl. The large dog crouches at obedient heel at the young man's heel, his ears back, his tail tucked, wary and worried. They have just raised the worn knocker, bat-shaped and brazen, and allowed it to fall with a heavy and reverberating thud against the door.

Puffing and stamping, they wait, but not for long. The door creaks slowly open, and they are admitted by an as yet unseen host to the inner sanctum of the castle's interior.

The door slams to into the wind behind them, and suddenly they are faced with their host, tall, dark, coldly handsome, dressed in formal evening wear, draped in a long cloak, carrying a flickering lantern, intense eyes, a regal beak of a nose, a cruelly inviting, sensual mouth, the lips looking almost as if they have been painted into place.

He speaks, then, his voice at once sinister and soothing, like the icy death by freezing that awaits them outside the castle door, "I am the Voivode Vlady," his eyes widening, one of them burning as if a small light were focused on it from somewhere in the upper reaches of the dark hall, "I bid you welcome."

They mumble appreciations, too cold to be warm in their remarks, and are led by their host, moving so slowly that they almost feel that they are in a dream, a dream given them by a soothing subconscious to ease their freezing in some snowbank far from shelter or safety. They climb a curving and crumbling flight of stone stairs, past a spider spinning his web for the unwary fly, past what almost appear to be armadillos scuttling into crevices and rat holes in the walls, until finally, footsore and careworn, they reach a large dining hall, a fire flaming up in its stone fireplace by which the large dog settles, a large table laid in white and gold, tall candles, comfortable wing-backed chairs, a museum of sorts in one far corner, glass cases and all.

Beckoning to them, their host repeats his name, "I am the Voivode Vlady . . ."

"Of course, and of course," bursts out the tiny old man in the round glasses, his entire face as blue as his eyes except for the tip of his pointed nose, which is dead white. "How rude of me, of us, of me. I am Sir Hugh Fitz-Hyffen, late of England, and this is my old friend and companion." Gesturing with his mittened hand, he taps the end of his nose, which snaps off like a piece of chalk, and he stops speaking and stares at the icy chip in his furry palm.

"I," says his young male companion, taking up the task of the amenities, "am Partridge Quayle, also of the United Kingdom, and," bowing slightly to the young lady, as does the imposing Voivode Vlady, "this young lady, of, shall we say, the East, is Miss Fang-Yugh."

"You're most welcome, and your unexpected, if delightful, presence here in these seldom traveled parts?" their host responds.

"Traveling," young Quayle replies. "Following, let us say, our heart's desire."

"Let us do say, then," says the imposing dark man, the fire flashing red in his wide and widening eyes, "that I quite understand. And, now, you must permit me to offer you some wine to warm you after your wintry wanderings."

He leaves, silently and gracefully, and the young man sets about stripping off his heavy coats and those of his companions. Sir Hugh absently places the cold tip of his nose in his mouth in order to free his hands for the disrobing, and when the Voivode Vlady returns, he finds them all sitting around the table, thawing in the fire's glow, smiling up at him, the girl ravishingly and exotically beautiful by candlelight, Fitz-Hyffen sunk deeply in apparent thought, the two other men politely silent and attentive.

"I hope," says the Voivode, "that you will find the wine suitable to your needs," pouring his way around the large table. Four glasses filled, he pauses, bows slightly, and smiles his unsettling smile.

"You will join us?" says the beautiful Fang-Yugh softly.

"I never drink," the Voivode responds, pausing as if the pause carries great meaning of itself, then continuing, "wine."

Before anyone can say anything further, Sir Hugh pops suddenly alive as if he were operated by a taut spring just released, crunches something in his mouth, swallows, gasps, a startled look in his eyes, takes up his wineglass, and drains it in a trice.

The Voivode nods graciously, begs them take full advantage of his hospitality, and leaves to see about further refreshment.

"Refreshments, indeed," mutters the plump old man to young Quayle, "from the looks of those red stains on his shirt front, he doesn't drink wine, ho, ho, at least not in public."

"Not so loud," says Quayle. "We have no choice but to accept his hospitality, and we may not," and he, too, pauses significantly, "be his only guests."

A draft sucks through the vast room just then, causing all four guests to shiver for a second, as though a goose were stepping stiffly over their graves.

"Let's look at the museum, then," suggests the recovered old man, and the four travelers wander across the elaborate carpet and stone floor to the dark end of the room where the glass cases stand, the other corners of the room so dark as not to be there at all, Sir Hugh scrubbing at the itching nub of his thin red nose.

What they find in the glass cases strikes a coldness into them deeper than any draft could do, for they contain only six objects, four in the first case and one each in both of the other cases. The first case contains four burnished and worn silver hands, graduated upward from the small hand of a child to the large heavy hand of a fully grown man, laid out on blue velvet, gleaming like moonlight in the reflecting light of the fire, a tiny eagle and swastika stamped at the base of each hand.

The second case holds a large yellow diamond, the largest such stone two of these travelers have ever seen in their entire lives. It too nestles in blue velvet and burns in the faint light from the fire.

The third case contains only one object, too, a golden domino, a mask so intricately cast and formed that it seems almost to be half a face. Something that can only be called power radiates from it through the four still figures before it.

They turn away in awe, only to be startled anew by the figure of a man, seated at the table, immaculately attired in evening clothes like their host, but a tiny man, twisted, as though he were a normally formed man being viewed through a distorting lens, even his head twisted and warped. He turns to them, the stubble on his chin casting a permanent shadow across the lower half of his face, his eyes buzzing with the intensity of his hate.

"Sir Hugh Fitz-Hyffen, I believe," he says, his voice corroded like the edge of a discarded razor, ragged and sharp, foreign but familiar.

"I don't believe I've had the pleasure," responds Sir Hugh, removing his glasses, wiping them on his sleeve, his left eye wandering away to the waning fire while the right continues to peer at the small man, bringing the left eye to attention by replacing them.

"O you have," replies the man. "I am Otto Vuelph, so called, and we have indeed met, met indeed more than once," his voice sliding the last syllable out into a lingering hiss.

Sir Hugh peers more closely at him.

"Sir Hugh," says his companion, "wasn't it in . . . ?"

226

"No," says Sir Hugh, cagily, "I think it was in Yorkshire in, was it 1915? Or, possibly in America, in, say, 1941?"

"Then you do remember," says Otto. "How touching to know that you do remember. But there have been other times, many other times."

Sir Hugh notices as he listens the spread of meats and cheeses, brown and white breads, hot mustards and bottles of beer, laid, all of them across the wide table, and, motioning with his busy elbows to his friends, he digs in, stuffing food into his eager mouth even as he begins the composition of a massive sandwich, managing also to say between mouthfuls to the smirking Otto, "Please, if you will, refresh my memory."

"We met," says the obliging Otto, "once in London. I think I was going then by the name of Otto Luker. We engaged in a small transaction, the full nature of which I don't think you realized for some time after that."

Sir Hugh chews on, nodding for him to continue.

"And we once sat across from each other on a delightful transatlantic flight. My plans for our further meetings on that little gambol were spoiled by an overeager stewardess and the juvenile authorities in Reykjavik who reached the curious conclusion that I was a stowed-away runaway. You were gone to some sunny place or the other (I failed to find out which) before I managed to set matters, shall we say, straight.

"And I'm sure you remember the charming play you attended in Paris, that experimental delight by O. T. Loup-Garou, *Chomp*, the tale of a man who decides to eat himself. Don't you remember how his warm parts were passed around the audience before he dug in himself, as it were? O I was there, and I had hoped for you to join our little troupe in a very important part, or parts, but again you seem to have slipped away."

Sir Hugh settles back in one of the wing-backed chairs, replete and relaxed, ready now for what may come. And it does come as Otto continues, spittle forming in white pools along his lower lip in his rising excitement, "And there was, you might say, I would, one other time. I was once very close to you, Sir Hugh Fitz-Hyffen, yes, very close to you."

"I suppose," interrupts Party Quayle, "since you know one of us so well . . ."

"O," says Otto, looking hard at Fang-Yugh, who blushes to the tone of a warm peach at his gaze, "I know you all very well, don't I, my dear?" He laughs with the sound of a dozen old men hawking up their last deadly rattles. Quayle clenches his fist. Sir Hugh motions him to stay calm.

"Yes, I know you, and you know me. You've seen my calling card, or should I say coin. I left the same one for a certain Adolf when I absent-mindedly wandered off with one or two of his little treasures. A copy, to be sure, of a missing original, emended a little bit, but emendations are one of my hobbies. Making things change is one of my few pleasures."

"Yes, Herr Vuelph," says Sir Hugh, his voice, for all its being nearly worn away with years, firm and steady, his gray hands gripping the arms of his chair, his lively tongue licking at the mustard around his lips between words, "we know everything about you that we need to know."

"I trust," says Otto, "you have kept your coming here a secret."

"No one knows who shouldn't know, that much I know and you know, too."

"O no," says Otto, "there is much that I don't know that you know," and then, very calmly, almost as slowly as if it were the Voivode speaking and not Otto, "but there is one thing that I do know that you do not know."

"And that?" says Sir Hugh, arching the sparse white sprinkle of his eyebrows.

"And that," says Otto Vuelph, his voice now as cold as the icy outdoors beyond the stone castle walls.

The dog, which all this time has been sleeping silently by the open fire, suddenly screams a horrid scream and leaps across the room, scrabbling on the stone floor, sparks dancing along his singed hairy tail.

"And that," says Otto through the din, "is that, Sir Hugh Fitz-Hyffen, I am your son."

* * * *

It is a single substance, a single surface, curving, swaying, rippling like a silk banner floating on the wind, gold and vermilion, humming in a sort of runic rime, alive in all of its particularity, its particular singularity, electrical and atremble, the essence, the fact, the ground, the field.

* * * *

EZRA POUND: Time, space,
                 neither life nor death is the answer.

* * * *

Berlin, April 10, 1965 (Reuters)
Otto, a lone Mediterranean octopus captive in West Berlin's aquarium since September, is eating itself to death at the rate of half an inch a tentacle a day. An aquarium official said the octopus apparently was suffering from some unidentifiable emotional upset.

* * * *

ALBERT EINSTEIN & LEOPOLD INFELD: In our case the reader is also the investigator, seeking to explain, at least in part, the relation of events to their rich context.

* * * *

RALPH WALDO EMERSON: The individual is always mistaken. He designed many things, and drew in other persons as coadjutors, quarrelled with some or all, blundered much, and something is done; all are a little advanced, but the individual is always mistaken. It turns out somewhat new and very unlike what he promised himself.

* * * *

You are somewhat and not a little puzzled, in the dark, staring out at the scene. Otto is exultant, strutting his crooked way back and forth before the fire, ringing his voice into the still muddy shadows of the enormous room, waving his uneven arms, even leaping high into the air once in an aerial somersault, smacking back to the stone floor on his polished patent-leather pumps.

Sir Hugh Fitz-Hyffen is sitting in a wing-backed chair, upholstered in rich red velvet, sitting fixed, his eyes open but unseeing through the thick glass circles of his spectacles, as still as a photograph.

"I have something else to show you," says Otto to the remainder of his audience. "O yes, yes, many things, things to interest and amaze you."

He steps to a darkened section of the room and returns, almost in a prance, with a drab musette bag slung over his shoulder and, clutched in his hand as if he were afraid it might take wing, an ormolu image of a bird, its black and yellow and blue-green paint flaking.

Fang-Yugh inhales sharply, and Otto responds, "O yes, my once and future petling, mama's yellow tit, and now we know where mama went when she ran away, and, my late loveling, who your mysterious and missing papa is, o yes, my dearly beloved lass." Fang-Yugh stares at him, her features inscrutable, her hands like bird's claws clutching at the arms of her chair.

"O yes," Otto continues, perching the tit on the table top, swinging the battered musette bag down beside it. He pulls up the flap, revealing the stenciled G.Q. inside and a stack of pulpish paper, gaudy magazines with a familiar face, known to young Quayle from a thousand photographs, a thousand similar covers. "O yes, the last remains of dear departed granddad, his final solace before he, shall we say, went to earth. I knew your mother, too, sweet Mary, well, yes, very well."

Young Party springs from his chair, fists clenched, but soon returns to it, his eyes riveted on the gleaming Luger in Otto's tiny warped fist.

"O yes," says Otto, "it's a smart child indeed that knows its own pop, o yes."

He begins to laugh again, waving the large gun, gurgling his expletives out into the still air.

"O yes," he says, this time tossing the torn and tattered remains of a magazine, a physical-culture magazine from the look of it, onto the table top beside his other exhibits. "Here's something you might enjoy reading, the last issue of *Pudd*. I had a little something to do with that rag's unseemly end. Sorry so many pages are missing. The need, I assure you, was extreme." More strangled laughter, splashing around the echoing room.

"And this," he says, dramatically lifting the silver cover of a virginal serving dish, revealing a cheap scrapbook, stuffed with tags of paper, the orts and shards of someone's compulsive collection, "is the key to it all. You've seen the hands and the stone and the mask, o yes, the mask. But this is the key to them all, the Longinus Papers, the secrets of the Old Ones, the alarm bell to awaken slumbering Newarkk. It's all here, and now I have all the pieces of the puzzle, and best of all I have lovely you. You'll be such a help to me.

"Ph'nglui mglw'nafl Cthulhu R'lyeh wgah'nagl fhtagn!"

At the sound of those chilling syllables, Sir Hugh comes into focus. He snaps alert and says, suddenly as if he were spitting, "Son!"

"Son," shouts Otto, whirling like a ballerina, "son, conceived of a serving girl (you remember that lupine night) in the household of the Baroness Trutz-Drachen, named with typical discretion Otto Vuelph by my mangled mama long years ago. And I've followed in your footsteps ever since, dear papa."

"Then," mumbles Sir Hugh, his face slipping like mud on an underground-spring-fed hillside, "I have progeny, I have progeny in this room."

"You certainly do," replies Otto, "you certainly do."

"In fact," says Sir Hugh, "more than one." He glances across the table to Fang-Yugh, who is crouched fetchingly in the comforting arms of Party Quayle.

"What do you mean?" says startled Otto.

"I mean that those children are mine. I fathered young Quayle in December in Denver or some such high place, and the sweet girl is the side effect of my efforts in Sheffield to penetrate the yellow peril," says a suddenly confident Sir Hugh, his old friend's mouth popping open in stunned amaze, where it remains for a long time to come.

"Impossible," cries Otto, "their ages, my knowledge."

"Believe," says Sir Hugh, "what you see," his eyes cobalt blue, echoing in the eyes of the horrified young lovers holding each other even more closely across the table.

"But," says young Quayle, "my father is Mallory Quayle. I was born shortly after he moved back to London after America proved too full, he said, of sneaky surprises."

"Believe," repeats Sir Hugh, "what you see."

Otto's face twists like a discarded oily rag; his finger tightens on the Luger trigger.

At this tense moment, you are startled to see the Voivode Vlady enter the room through an arched doorway, his face paler than before, even his lips blanched and arid. Otto looks that way, too, and is startled himself to hear a tough voice say, "Drop the gun, Otto, the jig is finally up!" The voice seems to come directly from the unmoving lips of the Voivode, but, as a figure, a .45 in each hand, steps from behind the tall cloaked figure, it proves to be the voice of an absolute stranger.

Sir Hugh's face falls even faster than before.

"Who," says Party Quayle, "are you?"

"If it takes a smart kid to know his own dad," says the tough voice, "I guess it takes a real genius to recognize his own grandfather."

Sir Hugh's friend pops his mouth shut, then opens it again to say, "Gridley Quayle!"

"None other," says the elder Quayle with a grin.

"But . . ." says Party.

"But . . ." says Otto.

"But . . ." manages the recovering Sir Hugh, drawing his wandering features together.

232

"Gridley Quayle," says Gridley Quayle, "still on the case. Forced that wog Aliynfri to lead me here. Decided to blow my cover and wrap things up."

"Aliynfri?" says Sir Hugh.

"Yeah, but he died on the trail, a lesser breed."

"Ahem," says Sir Hugh's friend, eager to explicate.

"Not now," says Sir Hugh.

"And, as usual," says the elder Quayle, "it looks like I've arrived in the nick of time."

"Nick?" says the Voivode. "What do you know of Nick?"

He turns to stare at his captor.

"Watch it," says Quayle.

Furrowing his brow, widening his eyes, raising his right arm with the hand bending gracefully down and forward, the Voivode stares at Quayle's eyes, his tongue licking his lips, then retreating as he says, "Come here."

"Don't look at his eyes," cries out Sir Hugh.

"Come here," says the Voivode Vlady.

"Go to it, Vlady D," says Otto.

"Come here."

Quayle wavers. His eyes glaze over. He steps toward the towering Voivode, extends his hands, and offers his guns. The Voivode takes them and turns, an almost childish glee on his face.

Then he looks at Sir Hugh and says, "You are a wise man, Fitz-Hyffen . . . for one who has not lived even a single lifetime."

Otto laughs again, the sound of a stopped drain opening. He waves the Luger in the air again, confidently and menacingly.

You feel the hairs on the nape of your own neck begin to prickle and rise. You hear Sir Hugh's voice, calm but serious, asking the room at large, "Does anyone happen to have a crucifix or possibly some wolfsbane, perhaps a piece of the host?"

He darts his hand around the table top, clutches the tattered magazine with its repeating harrowed face, page after page, but as he does there is a snap, a flash of light as if you had flicked a wall switch and the ceiling lamp had popped into sudden and suicidal light, as if the film had snapped in the projector and the bare arc light had dazzled onto the screen, as if lightning had struck the castle walls.

The room is in darkness, pitchy and total, all candles blown, even the fire in the fireplace puffed out.

"O no," says Otto. There is a scuffling around in the dark. The air is icy cold. A muffled snort. A sob. Someone, something pushes past you in the dark. You dare not make a sound.

Visions. Visions. Visions.

Snow. The leaves of the tree. Its white blooms.

The sun crawling up in the west like the end of days.

A silhouette in the rising sun, the setting sun.

Your fingers touch a hand, her hand.

Her skin is pimpled like a goose.

Three bare women weaving a net of flesh in the air.

You are alone. You are cold. You are in the dark.

Facts. Facts. Facts.

And there is light. Sir Hugh pops his last Ohio Blue Tip on the worn tip of his thumbnail. He touches it to the tattered remains of the stained magazine. It ignites with a hiss, a thin scream.

At the sight of the first edge of true flame, the huge dog which has been crouched, trembling like a wet pup at Sir Hugh's feet, shrieks again, leaps out from under the table, slamming chairs to left and right, scrabbling again on the stone floor until he slams into armed Otto, knocking him sprawled and akimbo, his Luger arcing lightly into the waiting hand of Gridley Quayle.

The magazine burns brightly in the cold air, and just before it touches his finger, Fitz-Hyffen tosses it into the waiting fireplace, which bursts again into eager flame, the magazine leaving an arched trail of white smoke, pure and sweet-smelling with only the faintest acrid edge, an incense of innocence.

The large dog, growling deep in his throat, drags the snarled Otto into the muddy shadows at the rear of the room, and as they disappear into that dark, the Voivode disappears as well into a sort of blur, a fuzzy misfocus, a smudge of dust on the projector lens, and then, where he was standing, a magnificent wolf appears, red-eyed and bushy-tailed, erect and dancing, howling night music on its lips, twirling a gay fandango across the gleaming stone floor, through the door, and into the outer darkness.

Gridley Quayle moves as if to follow him, but Sir Hugh says, "No, no, it is finished, let him go."

You relax in your puzzled position and settle back to watch the denouement.

"There remains," says Sir Hugh, "the denouement. The division of the spoils."

"But, Sir Hugh," says Party Quayle, still entangled with the shaken Fang-Yugh, "you can't leave it at that. We must know, I mean, about our, I mean, our relationship."

Sir Hugh seems to be distracted, listening perhaps to the greasy crunch and grumble of the dog's dark activities in the corner, mumbles only, "Absalom, Absalom," then looks up, sees the knotty pair, seems to have heard what has been said, says, "O don't worry about a thing. We are all brothers. It's always incest," then notices the dismay on their young faces, the doubt on Gridley Quayle's, his finger on the Luger's trigger, adds, "All a ruse, all of it. Otto's father was a handicapped Hungarian servant, no more a Vuelph than you or I, spent his last days, at my whispered suggestion, in the Berlin Zoo. His mother, poor thing, we had long intercourse through much of the affair, died bare on a bearskin not long after, but that was in another country. And you are wise children, you know enough to see that what you believe is what you see. I am, as you know," nodding to his ancient companion, "childless and ever shall be."

He turns, then, the subject dropped as if never again to be raised, to the spoils, the hands, the tit, the mask, the stone, the scrapbook.

"I believe I'll be taking these along to my son Mallory," says Gridley Quayle, opening the case containing the silver hands of Otto, stuffing them into his recovered musette bag, wrapping them in the soft pages of his own life's story. "May make up for a few things, eh?" he adds, winking at his unheeding grandson, still wrapped in the warm mysteries of the East.

"And," says the now mobile Sir Hugh, opening another glass case, "I'll be taking this," tossing the yellow gemstone in the air before pocketing it. "Old Guy would like it this way. I was first in on the case you know." Quayle does not protest.

Young Party and Fang-Yugh, parted at last but still touching, join the party at the cases. Fang-Yugh is holding the ormolu bird, her own by undeniable right, and young Quayle removes the mask from its case, the object of his own quest.

"Let me wrap that for you," offers Sir Hugh, taking the mask and carrying it over to the table. He first wraps a pewter plate in a linen napkin, "trying it for size," then wraps the gleaming domino in another identical cloth. Young Party, staring deeply into Fang-Yugh's blue-flecked almond eyes, accepts the bundle Sir Hugh offers him without looking up, mutters a simple "Thanks," and pops it into some large pocket on the inside of his Norfolk jacket.

"And only this remains," says Sir Hugh, as the large dog walks into the firelight, licking its grisly chops. "Otto was a fraud, and this," raising the object of his remarks, the thick battered scrapbook, in his hands, "is just as much a vulgar hoax, but too dangerous to leave lying around."

He heaves it into the fire, where it bursts into a gaudy multi-colored flame, filling the room with the raw smell of burnt sulphur; one page, lined and interlined with two lines of Latin, separates unscorched from the igniting pages and floats like a hummingbird or a promise on the rising air up the chimney and into the blank, snow-swirling night with its invisibly circling stars.

"It is all over, come to an end," says Sir Hugh, "and just as well. It's time for bed."

He turns to his plump and worried companion and says, "Let's not disturb anyone further."

He picks up a napkin-wrapped bundle from the table, a gleam of rich yellow flashing from it for a second into your eyes, pats the familiar lump in his pocket, and, arm in arm with his old friend, heads for the door, an old man moving with an old man's unsteady

236

steps, over the hill, off to a deep sleep, experiencing the final end of things in small.

He pauses just as they reach the door, looks directly at you, and winks one cold blue eye.

And then he is gone for good.

* * * *

CHUANG TZU: Where is there a reason to be discouraged?

The essential fact to be remembered, now that the experience is ending even as experience continues, is that you have seen far more than you have understood, but that you are able, if you will, to believe as much as you have seen, therefore the only appropriate guide to action in the weave of fact and observation is the act of seeing itself, if it is understood that seeing and believing are the interchangeable elements of the same fundamental activity.

The essential fact as experience continues is that you have seen, therefore the only action is seeing, if seeing and believing are interchangeable.

The essential fact is that you have seen, therefore the only action is seeing.

The fact is seen, therefore action is seeing.

fact is therefore action is

is therefore is

is   is

is

IS